MW01068179

Old Country Fiddle Stories

Heath Dollar

©2021 by Heath Dollar
ISBN 978-1-68489-893-0

All rights reserved. No portion of this book may be reproduced, stored in a retrieval system, or transmitted in any form or by any means--- electronic, mechanical, photocopy, recording, scanning or other--- except for brief quotations in reviews or articles, without the prior written notice of the publisher.

Red Dirt Press
1831 N. Park Ave.
Shawnee, OK 74804
www.reddirtpress.net

For Martina, my *báječná ženská*

Contents

Third Fiddle
★ ★ ★

Cora Mae Atkins had just turned thirteen and was growing so quickly that it seemed like her mama had to let the hem out on her favorite calico dress about once a week. Upon each of Cora Mae's knobby knees she donned a flesh-colored band-aid, and her light auburn hair was cut a bit unevenly. Her mother wanted her to be a musician, and though Cora Mae liked music fine, she did not particularly care for playing it.

Cora Mae's mother, Tilley Bee Atkins, played piano at Second Baptist Church and kept an old upright Baldwin at home so that she could practice songs such as "The Old Rugged Cross," "The Solid Rock," and "Onward Christian Soldiers" for the Sunday service. Mrs. Atkins relished every opportunity she had to touch the ebonies and the ivories, though her daughter lacked such enthusiasm. Cora Mae, in fact, disliked playing piano so much that, in an act of clear-eyed pragmatism, she had cut the tips of all her fingers with her father's pocketknife to avoid having to practice. Whenever the piano teacher, who had been hired when Cora Mae's mother lost patience, arrived at the house to teach private lessons, Cora Mae promptly presented her daintily cut digits and was granted what the piano teacher called temporary clemency. Cut fingers served as an easy alibi, and the music teacher at least pretended to believe that the little cuts were an accident, and Cora Mae never had to play.

Tilley Bee, who had long hoped that her daughter would one day join her on the piano bench at church, attributed her daughter's disinterest in playing music to adolescent angst, an affliction that would pass as surely as acne. But angst was only a contributing factor. The main issue was that Cora Mae happened to have a different passion. Ever since her father had made her and her sister spend some family time watching a Spaghetti Western about the outlaw Belle Starr rather than the dance contest the two of them had wanted to see, Cora Mae had dreamed of becoming a professional gambler. After seeing that movie on the Cowboy Channel, Cora Mae dreamt of dealing blackjack while wearing a black silk dress and a necklace that matched the cute little pearl-handled pistol she would have strapped to her left hip. She could imagine herself cutting the cards, shuffling them in a beautiful, orchestrated flurry, and dealing them one by one on a green velvet table as the steamboat on which she was traveling rolled down the Mighty Mississippi.

Her younger sister, Virginia, however, did enjoy playing music, and she could often be heard playing their daddy's fiddle, which she had acquired when Daddy quit playing for reasons he never told the children. Virginia could play "Three Blind Mice" by the time she was four, "Roly Poly" by five, and "Faded Love" by six. She also learned to saw out a little Mozart, but that was just because their mama wanted to show off to the neighbors. Cora Mae had been sentenced to violin lessons as well, and she even had a fiddle of her own, but rather than find an alibi like she had with the piano, she just sawed and grated when she practiced, if that is what that sadistic exercise could be called, for she garnered all of her passive-aggressive energy into her violin practice in order to punish her mother for forcing her to play. She had no apparent musical talent or ardor for the art form, but still she played, if only to get her mother's goat.

Now Cora Mae was standing under an enormous oak tree at the Waylon County Old Fiddle Geezer Society's annual diamond jubilee. Her sister, Virginia, had brought her fiddle and planned to play in the thirteen-and-under open competition. Virginia could do what she wanted as far as Cora Mae was concerned. She herself had pretended to forget her violin and now stood empty-handed in the shade. The fact that she wouldn't be playing burnt her mother's biscuit, but there was little that could be done at this point since they were a good twenty miles from home and the thirteen-and-under competition was about to start in a few minutes.

2

The only other contestant besides Virginia was a six-year-old boy with turd-brown hair who was missing a fair number of teeth. The boy, who was skinny, pale, and covered in freckles, shook and scratched like a birddog with fleas, and he kept rosining his bow in what appeared to be a deep obsession. He tuned his fiddle with a strange look on his face while standing alone a few steps away from the shade of the oak, and then he played a few bars of "The Farmer in the Dell," and Cora Mae thought he sounded pretty good for a rickety little boy.

Cora Mae, to her credit, was not plagued by jealousy. She saw the world as it was much better than most children her age and did not find herself threatened by other young people, and certainly not a freckle-faced kid who could play a handful of chords on a starter violin. However, she did see an opportunity. The sign on the registration table noted that a first, second, and third place prize would be awarded for each division, including the thirteen-and-under open division. The winner would receive thirty dollars. Second place would receive twenty dollars, and third place would receive ten dollars. The entry fee, she saw, was five dollars. She looked to her left and right. There were no other children lugging fiddles for as far as the eye could see.

"Virginia," Cora Mae asked. "Can I borrow your fiddle after you play?"

"Why?" Virginia asked. "You don't like to play."

"I do, too."

"You do not. You just like to make noises to irritate Mama."

"I'm not saying I play well, but I do play. Can I borrow your fiddle or not?"

"Of course, you can. You're my sister."

Cora Mae smiled. "Thank you, Virginia. You're a good sister."

"I know."

"You don't have to be stuck-up about it."

"It's not stuck-up if it's the truth."

"Maybe not. Either way, thank you for letting me play your fiddle."

Virginia grinned and opened up her case. Cora Mae took a five-dollar bill out of the pocket of her dress and went to the registration table to pay. She unfolded the bill and laid it flat on the table. She then filled out her registration form and handed it back to the heavyset man in suspenders and a straw hat who was sitting in a folding chair. Once Cora Mae walked away from the table, two frumpy old ladies and a skinny old man leaned over her registration form like buzzards on a dead armadillo. After a couple of minutes, the old man from the fiddle contest walked over to the oak tree, stood up straight, and then began to speak.

"Welcome to the Old Fiddle Geezer Society's Eighty-Seventh Annual Diamond Jubilee, folks. For our first competition of the day, we got our thirteen-and-under division. Three contestants, Virginia Atkins, Caleb Reichenberger, and Cora Mae Atkins, will be vying for the prize. I'd like to thank all of these fine young people for coming out and sharing their musical talent. The young are the future, and we're real proud of every one of y'all. First up is little Miss Virginia Atkins, who'll be playing 'The Arkansas Traveler.' Virginia, can you take a place near the old oak and play for us?"

Virginia, who always did her best to please adults, stepped under the tree, raised her fiddle and her bow, and waited for her cue, which the old man gave with the nod of his noggin. She began to play "The Arkansas Traveler" even though her family was from Texas, and then she slid into the reel for which she was named, and then weaved back into the original song. When she was finished, there was a smattering of claps, and she started to grin, her long dishwater blond hair flapping in the wind. She gave a slight curtsy, her green eyes sparkling and her lips curling into an easy smile as she gazed at the judges' table.

The Master of Ceremonies resumed his position under the tree.

"Next up is Caleb Reichenberger from Limburg, Texas. This little fella will be playing... Caleb, what are you playing?"

"I'm playing the 'Beaumont Rag,'" he said and then drew his fiddle to his cheek.

A deep breath later and Caleb was fiddling hard and fast, his instrument occasionally screeching like a freetail bat on fire, and his tone, by anybody's survey, was awful at best. But still he played, and he hit the notes the best he could. When he finished, there was vigorous clapping from a contingent that was very likely his family, considering that the majority of them were freckle-faced with turd-colored hair and grinning from ear to ear.

"Next up is Cora Mae Atkins," the announcer said. He gave her a gentle nod as if he figured that she was shy, and then he stepped out of the way. "What are you playing, Cora Mae?"

At first Cora Mae started to panic. There was a crowd of people moving toward her, and her first instinct was to start running as fast as she could. There were probably more than a dozen people now standing there looking at her, including the little boy who had just played and her younger sister, who didn't appear too concerned about losing. Her father, she could see, was standing back with his arms folded and with one hand on his chin like he was thinking about supper or something. Her mother, in a denim dress and boots, stood directly in front of her smiling like it was Christmas.

Although she had changed her mind about being in the contest, Cora Mae figured that she had better play since she had already paid her five dollars, which had taken her three weeks of chores to earn. Cora Mae had not told the announcer what she was going to play because she really didn't know, and in the end, when the bow touched the strings, she started making awful, high-pitched sounds that caused a couple of birddogs waiting for their masters in the back of their trucks to start to howl. The judges wrinkled their noses and squinted. Her sister, she could see, was wincing like her mama was about to hit her with a flyswatter. Her father took a chew of tobacco and made the same face he made when someone asked him if he had killed anyone during the war. Her mother, who was standing front and center, looked like she might march right up and swipe that fiddle out of Cora Mae's hands.

Cora Mae started to grin, and then she slid her cut-covered pinkie down the fingerboard to play the highest note, if a note is what it could be called. The dogs in the parking lot went crazy, and she could hear the howls of dogs from the farmhouse down the road now. She played that note as long and hard as she could, sliding her bow faster and faster and faster until bow hair began to fly. Then, when her arms started getting tired and her fingers, which had not all healed from the little cuts she had made, started to hurt, she ended on four quick strokes of something she thought might be a chord. Then she saluted the crowd with her bow and gave the fiddle back to her sister. A few people clapped, but most just stood there in astonishment.

"What do you call that?" the Master of Ceremonies asked.

"It doesn't have a name," Cora Mae said, "but if it did, I would probably call it 'Fiddle Player's Pain.'"

The crowd milled and talked while the judges tabulated the scores. Cora Mae stood off to the side, and her sister was now talking to her father and mother. After what seemed like very little deliberation, the Master of Ceremonies resumed his place beneath the huge old oak tree.

"Ladies and gentlemen, we have our results. The third-place winner, who will receive ten dollars and a certificate, is Cora Mae Atkins."

A few people clapped with bewildered looks on their faces, and Cora Mae strode confidently up to the Master of Ceremonies, shook his hand, claimed her prize, and stood there beside him.

"Second place, who will receive twenty dollars and a certificate of achievement, is Caleb Reichenberger."

The group that appeared to be his family started hollering his name and clapping like he had just scored a touchdown. The little boy walked up, limply shook the judge's hand, took his prize, and then stood next to Cora Mae.

"And the winner, I am proud to say, is Virginia Atkins," the Master of Ceremonies said. "She done us proud with her version of 'The Arkansas Traveler.'"

Virginia rushed to the grassy space that served as the stage and shook the MC's hand profusely. Then she smiled, bowed, and claimed her prize. People in the audience started snapping pictures, and all three of the winners stood up straight and smiled. Cora Mae imagined that some people would have been embarrassed had they just gotten beat by a six-year-old boy who looked like he would have a rough time eating corn-on-the-cob, as well as by his or her own little sister, but she wasn't. Cora Mae Atkins was on her way to becoming a professional gambler. Today she had learned how to play the odds and how to put up a good bluff, and she was happy, as well as proud, for, with a gambler's eye for an easy game, she had just doubled her money.

Ink upon the Furrows
★ ★ ★

Daniel Zima pushed his walker across the linoleum toward the converted janitor's closet that served as his office. Daniel had been the publisher of the *Texaský rolník*, the *Texas Farmer*, for the last four decades and had written for the paper since he was twenty-four, back when his father's name appeared at the top of the masthead. His father, Dalibor Zima, died of a heart attack when Daniel was forty-five, and though his father had bequeathed the paper to him, Daniel didn't want it. He didn't want to run a newspaper. He even tried to sell the *Farmer* but had no takers. But then, who would want to buy a Czech-language newspaper in the middle of Texas? That was forty years ago, and somehow Daniel had managed to keep the weekly paper alive.

Now he did not know how much longer he or the newspaper would survive. He was down to thirty-seven subscribers, and of those, seven resided in the same nursing facility as he did. If he could somehow outlive his old-time readers, they would never have to know life without the *Texaský rolník*; and then, when Daniel's time arrived, he would have the final issue, which would lack only the closing details of his obituary, waiting on his desktop ready to print. That issue would also include his farewell, which he imagined would only be read by a handful of Slavic studies professors from universities large enough to have such a major and maybe a couple of graduate students whose master's theses would be disrupted by his ascent into heaven.

Daniel found it all rather amusing, for these folks treated him like some kind of oracle despite the fact that he tended to spell Czech words phonetically and wrote like a Bohemian Will Rogers, though not for comedic effect but because he didn't know how to write any other way. Still, considering that neither he nor most of his readership had received much formal schooling in the *mateřský jazyk*, the mother tongue, he never got too worried about spelling and such. Truth be told, the closest he himself had ever come to instruction in his native tongue was while attending Saints Cyril and Methodius Catholic Church in the little Waylon County town of Krasna Lipa, which continued to conduct mass in Czech, though many parishioners found it no more decipherable than Church Latin.

Since he was already saving on postage, Daniel thought it proper to hand-deliver the paper to the readers in his nursing home. All of these readers were women, and he imagined that he was one of the last male speakers of Texas-Czech alive. *Bez práce nejsou koláče*: without work, there are no kolaches, and the men had worked hard in the fields and worn themselves down, though he himself was not in much better shape. He had broken his hip about a year ago while trick-riding on his walker, which he called the Silver Stallion, and he had never truly recovered, but at least he hadn't died of a blood clot or pneumonia in the weeks after surgery.

He and the newspaper were both lucky to still be here. He attributed his own longevity to hard liquor for the parasites and the strong pioneer heart inside his chest. However, he attributed the newspaper's century of success to a formula. The front page always included a lectionary from the Catholic Church and a news story, which, over the last few years, had more often than not been the obituary of one of the last members of the Czech-speaking community. The inside pages featured a calendar of events that included polkas, chicken dinners, and church picnics, which had driven circulation for decades. He sold advertising space to Novacek Nursing Home, where he lived, to Milosh's Czech-Tex Restaurant, and a variety of small businesses including a roto-rooter man and a funeral home. Daniel, of course, translated the ads into Czech at no additional charge.

The language had lasted more than a century and a half in Texas but now was dying out. Even the companies that advertised in it rarely had an employee who could exchange more than civilities in the language of their progenitors. It made Daniel sad, but there was little he could do at this point. He was among the last of the old-timers.

Daniel took the photocopied newspapers from the copy machine. Before moving to the nursing home, the newspaper had always been sent to a printer, but now it was too difficult for him to get back and forth. And since circulation was so low, it was just as easy to photocopy the newspaper and mail it to his subscribers, the majority of whom lived in little towns like Schulenburg, Shiner, and West. The only place that sold the paper on the stand was the cultural center in La Grange.

Daniel, like most of his subscribers, had been officially retired for years. And knowing what it was like to live on a fixed income, he had not raised the annual subscription rate in twenty-five years. These days, the revenue from the newspaper did little more than cover his toiletries and other sundries, which was fine with him, for he wanted no truck with the taxman. The true profit of the newspaper, he had found, was that it provided him a reason to keep living.

His wife, who was bright, vibrant, and energetic, had died unexpectedly eight years ago. He himself had been experiencing health problems for years, and he would have never dreamed that he would outlive his wife—until he did. Life had changed in a split second, and it had left him reeling, though this was certainly not the first hardship he had faced. They lost their son in Indochina, in a war he thought unnecessary, though he would never say that aloud. And, of course, his parents were long gone.

But still, his daughter, Liliana, was close by. She worked the night shift as a nurse at Waylon County Hospital, and though she visited once or twice a week, Daniel still felt empty sometimes. His old friends and his other relatives were gone. He knew many people in the nursing home, but it wasn't the same. The people he had known from childhood until the sad day of ashes and dust populated his mind. No phone call could reach them. Letters would return to sender. He wrote their obituaries and mourned. He considered the obituary in the *Texaský rolník* the final rite.

Daniel spent much of his time in reflection. He loved thinking about the old days, especially days he spent with ink on his hands. He remembered the ink between the furrows of his fingerprints. He remembered the old hardscrabble farmers joking about him not being a farmer though he published the *Texas Farmer*, and he would show them his hands, show them the ink on his fingers. He told them that he planted ink and grew a sense of community. That was his pat response, and the old farmers would laugh and ask him to join them for *par piv*. This was a joke that could not be told in English because it was a language trick. In Czech, the word *pivo* means beer. When counting, the word *pivo* is used for one beer. *Piva* is used for two to four beers, and *piv* is used for five or more. With *par* meaning two, *par piv* could loosely be translated as "a couple of five beers." It was a good joke, and one that was used regularly in the town of Krasna Lipa in the old days.

With a stack of newspapers in the canvas sack upon his shoulder, Daniel started down the hall. The first place he stopped was Mrs. Kohout's room. He and Mrs. Kohout, who was thin, small, and shrunken, had both attended Saints Cyril and Methodius. They had been to the same beer bash weddings and attended the same Fifth of July picnics with their families to celebrate Cyril and Methodius' feast day on the liturgical calendar.

"*Dobrý den*," Daniel said.

"*Dobrý den*," she replied. "What's in the paper this week?"

"You'll have to read it. If I tell you, then there's no use in you subscribing."

"I like the way you read."

"You like not having to put on your bifocals."

"I'm self-conscious about them."

Daniel wanted to tell her she was pretty either way, but he did not want to seem improper. He had been friends with Mrs. Kohout's husband, Stan, and he didn't want his meaning to be misunderstood. He only wanted to make her feel good. He did not want her or any other resident of the nursing home to think him a cad. To remain above reproach, he read her the lectionary, which came from the book of First Maccabees. He read the story of a king who made an alliance with the Gentiles at the cost of his people's customs.

Mrs. Kohout smiled a gentle smile.

"*Děkuju*," she said.

"*Neni za co*," Daniel replied. "You are perfectly welcome."

Daniel gripped the handles of his walker and moved forward. A couple of doors down, he stopped at Mrs. Kovar's room.

"The Pony Express is here," Daniel called.

"*Daneček*," Mrs. Kovar said. She always called him *Daneček*, even though he didn't like the nickname. "*Daneček*, what is in the paper?"

"You'll have to read it."

"I will. I have an idea for an article for you. You should write about the people that keep parking in the handicapped spaces over at the Hoggly Woggly."

"That sounds like a letter to the editor to me."

"I have already written it."

Mrs. Kovar presented him with two handwritten pages in Czech lambasting the people who parked in the handicapped spaces without a sticker at the Hoggly Woggly. Daniel figured that at least half a dozen subscribers should start their own newspapers considering the length of their letters to the editor. But he appreciated those sprawling letters, especially in August, when news was so slow that he almost wished for a grass fire or two to have something to report. Long letters meant fewer column inches for him to write. However, he was careful not to let those harangues go on too long. His readers could only take so much.

Daniel tipped his straw hat to Mrs. Kovar and rode the Silver Stallion to the end of the hall to deliver the paper to Mrs. Bily. Mrs. Bily, who had worn red polyester dresses and a beehive hairdo like Lady Bird Johnson for the past five decades, never left her room without makeup. And were it not for Alzheimer's, she would still be living at home. Her children had put her into the nursing home for her own safety after she flooded her house with bathwater, buried her jewelry in the backyard, and had been found sitting in her car on a dirt road in Bigfoot Wallace County with no recollection of how she got there and no memory of where she lived.

"Have you seen Eugene?" she asked.

Daniel gave her a sad smile. Her husband, Eugene, had been dead for at least a decade.

"I haven't seen him," Daniel replied. "*Dobrý den. Jak se máš?*"

"I am doing well. And you?"

"Great. I am always happy when I can deliver the paper."

Mrs. Bily took the newspaper he offered, though with a perplexed look that she tried to hide with nonchalance and confidence. Daniel had lived a long time. He knew the expressions people made when trying to disguise their loss of memory, when they were trying to hide all they had forgotten. Someday soon he too would be forgotten, but week after week he tried to preserve life, language, and culture for his father, for the old-timers, and for the paper itself. The paper, as he saw it, was a member of his family. It had its own personality, its own idiosyncrasies, its own strengths and short-comings. It gave him a sense of pride akin to that which a father has for his child. It made him smile warmly when he held it in his hands.

Daniel knew he was fortunate. His life could have taken such a different direction. His father had died in the middle of Daniel's midlife crisis, and in the weeks before his father's passing, Daniel had told everyone who would listen that he did not want to be tethered to this town, this region, and this old way of life. And now here he was.

He could have moved away and been an outsider in an alien land. But he had been forced to look inward at all that was around him. He had tried to sell the newspaper, but half-heartedly. He could have found a buyer if he'd looked hard enough. He could have taken that money and moved away, but something had stopped him. He was not the kind to use the word destiny or even believe in it, but he believed this had all happened for a reason. And he was glad that it had.

Once the rest of the papers were delivered, Daniel made his way to the nursing home's front entrance, where he sat in a parlor chair and waited. He had been interviewed for newspapers, journals on applied linguistics, and junior high projects. He had been interviewed for dissertations and local radio shows, and he had been referred to in countless publications. But still he kept waiting for someone to come. He kept waiting for someone to walk through the nursing home door asking for him. He was tired. He was so tired. And he needed to hand the paper off to another person. He did not want it to die with him. Surely a young person, a young person wiser than he had been, would see the value in printing this paper, would decide to dedicate his or her life to this newspaper. And every day he waited near the door, never wanting to pass beyond the threshold into the August heat. He waited, looking out the plate glass window at the field across the street, thinking about the farmers, the ink beneath his fingernails, the furrows upon his hands, hoping that someone young and hopeful would walk through that door, say *"Dobrý den,"* and ask about buying a newspaper.

The Flag Salesman
★ ★ ★

Prairie Dog Brown stood on the side of the road next to his truck surrounded by thirty flags that were flapping in the wind. He had American flags, Texas flags, Come and Take It flags, Don't Tread on Me flags, the Confederate battle flag, the Christian flag, the Goliad flag, and a flag featuring the head of Willie Nelson with a huge leaf behind him that made him resemble a saint from the church of the blessed skunkweed.

Prairie Dog was mighty happy because there was a good steady breeze blowing, and the flags were flying on their poles with an adequate amount of drama. He stood up straight with his chin held high, turreting his head from Mason to Dixon, his eyes inquisitive, his nose testing the breeze. Standing there in his clean, faded jeans, a plain white T-shirt, and scuffed, but well-treaded, work boots, he lowered the brim of his Waylon County Feed and Seed hat to better shade his silvery-blue eyes. From beneath the canopy of the feed store brim, he tried to guess the length of the long lanky shadow that stretched across the gravel before him.

A few steps beyond his shadow, cars passed on either side of the highway, their drivers gunning the throttle on the straightaway, passing him by without so much as gliding a toe from the footfeed or tendering so much as a glance; but he was not discouraged. He spent plenty of Saturdays out on the highway selling flags. He had a regular job, after all, and selling flags just got him out of the house when he needed an excuse to get some time alone. He made a few bucks here and there, which paid for fishing lures and boxes of shotgun shells, but what he enjoyed most was the time to just sit on his tailgate and think about whatever he wanted to think about.

He wouldn't be thinking about anything too deep, though. He had no interest in contemplating existence or anything like that because whatever was was and whatever wasn't wasn't, so he saw no point in thinking about it. But he liked to let his mind ramble around, to let it graze and wander the pasture. He wouldn't let it go far. His mind had enough room to stretch its legs, but there were fences to keep it from wandering off.

A silver pickup pulled onto the shoulder, and a young man who looked barely of bar-going age stepped off the running board and down to the ground.

"Howdy," the man said.

"I'm good," Prairie Dog said. "Fine as fur on a bullfrog. How are you doing?"

"If I was doing any better, I'd have to be twins."

The young man, who was built like a bullrider, walked among the flags. He wore a pearl snap shirt and kept his hair cut short in the style of a 1940s rancher.

"You ain't got no Mexican flags, do you?"

"Nah, I don't carry 'em."

"Canadian?"

"Ain't got none of those either."

"Do you have a rainbow flag?"

Prairie Dog eyed him with suspicion. He wondered if this ol' boy stopped on the side of the road with the singular purpose of making fun of him.

"Nah, I ain't got one. But I got a Texas flag. I've even got a Burnet flag, from the Old Republic. Blue background, yellow Lone Star in the middle. The letters of Texas going between the points of the star. Looks pretty damn cool in my books. Just got them Burnet flags in, too. You'd be the first one in town to have one. You'd be starting a trend."

"That ain't what I'm looking for."

"Well, I got the Stars and Bars, as you can see, and then there's ol' Dixie, of course. A lot of folks like to buy Dixie and the Christian flag together. But Dixie sells like hotcakes on its own, and so does Old Glory. I can hardly keep those two in stock."

The young man leaned against the truck.

"If you don't have any rainbow flags, Mexican flags, or anything like that, do you at least have an old Russian flag? You sure you don't have an old hammer and sickle flag somewhere?"

Prairie Dog looked either way down the highway to make sure there weren't any cars coming.

"I got one behind the seat of my truck. I don't put some of the flags out in case someone gets the wrong idea."

Prairie Dog slid his hand behind his bench seat and produced a flag. He quoted his price. The man smiled and handed him the money.

"I know it ain't none of my business," the roadside salesman said, "but you ain't a communist, are you?"

"Let's just say that I am a weary neighbor."

The young man took the flag and drove away. Prairie Dog felt kind of guilty about carrying the old CCCP flag, but business was business, and, hell, even the president wanted to have the current Russian autocrat's adoptable babies, so selling that Russian flag could not be completely bad. At least he wasn't selling those damn Hitler flags. He had a set of morals, for God's sake.

While he was thinking about all of this, Prairie Dog sat on the tailgate of his truck cleaning gunk from beneath his fingernails with his pocketknife. There was always gunk beneath his fingernails. He repaired lawnmowers for a living, and there was always oil or grease caked up somewhere for him to get under his fingernails. His wife hounded him about it, gave him manicure brushes for Christmas even, but he thought that using a manicure brush was too candy-ass for a man, so he dug underneath his fingernails with a pocket blade, with marginal results, which was fine by him. At least he wasn't a candy-ass.

More vehicles whizzed past. The rigs rattled Prairie Dog's truck, and the pickups a bit less so. The cars simply made a sound, and that was all. Prairie Dog didn't wear a watch, but he could tell by holding his hand up between the horizon and the position of the sun that it was about an hour until sunset. A hand's width was about an hour, and he would leave when the sun was two fingers from setting. Prairie Dog had sold only one flag all

17

day when a huge black pickup with a skull in a cowboy hat airbrushed on the door came to a stop. A man with a big wooly beard wearing a leather vest, jeans, and a pair of crocodile boots jumped out of the cab.

"Hey, Prairie Dog," the man said.

"Howdy, Buckshot," Prairie Dog replied. "If it ain't my best customer. Good to see you there, pardner."

"Hell, Prairie Dog," Buckshot said, his eyes coyote-wild but focused. "My goddam neighbor hung up a damn commie flag today."

"Are you shitting me?"

"Nah, I ain't shitting you. I gotta counterbalance that crap. Mutually assured destruction. You know what I mean?"

"Does he got other flags hanging up as well?"

"Nah. That's the only one. Damn pansy ain't got but one flag up. He hung it from the roof next to his kids' basketball goal. And they can't shoot a lick, by the way. Always missing the backboard. They probably couldn't make the peewee team. Anyway, that ain't the point. I need more flags. I think he's mocking me."

"What flags do you got already?"

"I got a Texas flag, a Confederate battle flag, an American flag, a Come and Take It with a cannon, a Come and Take It with a machine gun, a Fifth Cavalry flag, a Don't Tread on Me flag, and a Dale Earnhardt flag all in my front yard. I even have a statue of Stonewall Jackson on horseback in the middle of the yard. I wanted a metal one, but those damn things are expensive, so I got a concrete one and spray-painted it bronze. It looks bad-ass. It's standing right next to my statue of Davy Crockett in his coonskin cap, which I painted in full color. He's pointing his long rifle toward the holly bushes. Damn near looks real. So I got my place looking good, looking like it should, and then here comes the asshole next door. He ain't got nothing but mowed grass, daisy flowers, and some fancy-looking bushes that he clips all the time. Then, suddenly, today he thinks it's a goddam pissing contest. Bigger'n Dallas, this ol' boy hangs a Russian flag, the one with the hammer and the sickle, right in front of his house. Well, that ain't American. Americans love freedom of expression, but that ain't an American expression. That ain't something somebody should be displaying. Love it or

18

leave it, like ol' Merle says in the song. If you're runnin' down my country, hoss, then you're cruising toward a country ass-whipping. So I'm going to overwhelm him in a neighborly way. I'm gonna fly so damn many flags that I break his spirit. And even if I don't break his damn spirit, I'm gonna fly so many flags that nobody is going to even notice his piddly-ass commie flag. That's the way to do it."

"Well, what ain't you got?"

"I ain't got a Confederate national flag. Give me one of them."

"You want the Christian flag, too?"

"I'm a Christian, as you well know, but I don't want to advertise it like a Pharisee."

"A lot of the ol' boys that buy 'em only wave 'em at night."

"Really?"

"They burn crosses in the yards of folks that are different from them and carry the Christian flag and ol' Dixie."

"That don't sound real Christian."

"That ain't none of my affair. I just sell the flags."

"Well, give me a Christian flag. I'll fly it day and night. Do you have any red flags?"

"Red flags?"

"You know the flag. The flag of no quarter. The flag Santa Anna showed the defenders of the Alamo."

"I got one behind the seat of my truck. I'll go get it. I don't fly it so folks don't get the wrong idea."

"Throw in a couple more of them Stars and Bars and three more Come and Take Its, the one with the machine gun."

Prairie Dog put all of the flags into a paper grocery sack. The sun was one finger from setting. Buckshot paid him with a stack of crumpled bills and climbed back into his pickup.

"Have a good'n," he said.

"You, too," Prairie Dog Brown told him, his fingers fondling the bills within his right front pocket. "Hope you enjoy the flags."

"You know I will. Everybody will. Don't tread on me is all I can say."

Prairie Dog nodded.

19

"Take care, Buckshot. See you soon."

Prairie Dog watched the man in the crocodile boots put his truck in gear and drive away in a Dixonward direction. Then, in the growing darkness, he took a notepad and a pencil out of his glove box. On the first page, he wrote "5 Rainbow flags, 5 Mexican flags, and 5 Maple Leaves." If he was lucky, his order would be there before next weekend, when he would set up along the highway and sell those flags like hotcakes.

The Pregnancy Test
★ ★ ★

Jennifer Turner stood in the express line at the Hoggly Woggly waiting to buy a pregnancy test. She was second in line behind an old woman who was five items over the limit and seemed to have a coupon for every single thing she was buying. With a slim, manicured hand, Jennifer lay the little box on the conveyor and, standing there between the candy rack and the cash register, took a quick glance in front and behind her. She had just finished cheer practice and was wearing a tight velour sweatsuit that tended to draw attention. Normally, she liked the attention, enjoyed the power she held over all of those gawking boys, but today was not the day. Today she felt a bit self-conscious. She felt insecure, a feeling she was not altogether used to.

Jennifer stood there with her ankles crossed, pretending to be looking at her cell phone. She did not flit her ponytail from side to side. She did not swivel her shoulder blades. She did not strike a flattering silhouette. She just stood in line hoping to God that she wouldn't be seen by anyone she knew. She would have ordered the pregnancy test online, but she was not old enough to have a credit card. And if she ordered the test using her mother's account, there was no hiding the charge. She did not want a soul to know that she was not a virgin, much less that she thought that she was pregnant, so she couldn't have asked an older friend to get the test for her either.

She wished that she would have bought some of those little rubber party hats for Tommy, but she would never have dared stand in line to buy something so embarrassing. Now, she had no choice. She had to stand in line waiting to buy something even more embarrassing. She had to know if she was pregnant. There was no choice. She had not had a period in eighty-four days. She had been exercising and eating right and was very light right now because she was a flyer for the cheerleading team and needed to weigh ninety pounds, so it was possible that her body mass index was really low and that that was what had caused her not to have her period, but she had been with Tommy five times between the twelfth and fifteenth days since her last period. She knew this because she marked her calendar with a little heart each time they made love. She should have thought it out better, but she couldn't help it that fall break landed halfway between periods.

The old woman in front of her, a thick woman with auburn hair wearing grandma jeans and high-end running shoes, fished in her purse for another coupon, one which would save her ten cents on blueberry yogurt. She handed it to the cashier and waited for the woman to finish ringing her up.

"These are supposed to be twenty cents each," the old woman with auburn hair told the cashier, pointing to the line for lemons on her receipt.

The cashier, a middle-aged woman in cat-eye glasses, squinted at the receipt through her trifocals.

"Ma'am, those are five for a dollar. If you buy less than five, they're twenty-five cents each."

"That doesn't make sense," the auburn-haired woman said. "They should all cost the same even if you only buy one. Let me speak with the manager."

Owen, the assistant manager, came over from the service desk before the cashier could even say "Code Blue" on the PA system.

"How can I help you, ma'am?" Owen asked.

"I want to be charged the sale price for these lemons. Just because I bought four shouldn't mean that I pay more for each one."

"Ma'am, we can honor the sale price. That's not a problem. Please follow me to the service counter, and I'll reimburse you from the cash drawer."

"But I want the money back on my card. Can I not do it here at the register?"

"No, ma'am. I'll need you to go with me to the service desk."

"But I bought the lemons here."

22

"I understand, ma'am. Please come with me to the service desk, and we'll get you taken care of."

Jennifer looked at the cashier and then at the assistant manager. She knew them both by sight, although she did not know their names without looking at their name tags. She didn't think they knew who she was either, other than the fact that she was a cheerleader and came into the store sometimes. If they had kids at Warnell High, she would have already known. She knew everybody at school, and everybody knew her. She was popular, and she would be surprised if she was not named the homecoming queen her senior year. She prayed to God that she was not pregnant. Pregnant girls are never the homecoming queen. And if she thought about it, well, if she really was pregnant, next fall she would already have a baby. What would people say? Her mother, she knew, would kill her.

No, she did not think the cashier or the assistant manager knew who she was, which was good. Usually, she was proud that most of the people she encountered knew who she was, but today she considered herself fortunate that no one had recognized her. The old auburn-haired woman glanced at the little pink box on the conveyor, looked Jennifer in the eyes, and then looked back down at the pink box with disgust. Judging from the way the woman looked at Jennifer, she might as well have shouted, "Slut." The message on her face could not have been more clear.

The old woman looked a lot like one of Jennifer's less popular classmates, a girl in the genetics club, but Jennifer was sure that this woman could not have possibly known who she was. Jennifer was thankful for that. And she was also thankful that a Spanish-speaking woman and her three elementary-age children, none of whom she had ever seen before, were now behind her in line and would obstruct the view of anyone who might pass along the polished linoleum no man's land beyond the candy rack.

The auburn-haired woman gave Jennifer another quick, poisonous look and then followed the assistant manager to the service desk. The cashier pushed the button that moved the little pink box toward the register. She gave Jennifer a blank, inaccessible look, and then her face, which always seemed fixed in a state of sad, abject depression, changed to a neutral expression. The expression caught Jennifer off-guard. It was not a face of scorn. It was not a face of righteousness. It was a face of encouragement. The woman, as long as Jennifer could remember, had always seemed sad. And now, she gave Jennifer an expression that from most people would have seemed neutral at best, but from her appeared to be a hopeful smile.

Jennifer didn't know what that smile-like expression meant. She didn't know if the woman was hoping she was pregnant, hoping she was not pregnant, or if she was just trying to be nice. Understanding people was Jennifer's forte, her English teacher once told her, but still she could not figure out the cashier's smile. She searched the woman's face, followed its every line and wrinkle, but could not come up with a clue.

After the conveyor stopped, the cashier picked up the little pink box with her left hand. There was no ring on her wedding finger. Standing near the bagging area, Jennifer saw Mia Houston, the head cheerleader, walk into the grocery store's pneumatic doors. Behind her were Beuna Green and Josephine Long, who sang in the church choir with Jennifer's mama. Jennifer had known Josephine and Beuna her entire life, had eaten their cobblers, had listened to them sing, had hugged them after her baptism in the Blazeby River. Please, God, she thought. Don't let any of them see me. And if they do see me, please, God, let them think that the little pink box is allergy medicine. Everyone around knew that she had allergies. Everyone. People always talked about her cute high-pitched sneeze. She sneezed like a princess in a Disney movie, they said.

Jennifer hid behind her phone, and she tried not to whip her ponytail around like she usually did. She just stood there looking as boring as she could. She even tried to stand in a way that would make it difficult for anyone to know that she was a girl. But she was a girl. She loved being a girl. And her daddy loved his girl. He hugged her and kissed her forehead and told her what a good girl she was. He stroked her forehead with his thick, strong hands. He told her that she was his precious butterfly, his little sweetie, his little golden princess. He told her that she made his life worth living. He told her that he lived for her and her mama, that he was proud to go to work every day to make them happy. He loved her as much as a daddy could love a daughter.

But what would her daddy do to Tommy if he found out? Would he break his legs? Would he snap his neck? Would he do something even worse? Although he was the biggest, sweetest daddy a girl could ever have, Jennifer knew that her daddy could snap Tommy's neck and even more because he loved her so much. After all, her daddy had fought in a war for his country. He had done things he would never tell Jennifer or her mama. Jennifer knew that. She may have been a cheerleader, but she was not dumb. She had intuition. She could read people. And she had seen enough to know that her daddy had not just sat around Iraq playing cards like he claimed and that the Warnell Wardogs letter jacket Tommy wore everywhere he went would not save him were that little plastic indicator to turn pink.

Jennifer prayed that the item would scan. She prayed that there would be no problem with the bar code. She prayed that the cashier would not have to ask the bagger to go to the pharmaceutical section and do a price check. She prayed that there was not an age restriction on who could buy a pregnancy test like they had with wine coolers and beer. She prayed that she wouldn't be carded. She prayed that there would not be a problem with her purchase.

Jennifer was relieved when the checker gave her the total. She paid with cash and quickly grabbed the little plastic bag with the pregnancy test inside and slid it into the right front pocket of her hoodie. The cashier, whose face almost smiled a sad smile, handed her the receipt.

"Have a nice day," the cashier said with a hopeful inflection on the last syllable.

Jennifer tried to smile back.

"Thank you. You too."

But she did not walk away from the bagging area. She stood still a moment waiting for the people she knew to disappear into the produce department and become consumed by avocados and bananas and Caesar salad mix. Had Mia seen her? She hoped not. And if she had, even the JV cheerleaders would know by sundown. Had the women from the church choir seen her? That worried her too. Beuna and Josephine had headed in a beeline straight toward the sweet potatoes, so maybe they hadn't noticed her. Either way, she had better get moving. They could be in the express line before she knew it.

Jennifer did not know if she was pregnant or not, but she needed to know. Not knowing was worse than knowing, she thought. There was nothing worse than not knowing. And her belly would swell soon if she was pregnant. What if she was not pregnant and someone saw the box and started a rumor that she was? It was better than being pregnant, she figured. But it still wasn't good. She had to know. She had to know if anyone had noticed her. She had to know if anyone had seen her buy the little pink kit. Jennifer headed for the doors on the far side of the store, over by the pharmacy, where the old people entered, where she had less of a chance of knowing anyone. She hoped with all her heart that she could get out of the store and to the handicap space where she had parked for a quick escape without being noticed, and she prayed that the little plastic prophet wouldn't turn pink. After exiting the sliding glass doors, she surveyed the parking lot and then almost ran to the cute yellow pickup truck her daddy had bought her. She could almost cry. She prayed that she wasn't pregnant. She prayed that she hadn't been seen. But, as always with life, she would have to wait and see.

Hildegard of Limburg
★ ★ ★

Hildegard of Limburg played honkytonk versions of medieval hits on a lap steel guitar in the key of lost highways and cold, cold hearts. Alone in her old limestone house on the Roemer Escarpment, eight miles of dirt road away from the nearest farm to market blacktop, Hildegard recorded songs called virelays, songs that included stylized bird calls as well as rippling series of notes that flowed like gentle brooks and soft forest winds.

With her left hand sliding the steel bar and her pick-shrouded fingers plucking the strings, glissandos and vibratos were born of phosphorous and bronze. Hildegard enjoyed playing these musical vignettes, these character pieces, and she recorded each voice of each song on a different track to create her polyphony, each voice different, but still her own, each voice a different facet of one being ultimately to be heard in blissful commune with all the others.

On a computer with Eve's bite stamped upon its case, Hildegard recorded these sounds, this music. And once the songs were created and she was satisfied with the tracks she had made, she distributed this music to the outer world via the great digital highway in the sky. The cuckoo bird sounds of Europe had been transformed into the call of the mourning dove, and the sylvan breeze had become a hot Texas wind, and there was the rattling of mesquite beans on the scattered trees, and the occasional rush of the diamondback rattler's call for peace. Hildegard knew these sounds, had known them all her life, had perhaps acquired her ken of them through instinct after so many generations in this hostile place.

Hildegard was born in Waylon County, in the town of Limburg, which was settled by Germans the year Texas became a star on Old Glory. And Hildegard was a descendant of those settlers, immigrants who had crossed the blue Atlantic to arrive at Indianola and survive the wet cough and depredation and to somehow prosper and multiply in a wild, unforgiving land they had been told would be Eden. And her family had truly prospered, though no one would have known it, for they always remained frugal and sensible. Yes, they possessed vast holdings of land and resources, and they had lived and farmed in the same way for generations and were the sort of people who, no matter how much money they had, would not buy a new truck if the old one still ran.

But Hildegard, though she respected and appreciated the agrarian tradition, decided on a different life. After high school, she studied German folk melodies in Erfurt, where she, like Luther, grappled with the Devil. From there her path led to the Sorbonne, where she explored the ancient library and pored over the codices of Abelard and Machaut. But she disliked cold weather and missed her family, and one night Hank Williams and a bottle of absinthe convinced her it was time to go home. Upon her return to Waylon County, Hildegard resided with her grandmother, assisting her as she could, for her grandmother refused to live in town, much less enter a facility.

One afternoon while Hildegard was at the feed store, her Oma, at the age of one-hundred-and-one, climbed onto the roof to see if that morning's hailstorm would warrant a reshingling. Hildegard had promised to scale the ladder and assess the damage as soon as she got back from buying chicken scratch, but her grandmother, who was endowed with every virtue but patience, had slipped off the roof and flown up to Heaven before Hildegard could return from the feed store. So Hildegard had lived alone in her grandmother's limestone house ever since, transforming her grief and guilt into music that gradually began to resemble acceptance, music that became both clear-eyed and unsentimental, music that told the truth in time before slowly evolving into the sounds of cloistered devotion that could best be described as ecstasy.

28

These days, Hildegard's music blessedly sustained her, for most of her needs were covered by the Native Texas Lucrezia Borgia Society. Their patronage provided gas for her old four-wheel drive truck and the groceries she purchased at the Hoggly Woggly in town. Their money paid for electricity and a high-speed connection uncommon so far from any major road. At present, she was working on a Texas version of the Book of Psalms, that she, like Luther centuries ago, would set to the music of folk songs. Luther had translated the Bible from Koine Greek to the German vernacular, so, with the help of the Living God, Hildegard figured she could at least build a Book of Psalms that would dance across the Texas tongue when sung to the strains of "The Streets of Laredo." For her translation, Hildegard focused primarily on syntax and vocabulary, straying from the sort of colloquialisms found in guides to talking like a Texan sold in truck stops and tourist traps. And she, of course, used the word "y'all" to express the second person plural. Hildegard had not mentioned the project to anyone, much less released any of it, for she felt its distribution tantamount to sanctimony. This work, she felt, was a secret between her and God, and she would play these songs for the Lord and the Lord alone.

One controversial work that she had released was an album that contained lyrics advocating for the philosophical coitus of the Texas variety of Christianity and Tantric yoga. This album, according to one reviewer, was the modern equivalent to the work of Saint Thomas Aquinas, who built the bridge between Aristotle and Christianity. And though Hildegard's album had caused thunder and lightning in the firmament of the Academy, it had not stirred so much as a gentle wind in her native Waylon County. The work was unknown in the place where she lived, which is how she preferred it.

Hildegard herself, however, was not unknown. Anyone in town could describe her. Anyone could expound upon her ornately tooled cowboy boots and flowing cotton dresses. Anyone could talk about hair that was long and flaxen. Anyone, if being fair, would say that she was pretty. However, opinions varied on her eyes, which were described on a spectrum that ranged from enlightened to mad as birds. And she had lovers. These lovers arrived like pilgrims from distant lands, traveling the eight miles of unimproved road to the limestone homestead on their knees. These men were acolytes, and they would stay for some days before she sent them back home with a kiss and a blessing.

Hildegard of Limburg was happy with her life on the Roemer Escarpment, content to live her life in this land of thorn and waste. From her grandmother's window she could see the Milky Way glide the heavens while the coyotes sang their choruses, sang with call and response, and so, she too made her music, drew her bar across the strings and touched them with her picks, the sounds of wind and wilderness rising to the heavens.

Honkytonking with
the Silver Strings
★ ★ ★

"Play your damn song, Earl Todd," Wild Bill Lemsky said, pulling his bow across the strings. "It's your turn to be the band leader."

"Hold on there, hoss. Give me a second to sop up the moment with the biscuit of my mind. Ain't nothing wrong with me standing here at the mike holding my guitar and smiling at the audience a little while. I'll start playing in the Lord's due time."

The audience, which mainly consisted of older women in well-ironed dresses, laughed. All of the women were country and western singers, even if they mostly sang at home while cooking supper or in the choir up at church. Some were widows and had already outlived a husband or two. A couple of the women had left their husbands at home to watch sports on television. Others had husbands onstage. Every Tuesday, the women all sat in the four rows of folding chairs waiting for their turn to sing. Some could sing like Patsy Cline or Jean Shepard, and others just got up and made a joyful noise, as the music minister up at the church house sometimes said, but how they sounded was not what really mattered. The fact they were doing what made them happy is what was important.

The old women loved Earl Todd, and he was fond of them, too, though he always kept his distance, even if he did like to address them as "the beautiful ladies of the audience" whenever it was his turn to lead the band. His own wife had passed many years prior, and though he certainly liked to flirt with the ladies, he never thought it proper to court another woman after his wife had gone to be with Jesus. And, besides, if he married again, which one of them would be his wife once he got to heaven? It all seemed too complicated.

Earl Todd stood behind the microphone in a brown western suit, spit-shined boots, and a silverbelly cowboy hat, holding onto a pretty, blond Martin with extra-light strings that shined above his well-loved fretboard. Just when he looked about ready to play, he turned away from the microphone, covered his mouth, and coughed and coughed again. Then, when the rumble had subsided in his chest, he stood there casually with his knotted left hand resting upon the neck of his guitar, all the while gripping the mike with his right like he was the king of rock and roll.

"I'm ninety-nine years old today," Earl Todd said into the microphone. "Older than dirt. Younger than love. And I guess at this point I can play whatever the hell I want, because if you're this damn near a hundred, folks'll let you do as you please, which is one of the few perks of outliving most of your contemporaries."

The makeshift band sat behind him. Every Tuesday, whoever had the notion or the time came and played at the Krasna Lipa Senior Center. A few younger people were among the regulars. There was Arnold Spoetzl, who had a salt and pepper beard, on stand-up bass, and Royce Granger, the lanky electrician, on lap steel, alongside a dozen acoustic guitar players on social security. The guitarists sat in two rows facing one another with a long linoleum space in the middle. A harmonica player called Horsefly had started coming since he learned to play again after getting dentures. Earl Todd remembered him being better when he was younger, but new teeth meant a different sound, and Earl Todd was not one to judge. He had, after all, seen his own arthritic hands lose speed along the fretboard in the last few years. He could still play, and he was still pretty good, but he was not going to fingerpick or do anything like that. Besides, he was no Merle Travis when he was young, and he wasn't going to pretend to be one now. Truth be told, he could strum and smile, and that was all that he really needed. The music made him happy, and that was enough.

Although the other players liked to give him flak, Earl Todd was and always had been the leader of the band. He had started this little group some thirty years ago after the icehouse went out of business. He didn't know how an icehouse could have held on that long anyway. Refrigerators and freezers were widespread, and only a handful of obstinate, and oftentimes poor, old-timers still used an icebox instead of a refrigerator. The end of the icehouse meant the end of a place for Earl Todd to play with his friends. But Earl Todd had talked to the young guy who worked for the city and told him his idea to start a music night at the Krasna Lipa Senior Center. A music night sounded great, the kid said, but there could be no drinking like they did at the icehouse.

So Earl Todd settled for Tuesday night, the only open slot they had. Monday was craft night. Wednesday was an open church service. Thursday was the senior council meeting. Friday was bingo, and Saturday and Sunday were kept clear for holiday parties and the like. For the past thirty years, Earl Todd's favorite day had been Tuesday. He lived for Tuesday. He thought all week about what he was going to play. And though he was the undisputed leader of the band, the way he had everything set up was nothing like Bob Wills. With Bob Wills, it was always clear who was the bandleader. With Earl Todd's come-as-you-are band, someone walking in would be hard-pressed to say who was in charge. When Earl Todd set up the Silver Strings, as the band was called, he did it in a way that everybody who wanted a chance to be the star got to be the star at least for a song or two.

Standing there at the mike, Earl Todd thought that maybe he would play an old song by Hank Thompson or something by Lefty Frizzell. He might even croon a little Ray Price. On Tuesday nights, he and his friends only played the old songs, the songs from when they were young. They didn't play any long-haired country, any songs with rock solos or even any rockabilly. And they sure didn't play any hippie songs. They were purists, and they only played western swing and honkytonk proper, and even with that, they mostly played music from North Texas and Oklahoma. Not even that Bakersfield sound would do, though a Buck Owens song got slipped in every now and then. Of course, they all liked rock and roll. Nobody would dispute that. And they even liked the Beatles. At least the early

Beatles. The "Hold Your Hand" Beatles. They weren't too damn old to like that. But rock and roll is not what they wanted to play. They wouldn't be playing "Love Me Do," even if the harp part had pretty much been written by an ol' boy from Fort Worth, and they sure as hell weren't going to stand around like a bunch of damn doowoppers.

Although Earl Todd mostly concerned himself with music these days, he had always had to work. He'd picked far more cotton than guitar growing up, and he'd married young, had four girls, and had worked and worked. He had dreams of becoming a honkytonk star, but dreams didn't put beans and cornbread on the table. So he settled for regular work for regular pay and raised his family.

When he was younger, he tried to write songs, but he needed quiet, and his house was always full of clanging and banging, and his daughters loved and needed him, and so did his wife, so he played on the back porch after everyone went to bed, with his English pointer for an audience. But still he listened to the Opry, and he loved rock and roll, loved the story of Carl Perkins writing "Blue Suede Shoes," a story he could relate to. But Earl Todd's moment never came. He was just a back porch picker with a day job.

And then, when he retired, he started going to the icehouse to swap songs. He loved playing with the other ol' boys. He loved being accepted by them, respected by them, and he loved it when someone told him his playing was good. He'd never had any money and he'd never been paid to play, and he could have never even imagined being paid to play, for he was unable to associate getting paid with doing something he loved, so the admiration of others was more compensation than he had ever dreamed of. He'd played beside three generations of bird dogs on his back porch over the years, and the chance to play with the circle of pickers at the icehouse brought him great satisfaction.

So when the icehouse shut down, he knew that he had to do something. The first Tuesday night at the senior center, he was the only person to show up, and he just sat there in a folding chair playing and singing by himself so that his fingers would be warmed-up if anybody decided to join him, but nobody did. But that first night didn't discourage him, and the Tuesday night picking party gradually caught on. He bought a mike here, a combo there, a tweed amplifier, cables, an old PA, and a mixing board. After a couple of years, a band the size of the Texas Playboys showed up every Tuesday, although most of the people were guitar players. Earl Todd reckoned that every musician in Waylon County had been there at one point or another.

When they played, two rows of guitar players always sat facing one another strumming along to every song, their profiles to the audience. The bass player and the lap steel player were situated by the back wall facing forward, making the whole arrangement look roughly like a horseshoe. Closest to the stage was Mary Jean, who played mandolin, and Wild Bill Lemsky on fiddle. Horsefly, the harmonica player, sat on the front row of the audience until someone nodded him in for a solo.

"Earl Todd, you may very well be a hundred years old before you decide to play a song," Wild Bill Lemsky called.

Earl Todd stood there grinning and still holding the mike like the king of rock and roll. Behind him, somebody made a guitar bock like a chicken. The steel man played "Nanananabooboo."

"All right. All right. I'll play y'all a song," Earl Todd said. "This here is an old one. Hell, all of 'em are old ones. Well, this one ain't as old as some of 'em."

Earl Todd played "Satisfied Mind" with Wild Bill accompanying him on a long-stroked Bohemian fiddle. The guitars strummed as one, and Royce Granger climbed in on steel. Arnold Spoetzl played a wide rhythm on bass that let everyone inside. Everybody knew "Satisfied Mind," even if it seemed like everyone knew a different version.

Earl Todd sang into the microphone. His voice crackled like an old 78 record but provided the same effect of wonder. His voice was so real and so true. His beauty transcended the limits of age, the limits of his medium. Through the crackle of ninety-nine years, there came a song, stripped-down and honest.

The song ended on a slow, wavering note on the lap steel, and then everyone clapped. The room broke into an acapella birthday song, and then people in the audience stood up and headed over to the kitchen for coffee and upside-down cake and peach cobbler. The musicians placed their instruments in their cases or leaned them against their chairs. They had reached the intermission. Some of the old men headed to the bathroom. Everyone mingled and laughed.

Earl Todd stepped outside for a smoke. He still smoked unfiltered Lucky Strikes like he did back in the army. He lit his smoke with an old metal lighter he'd carried since the Eisenhower administration, and after three quick puffs to get the damn thing lit, he took a deep draw standing out in the parking lot. He always smoked in the parking lot at the senior center because there were too many folks on oxygen there for him to be smoking close to the building.

Two rows past the handicap spaces, Earl Todd leaned against Arnold Spoetzl's truck. Arnold was sitting in the cab next to Royce Granger, and the two of them were passing a flask back and forth.

"You sounded good tonight, Earl Todd," Arnold said.

"Thank you, Arnie. 'Preciate it."

"Yes, sir. Even an old fart like you can sound good on his birthday."

"Ah, hell, son. I been singing like an angel since you were just a twinkle in some hound dog's eye."

Royce leaned out the window and laughed, trying not to spit out his slug of whiskey.

"You want a pull, Birthday Boy?" Royce asked.

"I reckon I'd better have one. I hear it's a good cure for screw worms."

"Holy shit," said Arnold. "You got screw worms?"

"Hell no, Arnie. But an ounce of prevention never hurt. I hear it's good for a limp pecker, too. You might want to take another draw yourself."

Arnold cocked his bright red "Ronald Reagan Forever" hat and cackled.

"If popsicle sticks and rubber bands won't help, I'm pretty sure that a bucket of whiskey wouldn't do no better," Arnold told him. "But I reckon I'm kindly thirsty. Let me see that dadgum flask, Royce."

Royce just laughed and passed the flask out the window to Earl Todd, who took a long slug and handed it back to Royce.

"Now that'll put hair on your chest," Earl Todd said.

Royce tilted back the flask and then handed it to Arnold, who took a quick sip, getting some of it in his salt and pepper beard.

"You saving some for later?" Earl Todd asked.

"I reckon I'll lick my beard if I get thirsty."

One of the guitar players stepped out under the awning of the senior center tapping his wrist.

"Well, it's been real, boys, but I reckon we'd best go back inside and do our thing," Earl Todd said, adjusting his lapels.

Earl Todd looked across the parking lot and saw Wild Bill Lemsky and his wife sitting on the tailgate of their truck drinking beer out of a paper sack.

"Turn up that damn *pivo*, and let's go, Wild Bill. It ain't a band without your Bohemian fiddle. Petra, tell that ol' boy to chug-a-lug."

"I'll be there, boys. I'll be there," Wild Bill hollered.

Arnold, Royce, and Earl Todd walked back inside.

"How're your boys doing, Arnold?" Earl Todd asked.

"They're good. Mack just made varsity. Wallace is flying to New York for work next week. He's a big shot down in Houston, and they send him all over the place."

"That's good, Arnie. Real good. Sounds like everybody's doing good."

When they got back into the bright fluorescent light of the senior center, Imogene Phelps handed Earl Todd a cupcake.

"Happy birthday, Earl Todd," she smiled.

Earl Todd had always liked Imogene. She was funny, a great singer, and real pretty, too. And he was kind of flattered by the attention she gave him considering that she was almost twenty years younger. Granted, twenty years younger than him meant that she was around eighty, but everything was relative he reckoned. Had he not felt the way he had felt after his wife passed, he would have swept Imogene away and they would have been a country music duo for sure. But loving another woman would have made him feel like he was living in a cheating song, so he remained a solo artist, though he had to admit that he did indeed like the attention Imogene gave him.

While Earl Todd was sitting there eating his cupcake, Wild Bill Lemsky stepped across the stage and took his turn at the microphone. Wild Bill's family had been among the original settlers of Krasna Lipa, and one of his ancestors had even played the flute at the Battle of San Jacinto. More than a century and a half later, the family still spoke a little Czech, and Wild Bill knew the old Moravian folk songs and even the Tex-Czech music he had heard at the Swiss Alp Dance Hall down around Schulenburg when he was young. In honor of his heritage, every now and then he would lead an old Dolph Hofner song. Tonight he played one called the "Stara Kovarna," a Tex-Czech waltz about an old blacksmith shop, but only he knew all the lyrics, though a couple of the guitarists had heard enough Czech from their starenkas that they could sing a word or two every now and then.

After Wild Bill led the band, Imogene played an old Patsy Cline song, her sweet voice holding the notes long and pure, and Eunice Griffin sang "Second Fiddle to an Old Guitar" by Jean Shepard, who was famous in her day but now was not widely known. Somebody played "Honkytonk Blues" and then Arnold Spoetzl sang "Always Late" while Imogene showed her chops on the bass. Earl Todd thought the evening went exactly how it should. Although he found it amusing to crow about it being his birthday, he had also made sure not to advertise beforehand so that no one had time to arrange a party or buy him a present. Only Imogene had remembered that his birthday was this week. He liked attention, but not that much attention, and he really didn't like people making much of a fuss over him.

He wished that his four daughters could have been with him tonight, but he also understood that they all were living happy lives in other places. All of them had moved away from Krasna Lipa years ago, when they were in their twenties. One was in Chicago, another in Boston, and a third in a little community outside of Santa Fe. His fourth daughter only lived in Galveston, but she owned her own business and he didn't see her much. They all tried to come in for Christmas and the Fourth of July, but they had married men they had met in college and had moved to cities far away. The girls were thankful that they had been raised in a nice, quiet town like Krasna Lipa, and they would all like to retire there, but it was not much of a place to have a career.

Earl Todd loved them all, accepted their decisions, and was happy that they were happy. When it felt too long between visits, sometimes he caught a flight out of Austin and went to stay with his daughters, his grandchildren, and even his great-grandchildren, and they all treated him like a well-

38

loved king. He was happy about that. He was happy that he had a good relationship with all of them, and that he could talk to each of his daughters using the computer, that they could even see one another like they were on television. He liked that a lot. He felt lucky that he could see them and talk to them. And he also enjoyed sitting on his porch playing his guitar and singing songs. He was thankful that his hands were still pretty nimble and that he didn't have arthritis as bad as some of his friends.

As always, the night ended with a benediction. The musicians played "I Saw the Light" and "May the Circle Be Unbroken." Everyone in the room sang together. They sang loud, with soul and conviction. In the old days, at the Saturday night dances, the bands always ended with songs like these, songs that got everybody thinking about Sunday morning, songs to get the drunk ones thinking about church in the morning, songs to make the ones ready to fight remember that the Good Lord was watching. This Tuesday night, like all Tuesday nights, ended with a sort of honkytonk blessing, ended with songs of God's peace and love, much like the dances ended on the wild Saturday nights of their youth.

When it came time for the final number, Earl Todd stepped to the mike to lead "Amazing Grace." The group sang the first, second, and fourth verses like they did in the Baptist churches. Although he would not dare try to alter the tradition, Earl Todd never understood why churches left out the third verse other than for brevity's sake. When he sang, his voice crackled like a brittle old record, but it was firm, full of conviction, full of earnestness. His voice was beautiful, beautiful just as it was. It was real. It was hopeful. It was good.

Everyone clapped, and then Earl Todd shut off the mike. Wild Bill hugged him and told him happy birthday. Arnold Spoetzl patted him on the back and told him once again how much he liked to hear him sing. Everyone began packing their gear. A few of the younger men carried Earl Todd's tweed amplifiers to his truck. Wild Bill unplugged the PA. Earl Todd smiled and laughed. But then he started to shake a little.

"Are you okay?" Imogene asked.

"I feel a little hot, a little dizzy," he said.

Imogene sat him down.

"Let me get you some water," Wild Bill said.

He went to the kitchen and got a bottle of water. It was cold. Earl Todd drank some and put some on his forehead.

"You alright?" someone asked.

By now a crowd of musicians stood around him.

"I'll be fine. No need to make a fuss."

Earl Todd's eyes closed, and he sat in the chair like he was sleeping in church.

"Somebody call an ambulance," Arnold said. He put his hand on Earl Todd's cheek.

Earl Todd looked up, though everything seemed blurry beneath the senior center lights. The first time he was in here, he played in one of these folding chairs all alone, and tonight he was surrounded by friends, surrounded by musicians. He closed his eyes again. He could hear someone singing the third verse of "Amazing Grace." Everything seemed so easy, and he was not at all afraid. It was easy since he felt like he had lived a good life, that his life had been fulfilled, that his family was good and happy and successful, that he had nothing to regret.

"You would have almost thought he'd planned it," Royce Granger said. "He was never happier than he was here."

A siren could be heard outside. Heads turned toward the door. Wild Bill Lemsky drew his fiddle to his cheek and struck up an old-time tune.

Down at the Creek
★ ★ ★

Tyler spat a tight arc of tobacco juice into the creek and watched the minnows circle round and feed on it.

"If minnows like to dip snuff, I betcha crappie and bass like it, too," he said and then spat on the big yellow grasshopper that was flicking around on his hook before casting it into a deep hole beneath an old scrub tree whose exposed roots could be seen beneath the water.

Tyler stood on the bank bare-chested in a pair of cutoff shorts and muddy old tennis shoes slowly cranking the handle on his closed-face reel. His daddy had taught him and his brother how to fish with an open-face reel, but they weren't allowed to use such expensive equipment unless he was with them. And though Tyler preferred fishing with an open-face because it made him feel grown-up, he was fine with using his old spin-caster at Fiddler Creek because they had never caught anything bigger than pan-size there anyway, so fancy equipment was not even necessary.

Tyler's older brother, Shane, who was named after a movie cowboy, tied a hook to some eight-pound test line and clamped a couple of split shots about a foot above the hook with his teeth. He took a fresh grasshopper from the coffee can, baited his hook, and dropped the line into a deep spot just beyond the bank with his hands. He then held onto the spool of line and waited. Tyler fished this way too sometimes, but today he wanted to use a rod and reel. Hand fishing, or Indian fishing as they sometimes called it, was fun, but he wasn't always in the mood for it.

Tyler's pole began to bend, and he pulled fast and hard to set the hook and then frantically began to reel and reel.

"I got one," he said. "I got a big one."

His line drew taut and his rod tip bowed creekward for a couple of seconds before there came a snap and everything went slack.

"Looks like he turned and broke my dadgum line," Tyler said.

"Hell, you probably just got hung up on a tree root and it busted off that way."

"It did not."

"Bet you it did. But, hell, either way we got more hooks. You better tie one on."

About that time a couple of girls they knew showed up with a little freckle-headed boy. The older girl was carrying a package of bacon, the younger a spool of kite string.

"Y'all catch anything?" the older girl asked.

She was tall and really pretty, though Tyler tried to pretend like he didn't notice.

"Nah," Shane said, "but we just got here. Y'all going down to the shallows to catch some crawdads?"

"Yeah."

"There's some pretty big ones down there."

"I know it," the older girl, whose name was Audrey, said.

Shane turned his head, spat a brown stream, and then reached into the back pocket of his cut-offs and produced a can of cherry-flavored snuff.

"Y'all want a dip?" he asked.

"Not me," Audrey said. "Girls don't dip."

"I'll take one," her friend said. "This girl does."

She reached for the can, packed it with a quick crack of her wrist, and took a little pinch. Her face turned sour at first, but then she adjusted her dip and began to smile. At that point, the girl, whose name was Lulu, reached back into the can and pulled out a tiny pinch for the little boy, who was probably four years old, putting it in his mouth like he was a baby bird.

Audrey, standing tall and straight and poised, reached into the little purse she was carrying and produced a long, thin cigarette and a book of matches from the Pink Poodle Coffee Shop in Fort Worth. It took her three matches, ten hard puffs, and a handful of coughs to get it lit, but there she was standing on the creekbank smoking, looking, in Tyler's eyes, a lot like her namesake, Audrey Hepburn, whose movies he had seen at his grandmother's house.

"Y'all want to smoke?" Audrey asked, her left hand on her hip, ashing the cigarette with an elegant flick of her right thumb.

"Nah, we ain't allowed," Tyler said. "We'd get a whipping for smoking."

"That's too bad. I love smoking. It's so relaxing."

"Don't your parents get mad?"

"They don't know."

"Don't they smell it on you?"

"They both smoke like a freight train. They smoke in the house, so I smell like smoke all the time anyway. So they wouldn't know the difference. And I only take one cigarette at a time so nobody notices. My mama smokes menthols. I like those the best."

"Nobody smokes at our house," Shane said, "so we couldn't get away with nothin'. And our mama's got a nose like a bloodhound. She could smell a popcorn fart from a mile away."

Everyone laughed, especially the little boy who was trying to repack his dip with his tongue, though in the end, his mouth was full of tobacco grounds.

"And it don't even matter if she's upwind," Tyler added, though no one laughed but Audrey Hepburn, which was fine by him. He was glad that she could get his humor.

"You're pretty funny," she said, "for a little kid."

"I'm ten," Tyler said. "That's not little."

"I'm twelve though," she said.

Tyler sat down and tied a hook using a knot his daddy had taught him. He picked up the coffee can into the plastic lid of which he had stabbed a few extra airholes with his pocketknife and then opened the lid just enough to catch the first grasshopper that jumped toward the hole. He was now holding it by the back legs, and it spat its tobacco while he hooked it through the thorax.

"That's a big one," Shane said.

43

"Best kind," Tyler said. "It's one of them big yellow ones we caught in the sunflower field. They're better than them little green ones. The green ones are too tender. They come off the hook too easy when you get a bite."

Tyler slung a cast across the creek while his brother, who was now crouched beside the bank, worked his own line with a slow, even hand. Audrey Hepburn, who was standing far enough away to avoid getting hooked, took a deep drag from her cigarette.

"Y'all wanna go look at those dirty magazines hidden in the treehouse across the field?" she asked.

"We just came to fish," Tyler said.

"What? Are you chicken?"

"I'm not chicken. It's just that we're fishing."

"You don't like those pictures?" Audrey asked with a little wave of her menthol cigarette.

"We ain't supposed to look at 'em."

"Nobody's going to know."

"My mama would know."

"How would she know?" Audrey said, drawing out the last word like a rich girl.

"She'd see it on my face."

"Then change your face."

"I cain't."

"She won't know."

"She will too know. The last time I looked at dirty magazines, I came home and she asked me what was wrong. I told her I had a stomachache, and she gave me some Pepto-Bismol."

"You looked guilty," Shane said. "That was the trouble."

"I was guilty," Tyler said. "It was like I was King David from the Bible looking at that naked lady. We ain't supposed to look at naked ladies. It says so in the Bible."

"You can look at naked ladies," Lulu said. "You can look at 'em if you're married to 'em. And I think you can look at 'em in magazines 'cause that's just paper. It ain't real ladies."

Shane started pulling hand over hand then gave his line some slack when a fish ran with his hook. He grimaced as the line bit into his palms, for he was latched onto a big one for hand-fishing, and once the fish had run wide, had cut back and forth across the water half a dozen times, Shane began to haul it in, hand over hand, careful not to get a finger wound up in the line but also careful not to give too much slack. He pulled firmly and surely but not too fast as he brought the fish closer toward him.

"That's a big one," the little boy said while trying to wipe the tobacco off his tongue with a dirty finger.

"It's big alright," Shane said, giving a hard, fast tug that flung the fish to the bank.

The fish, which was flat-faced and gray, began to flop in the Johnson grass. It was now covered in dirt from tail to eye, kicking and flopping and fighting in the open air.

"What is it?" Audrey Hepburn asked.

"It's a trash fish," Shane said. "It's a buffalo, and it swallowed my hook." He reached for his fillet knife.

"Ain't no point in killin' it," Tyler said. "Let's try to get the hook out with these needle nose pliers."

"Well, see if you can pull it out then," Shane said.

Tyler grabbed the fish by its lower lip so it couldn't move. He reached into the fish's mouth with the pliers and went past its tongue and down its windpipe, or whatever it's called on a fish, and caught onto the hook, but it was in deep, and blood started coming out of the fish's gills.

"Dang it," Tyler said. "I'm gonna cut the line the best I can and let the fish go. That's the best chance it's got."

Tyler cut the line with his pocketknife. He then took the fish to the edge of the bank, leaned down, and lowered the buffalo into the water by the bottom lip, shaking it slowly to get it used to being back in the water, little clouds of blood now forming on either side of the fish, and then, like a fighter that had recovered from a hard punch to the jaw, the fish shook itself for a moment and then darted away at full speed.

"You think it'll live?" Lulu asked.

"It might," Tyler said. "At least it's got a chance."

"At least it's got a chance," Audrey Hepburn echoed.

Tyler liked that. He knew she understood.

"I should have gutted that buffalo and got my hook," Shane said. "We could have used that fish for cut bait."

"We got more hooks," Tyler said.

Shane tied a new hook on his line, clamped a couple of split shots about a foot above it, and ran a new grasshopper down the hook.

"This is one of them soft green ones," he said. "Fish like 'em. They tear 'em apart fast, but I'm hand-fishing, so I can hook 'em before they take my bait."

Shane threw his line into the water, the sunlight shining on the golden skin on his bare chest and reflecting off his sun-bleached hair, which was cut in a bilevel. Audrey Hepburn kind of looked at him, Tyler thought, but not that much.

"Y'all wanna fish with us?" Tyler asked, trying not to pick at the dead skin on his nose, which had gotten sunburned at the lake last week. "I can give y'all some line and everything."

"We don't want this bacon to go bad, so we're gonna go catch some crawdads," Audrey Hepburn said, "but thank you. That's real sweet."

Audrey Hepburn, Lulu, and the boy all walked the trail along the bank toward the little dam where the crawdad holes were. Tyler watched them walk away and wished he had agreed to go look at the dirty magazines with them, for his heart sank at watching Audrey Hepburn leave. Still, he loved looking at her, and it didn't really matter that her legs were covered in Calamine lotion, for her chigger bites, like the peeling skin on his nose, would be gone soon enough. He just liked looking at her. He liked how she looked in her pink shorts and royal blue softball jersey. He liked how the bottom of her number, number one, showed just below her long brown hair.

Tyler stood there looking at her, his rod and reel in hand, reeling slowly to keep the slack out of his line. And while he stood there watching, Audrey looked back over her shoulder. Maybe she was looking at Shane, Tyler thought, for he was her age, though Shane thought hunting and fishing were for men, and having a girlfriend was for sissies and dorks. But Tyler didn't care. He looked Audrey Hepburn straight in the eye, and she kind of smiled and almost laughed, like she knew a secret she would tell if he asked her enough times, and then she turned away, never missing a step as she headed in the direction of the crawdad beds.

And Tyler smiled to himself and thought. He thought about girls, and he wondered if it was a sin to look at dirty pictures since the girls weren't real, since the girls were only paper, and he wondered about Audrey Hepburn. He wondered if she would ever consider being his girlfriend. And if she wouldn't because he was too young, he wondered if one day, maybe sometime after he too turned twelve, he would find himself a girl like that.

Thanksgiving in an Arid Land

★ ★ ★

Handley Robertson walked a thicket of long-spined pear and grizzled mesquite to a dry creek bed where he intended to pitch camp. To his left, to the west, rose a rust-red bluff, a landmark to assure he did not lose his way. Ahead stretched miles of scrub and thorn and prairie grass. Arroyos dipped and hills climbed. He walked slowly, looking all around. He saw blood-berried juniper, cedar, and acacia, creosote and yucca and sideoats grama. He marveled at the strange buckling layers of gypsum rising and winking from the oxide dirt. Today was Thanksgiving Day, and Handley looked forward to spending it alone beneath the wide turquoise sky.

Last year he had gone home to Waylon County for Thanksgiving, but it had been too much for him. There had been too many people in his parents' house, too much food, too much football, too much sound. There had been too much of everything it seemed. To celebrate Thanksgiving, Handley did not feel that a celebration of plenty, of overabundance, was a celebration of God. He needed to celebrate Thanksgiving through austerity, the absence of prosperity, in order to remember what he had.

And so he hiked deep into the wilderness, into the home of bobcat, skink, and rattlesnake, where the carrion birds turned gyres above the moribund and the slow, and the red-tailed hawk and kestrel perched at the woodbreak waiting for mice and voles and wrens. Handley, with sweat upon his back, hiked until the sun was four fingers from setting and then climbed down a ravine toward the place where he had decided he would sleep.

The fine cinnabar sand was soft, an easy bed, so he pitched his tent and spread his night-roll. No wind blew, and no clouds loitered the sky, so he did not concern himself with a rain fly or extra spikes to secure the tent. Handley took a long pull from his canteen and ate a piece of sourdough bread with a slab of summer sausage he had cut with his pocketknife, a knife that once belonged to his grandfather, a knife that bore his grandfather's initials, the initials of the man who last year had left the head of the Thanksgiving table vacant, who had gone and crossed over to Paradise, to the streets of golden memory.

Handley sliced another slab of sausage and ate it in two bites, and then he wiped the blade clean on his pants leg and put the knife back in his pocket. This was his Thanksgiving meal, and he was grateful for what he had received.

Looking all around him, he considered the ancient tribe that lived among these hoodoos and canyons before the Spaniards or Comanches or Anglos came, the Folsom people, who left on this land stacks of bones with bison skulls atop them, remnants of rituals to the spirit of the animal perhaps, remnants of rituals to thank the buffalo for its place in the circle, or rather, perhaps, to thank the Great Spirit, though no one really knew, for this was a place where archaeology and fiction converged.

Perhaps Thanksgiving was best celebrated by giving thanks to all the beings that suffered or died for the meal. Perhaps it was best to honor and pray to the plants and animals that provided sustenance. Perhaps it was best to pray Godspeed and peaceful travels until the reunion in life's next cycle.

He thought about the time he attended mass in Spanish with his girlfriend, Paloma, in the town below the mountain where he earned his daily bread. He remembered the priest. He remembered how he mentioned *amor encarnado*, love incarnate, *carne* meaning flesh, meat, and so we ate meat, and God became meat, became the Body, the Blood, and was taken and consumed in the name of Love. Were the Son of God and the Great Buffalo one and the same? Holy beings who offered their meat, their lives, for the nourishment of others? Holy beings who made a sacrifice beyond simply death, a sacrifice of unfathomable intimacy, the sacrifice of giving one's very muscles and bones and organs for another's enjoyment and survival, to allow another to taste one's liver and heart and flanks, to allow another to consume one's own body part by part by part. There is, perhaps, no greater sacrifice than to give one's very self. At first, Handley thought that even Jehovah, the Everlasting God, had not even offered His own bread and wine but then considered the Trinity, and how the Son was God, and so God, through the consciousness of the Holy Spirit that permeated the physical being of His Son, had in reality also sacrificed Himself.

Handley then thought about the piece of sausage he had just eaten, the animal or animals it contained, and even plants, were it to contain fillers, and he thought about how the animal no longer had a face or any other distinctive feature. It was simply protein, packaged in a form that distanced him from death and the animal that died for him. He was distanced from the life it lived, a life most likely enjoyed on the South Texas range before being loaded into a boxcar or onto a cattle truck and being hauled to a slaughterhouse to have a captive bolt pistol fired between its eyes. And then the body would be sawed apart and the flesh processed until Death, or even the identity of the animal itself, would be nothing more than a tangential thought, like the thought he was having now.

Perhaps Handley should have simply chosen to fast. He should have fasted. Like the desert fathers, the hermits whose words were translated by Thomas Merton, the Trappist mystic of Kentucky. In the consumer intensity of these days, he thought it best not to consume, for some lesson could surely be learned from that, for middle-class American life had become an interminable feast, a never-ending pageant of self-congratulation and narcissism in the name of piety. Thank you, Lord, for all you have given us, for the blessings you have bestowed upon us, the people pray as if the blessings and good fortune they have enjoyed are evidence of their goodness, their righteousness, their piety, a conclusion drawn from the homilies of the preachers of prosperity, the apostles of a gospel where Christ's words are written in green and Job is just a poor man from the wrong side of the Bible.

Handley thought about how all this frustrated him, how he himself had once been described as a Christian man with a Buddhist heart, though he did not think of himself as particularly Buddhist, other than the fact that he believed that each individual has his or her own path, and he did not like the term Christian, but rather considered himself a believer in Christ, for the term Christian now seemed to be too closely aligned with callous Samaritans and economic stances that threatened mite-less widows and children without fathers. Handley knew quite well that his blood kin, his aunts, uncles, and even his parents subscribed to this way of thinking, and though he truly loved them, he could not understand how they justified beliefs that ran contrary to what he had been taught on childhood Sunday mornings.

Handley, however, did not consider himself any more holy than anyone else. He himself had taken the Lord's name in vain, coveted his neighbor's wife, borne false witness, dishonored the Sabbath, and committed adultery, even though the arrangement was consensual with both the man and his wife. He had, after thinking about it, broken every commandment except thou shalt not kill, though he had killed deer and dove and quail for amusement rather than need, which was most surely a sin. So he was, he well understood, hardly a righteous man.

Handley looked up at the deep blue sky, prayed to his God, and then reached into the dust and prayed to the soil and the ever-giving Earth before praying to the unknown animal that had been transfigured into sausage. Hoc est corpus, he said without irony. And then he prayed thanksgiving to love incarnate, love turned into meat, and he would not eat again until morning, or perhaps later, until Black Friday, the antithesis of Good Friday, had ended, and then he would walk back out of the wilderness hungry and perhaps cleaner of spirit, mind, and body, perhaps better than he had been when he entered, and more thankful than he could ever imagine.

The Lord Ain't Willing, and the Creek's Done Rose
★ ★ ★

The rain crashed against the windshield of the old Lincoln Continental so violently that the sound nearly drowned out "The Old Rugged Cross," which was playing at top volume on the radio. Karl Feller, with his eyes in a squint and his jaw set tight, drove down a county road he had driven all his life, though he could not see where he was going. And though the windshield wipers could not keep up with the rate that the rain was falling, Karl still felt fairly certain that he and his wife were about two hills away from the high water crossing at Fiddler Creek.

"Myrtle, I reckon we oughta turn around," he said, his long, thin fingers clutching the steering wheel.

His wife, in a pink chiffon dress and costume pearls, twisted her lips slightly.

"We can't turn around. We have to go to church."

"We may have to watch church on TV this morning."

"You just don't want to go to church. You'll use any excuse you can find so you don't have to go to church."

"That's bullshit."

"There you are. Cussing on your way to the House of the Lord. That's a good example for your granddaughters."

"They ain't in the car."

"No, they're not. But that's no excuse. You should drive as if Jesus and

53

your granddaughters were all riding in the backseat."

Although he didn't say it, Karl didn't think he had enough seatbelts in the backseat for three granddaughters and Christ Almighty. But, then, he figured that if Christ wanted to ride with them, he'd do a loaves and fishes style trick and provide enough seatbelts for everybody.

"I'm ready to get to church and see our granddaughters in their cute little dresses we got them. I bet they all look so sweet," Myrtle said.

"I bet they do. But I think Fiddler Creek may be too high to cross."

"We can't miss church on Easter Sunday."

"If we cain't get across the creek, then I reckon we don't have no choice."

The car glided down the second hill, where Karl could see a yellow diamond-shaped road sign that he knew warned of high water, though he could not read the sign for the downpour. At the low spot at the bottom, where they always had to watch for deer when driving at night, there was a stream now coursing across the road.

"Easter or no Easter, that water's traveling pretty damn fast," Karl said.

"We have to go see those babies. And what would people think if we missed church on Easter Sunday?"

"Today they'd think we were sensible."

"Drive, Karl. We're going to be late."

Karl stopped on the road just shy of the moving water. He turned on his hazards so no one would hit them in the ass-end. Then he pulled at his clip-on tie like he was struggling to breathe. Although he often tugged at his tie, Karl enjoyed wearing one to church on Sunday mornings because it made him look important, like the bosses in the air-conditioned office up at the rock quarry where he worked until finally retiring eight years ago. At this point, Karl thought about removing his tie, but he figured that would piss Myrtle off. She would, without a doubt, use it to further her case about him not wanting to go to church.

Karl wished he would have gotten Myrtle under control fifty years ago, but he never did. He had always let her run over him. When he thought about it, he figured he had allowed her to behave that way because she was the most beautiful girl he had ever seen, and he never wanted to lose her at any cost, even if that cost sometimes included his dignity. He had been in love with her for more than five decades, and she had doled out her love like treats for a dog, little bites at a time, which left him constantly hungry, constantly starving for her love and her body. Yet she doled out those favors, that affection, at close enough intervals to keep him nearby. And when he was not at work, he never wanted her out of his sight, though still she did as she pleased.

Karl had let her throw dinner plates at him, had let her tell him what she was and was not going to do, despite the fact that she had no money or connections. All she had was her beauty and her will, and somehow that was enough. When they met, she was wearing a tow sack dress that her mother had made her, and now she had a closet full of fine, beautiful clothes. She had dresses and slacks and all kinds of accessories, clothes he had spent lots of money on, and though he was glad to have given her what he had given her, still he found it hard. She always seemed to want more than he could ever give. And yet he had given her all of the material things she asked for, a diamond ring so big that it intimidated other women, and men as well, and a brick house with an above-ground swimming pool, and that was not everything. None of it was sustainable, though it had somehow been sustained for years and years.

But then, maybe his allowing her to run over him had nothing to do with her beauty or her will, Karl thought. Maybe it was because he had lost both of his parents during the Depression and was raised by his aunt and uncle, which had always left him feeling like a walking imposition, a person for whom assertiveness could only lead to trouble. Even today he avoided conflict the best he could, though it was perhaps just a habit left over from his precarious childhood. Back when he was a boy, he was always the outsider in any dispute, even if he was blood kin. His cousins' parents would hardly be backing him in an argument against their own children. And he knew that his aunt and uncle had taken him on, grimly, out of a sense of duty, and though he had not always felt loved, he had been fed, and that was enough for a child born in the years when red dust rose like a storm.

"I'm turning around," Karl said, putting the car in reverse.

Myrtle reached for his shoulder.

"I will not cross the Jordan alone," Myrtle said.

"That ain't no Jordan. It's just Fiddler Creek. And only a fool would cross it running that high."

"The girls will be so disappointed if we don't make it to church. Drive."

"I ain't driving."

Karl looked into the rearview mirror hoping no one would hit them in the tail-end and ruin his Silver Star Medal license plate, which was, in his opinion, the only good result of the war he had fought.

"Myrtle, we done been married fifty years, and I have always done what you want me to do, but I don't think it's wise to drive through this high water."

The radio played "I'm Coming Home," and Karl changed the station for the first time in what must have been ten years. He didn't know how he'd listened to those same damn church songs for so long.

"What will people think?" Myrtle asked.

"From what I can tell, the Lord ain't willing, and the creek's done rose. And hell, I don't much care what people think either way."

"They'll take note. I just know they will."

No, they won't, Karl thought. They won't care, and if they do care they aren't worth worrying about anyway. They are dull, shallow, and narrow-minded. Such people will always find something to gossip about, be it his breath, his boots, or the feisty mare he could never seem to handle.

But he did hold the reins. He held the reins when it mattered. He held the reins when she threatened divorce two decades ago. He held the reins when she stomped and cried about wanting to change bankers. He held the reins when their youngest daughter became pregnant and wanted them to let her and her dope-smoking hippie boyfriend live there at the house until they got on their feet. Karl never let that happen, nor would he ever. He was not going to support some sandal-wearing candy-ass who was not man enough to solve the problems he had made for himself. That just was not the way Karl thought.

"Drive, Karl," Myrtle said.

Still, people always thought Myrtle wore the denim. They thought she made the decisions, and Karl resented it. He resented it. And he resented the hateful glances she gave him in public, with him too considerate to tell

56

her to go to hell. She had always been that way. He never liked to argue with other people around, so she had run over him in public although he held his own at home. He resented that. He truly resented it. He would give her what she wanted. He would give her what she deserved, and he did not give a damn if it was short-sighted. He would just drive into the floodwater. He would just drive into the stream, and if they made it across, that would be fine. It would be as if the car had been baptized in Fiddler Creek. And if they didn't make it across, then he had made the choice to be washed downstream.

"Drive, Karl," Myrtle said.

And so he drove. He drove slowly, and though he soon found himself pressing hard on the gas, the car was already afloat and traveling along the newborn river past cypress and cedar and oak. The car was moving quickly, and water was now entering the cab, the world outside the windows bobbing and bucking as the town car traveled with the wild current, the smell of gasoline from the flooded engine thick in the air as the water filled the floorboard and quickly rose up to the couple's knees as they sat strapped to the upholstered seats.

"Why did you go?" Myrtle screamed. "Why did you listen to me?"

"I did what you asked me to do," Karl said. "And nothing more."

The water, cool and fast, filled the car as it sunk.

The Dolph Hofner Hops Fest
★ ★ ★

Daniel Zima pushed his walker toward the wide-open doors of Panther Springs Hall on Farm to Market 1190 a few chug-holed miles outside of Krasna Lipa, Texas. Wild Bill Lemsky, who had picked him up at the nursing home and brought him to the dancehall for the Dolph Hofner Hops Fest, stepped cautiously along beside him, never straying more than an arm's length away. The dancehall had recently been renovated by a couple from Oregon, and Daniel, who was covering the event for the *Texaský rolník*, the *Texas Farmer*, newspaper, smiled as he crossed the threshold, though he smiled like a man who had encountered the ghost of someone he loved.

"*To není možné*," Daniel said. "I can hardly believe it. When I was a younger man, I spent many a Saturday night on that dancefloor over yonder."

"I'll tell you what. I chased my share of ladies and drank my fill of barley pop here when I was a pup. And I'm happy as a dadgum lark to see this place open again."

Although he did not mention it, for it was too difficult to say, Daniel had first danced with his future wife, Andulka, here at Panther Springs. The hall looked much like it did today, though there were no colored lights strung along the rafters and no Texas flag hanging at the back of the stage the night he fell in love with Andulka. Until being reopened a few months ago, the dancehall, which was all that remained of the old Panther Springs settlement, had been shuttered for almost twenty years, and Daniel thought it a wonder that these folks from Oregon had been able to bring it back to life.

For many years, Brangus cattle had grazed around the abandoned building or loitered in the shade of the nearby treaty oaks. And though the dancehall now stood alone, Daniel knew that it was once surrounded by a general store, a cotton gin, and a couple of smaller businesses. But a drought in the 1950s had, despite the word springs being in the town's name, caused the place to dry up and become deserted. Only the dancehall, which always purchased a quarter-page ad in the *Texas Farmer* to announce its monthly dances and special events, didn't go bankrupt. Then, in the 1980s, a tornado came and leveled the abandoned cotton gin, general store, and every other derelict building in Panther Springs, though by some strange miracle the dancehall was left untouched, a story which, of course, made the front page of the paper. After escaping that calamity, the dancehall enjoyed a good, prosperous decade and a half before the economic twister that arrived at the turn of the twenty-first century caused the ailing owners, after many weeks of soul-searching, to board up the windows and shut the place down.

Daniel took a seat at a long wooden bench and placed his walker, which he called the Silver Stallion, beside him at the head of the table.

"*Pivo* for you?" Wild Bill asked.

Daniel grinned and touched the brim of his old straw hat.

"I didn't think that was a question," he laughed. He reached for his wallet.

"Keep your greenbacks in that there moth trap," Wild Bill said, strolling over to the bar.

Daniel sat on the bench admiring the dancehall, which was essentially a long, rectangular barn with a polished wooden floor. On days like today, when the weather was good, the wooden flaps that ran the length of the building were propped open to let in sunlight and fresh air. In the past, Daniel remembered, there was a "Men's" sign above a door near the stage, but it simply led outside to a giant oak tree, where the men would go to perform the duties of nature. The new owners had actually built concrete and sheet iron facilities for both sexes not far from that old tree. And though Daniel was not always an advocate of so-called progress, he did feel that the addition of proper toilets was a move in the right direction.

Daniel took his steno pad out of the pocket of his checkered western shirt and began to take notes. Although he was the publisher, editor, and lone reporter for Waylon County's only Czech-language newspaper, due to his advanced age he did not always cover every story in person. However, there was no way he was going to miss covering the first annual Dolph Hofner Hops Fest. Dolph Hofner was a Texas music legend who played everything from Western Swing to honkytonk to the occasional polka, and Daniel had first danced with his future wife on a night when Dolph Hofner and his Pearl Wranglers were playing at this very hall. Hofner, a Texas-Czech boy himself, had been gone a few years now, though Daniel still listened to his music in the converted janitor's closet that served as the newspaper office at the nursing home where he lived.

Wild Bill returned to the table with a couple of pilsner beers. He handed one to Daniel, who laughed and raised it up for a toast.

"*Na zdraví*," the newsman said.

"*Na zdraví*," replied Wild Bill, and they turned up their bottles.

Wild Bill, who was long and tall with sharp features, looked down at the abundant recompense of case after case of ice-cold beer that was evident above his belt buckle. Sitting there on the bench, he proceeded to button the top button of his western cut blazer, which managed to cover the majority of his belly. After drinking about half a beer, Wild Bill checked his watch.

"Are you about to go saw on that fiddle?" Daniel asked.

"Not quite yet. The other ol' boys ain't even showed up for soundcheck yet," Wild Bill said. "I hope you don't mind being here a little early."

"Early's fine with me. In fact, it's probably better. I can take a few notes and get my story started. So, are you going to sing for us?"

"Mostly I'll be playing fiddle. But I'll sing the Czech songs since I'm the only one who knows all the words. I'll sing 'Stara Kovarna' and the 'Shiner Polka.'"

"Well, I'm looking forward to hearing you. And *děkuju*. I appreciate you bringing me with you."

"No problem at all. Glad you could come. And I'm looking forward to reading your story in the paper. Or hearing about it at least, since, well, you know, I'm fairly illiterate in Czech. Do you have any ideas about what you're gonna write?"

"Well, to start it off, I think I'll probably write about how every dancehall is unique, how each one has its own character and personality. Then I'll talk about how Panther Springs is no exception. I'll talk about how it's not tied to the church or a fraternal organization like a lot of other halls around here, which makes it kind of different."

"I think that'll be real good."

"I probably already told you this, but Andulka and I saw Elvis play here before anybody knew who he was. I'll mention that, too."

"Well, I'll be durn. I didn't realize you were at that show."

"Yessir, my wife and I were here that night. We saw Elvis play on that stage over there when he was touring with the Louisiana Hayride. And the next day, the day after the show, everybody who saw him play talked about how bad he was. Then, a few months later, when he was more famous than Eisenhower, we all talked about how great he was."

"Did he shake his pelvis?"

"He did. I didn't quite know what to think about that, and none of the other ol' boys did either. But the girls all watched him close, closer than we did for sure, though I don't believe any of them would've admitted to liking the way he danced. Andulka was the most free-spirited girl in the bunch, and not even she would admit it, though she did kind of smirk when she was trying to deny it. And then ol' Elvis became the King. Who would've thought?"

Wild Bill was taking a long draw from his beer when men with guitars slung across their backs came walking into the hall lugging amplifiers. Wild Bill smiled at Daniel and then stood up.

"I'll be back faster'n a minnow can swim a dipper," Wild Bill said.

Daniel Zima nodded. Even though it was early, he was worried that there weren't nearly enough people in the hall. If the hall was going to remain in business, they would need a lot more folks paying a cover charge and buying drinks. A couple of young tourists marveling at their lack of cell

62

phone reception sat at a table close to the stage. Across the room, a former high school football star in a black leather jacket drank beer at the bar, and Daniel wondered how many more beers he would race through before he would not be able to hold up a motorcycle, much less ride one.

Daniel understood why the couple from Oregon had decided to have the Dolph Hofner Hops Fest. They needed credibility. Daniel already knew what the letters to the editor would be like after he published his story. Readers would complain that the couple were outsiders, yet Daniel felt that without them, the dancehall might still be closed, and there would be no celebration of this great Texas music artist. There would simply be a boarded-up dancehall with skunks living under it.

The owners, who Daniel recognized from a picture in the local English-language paper, the *Waylon County Messenger*, were talking with the band. Both were about thirty-five years old. The woman was dark-haired and beautiful, and the man, who was red-headed and stocky, wore a button-down shirt with sleeves rolled up to the elbow, revealing massive forearms covered in a byzantine network of green-tinted tattoos. The couple appeared to have an easy-going, unassuming relationship, a relaxed sort of love that reminded Daniel of his relationship with Andulka. He liked seeing how they interacted with one another. They were a team, partners for life it seemed, and considering that this was the dancehall's first big event since reopening, Daniel knew that the couple, despite appearing very laidback and composed, had lots of work to do, so he would wait until the bands had finished playing and the patrons had gone home for the night before approaching the couple for an interview.

After sound check, Wild Bill brought the old newsman another beer, and Daniel, though he enjoyed an ice cold *pivo*, wondered how difficult it was going to be to make it to the outside facilities on his walker. He decided that he had better practice moderation, so he sat on the bench and nursed his beer as the crowd slowly drifted in.

By the time the sun began to set, the place was almost packed, and when Wild Bill's band started playing the "Alamo Rag," the dance floor filled with people young and old. Daniel was happy to see this. He was happy to see the carousel of dancers moving around the floor. There were people in boots and tennis shoes and even sandals. Daniel was happy to see love both young and old upon the dance floor. He thought about his own wife, a woman he had lost eight years prior, a woman who had been vivacious and beautiful, a woman who had a shining, gorgeous soul, who had somehow left this Earth far before her time.

Daniel looked up at the stage where Wild Bill was easing along on his long-stroked Bohemian fiddle and smiling at the couples now sliding across the sawdust. To Daniel, it felt like the old days, the days when every farmer in Waylon County would be there with his wife, dancing and drinking and laughing. Though Daniel's wife was gone, he could somehow feel her presence. Daniel stood up and grabbed his walker. And he danced. He danced where he was standing, one foot past the other in a heavy-footed shuffle, and he thought about Andulka, and how she guided him across the dance floor, always making it appear as if he were leading as they danced deep into the night.

He missed her. He missed those old times, and he was thankful to the couple from Oregon who, even though their name was not Novak or Zima or Kovar, were vital to the preservation of the local culture and would help perpetuate it for generations to come. Daniel was thankful to have a chance to be in the dancehall again, to remember his first dance with his future wife, to have the opportunity to honor her memory, to cherish it.

Daniel sat down at the long bench and began to write. He wrote about all he saw, all he heard. Wild Bill drew down on the first verse of the "Cotton-Eyed Joe," giving Daniel a nod and a wink. Young, middle-aged, and old all danced around the hall. There was laughter and joy and beauty. Daniel wrote and wrote. He wrote with heart and conviction and joy, for he felt that his wife, his sweet Andulka, was with him and that the old times had somehow returned.

Buckshot McGee's Odd Destiny
★ ★ ★

"I hope I have enough beer to live through the apocalypse," Buckshot McGee said as he sat in his easy chair stroking his wooly beard.

"I hope so, too, dear," his wife, Becky, told him while sanitizing the doorknobs with a mixture of rubbing alcohol and tap water, "but I'm more worried about toilet paper. We only have one roll of Fluff left."

"Baby, we've got enough asswipe to live through two apocalypses," Buckshot replied and then spat tobacco juice in the direction of the brass spittoon on the floor beside him.

Becky, straightening the hem of her polka dot house dress, started chastising him for missing the spittoon, but her voice could not be heard over the machine gun a supermodel in pink camouflage was firing at feral hogs from a helicopter on television.

"That woman, from a moving vehicle, that is flying no less, just hit a hog on the run at four hundred yards, and you can't even hit the spittoon beside your chair," Becky told her husband once the camera focused in on the splattered hog and cut to a hemorrhoid commercial.

"Didn't you hear what the chopper pilot said?" Buckshot told her. "That was four hundred and fifty yards, with a crosswind. That woman is a hell of a shot."

"And you can't hit a spittoon just below your chair?"

"Becky, please stop chewing on my ass. I'll aim better next time. And we've got lots of toilet paper. And ammunition, too. Got plenty of both to get us through the end times."

"Buckshot, these are not the end times. It's the flu. Just a really bad flu season. The commentators on the president's news channel said everything was fine. No big deal. And they know. If they didn't know, they wouldn't be on television. And if it were the end times, we wouldn't have enough toilet paper to live through one apocalypse, much less two of them. And the Bible doesn't say anything about there being two of them. There's only that one in the Book of Revelations. But either way, honey, regardless of all that, we only have one roll of toilet paper left."

"We only have one roll of Fluff. That stuff is like wiping your rump with a bunny rabbit. I ain't got no use for no damn Fluff. And you know damn well we got lots of asswipe. We got good deer camp asswipe. We've got half a bunker full of it."

"It's like sandpaper. I hate it."

"Sandpaper gets the job done. It might take off a little hide and hair, but it leaves you clean as a whistle. And well, the deer camp stuff is all we got, so after that roll of Fluff, you'll have to live with it. There's not a store in all of Waylon County with a single roll of anything on the shelf."

About that time Buddy and Dumptruck came sprinting from Buckshot's gun room. They were Buckshot and Becky's grandboys, and they loved their grandparents more than eating ice cream or even throwing rocks at passing cars. Buddy, a freckle-faced seven-year-old with a bowl haircut, jumped up into Buckshot's lap and inadvertently dropped a bony knee into his solar plexus before bounding back to the floor. Dumptruck, who was short and stout and sometimes soiled his pants despite being in kindergarten, came racing a few steps behind his brother. He also jumped up to hug his grandfather, and, in his excitement, stomped his grandfather's groin with both of his wide, bare feet, causing Buckshot to double over in his chair and swallow a fair amount of tobacco spit.

"You stepped on his tentacles," Buddy said. "Dumptruck, you shouldn't step on Papa's tentacles."

"I don't even know what that is," Dumptruck said, the grape juice stain around his mouth vaguely resembling a goatee. "You cain't step on something if you don't know what it is."

"You stepped on his dadgum tentacles," Buddy continued. "You gotta be careful. Memaw done said."

"That's right," Becky declared while picking up her flyswatter. "You boys need to be careful. We cain't have any more of that roughhousing. There's not an empty bed in all of Waylon County Hospital, so we cain't afford anybody getting hurt."

The boys stood still and faced forward as if they were standing in line at school. Becky, seeing that order had been restored, hung her flyswatter back on its nail beside the kitchen door.

"Papa, can we go out to the bunker and load some shotgun shells?" Buddy asked.

"Of course y'all can. But load double-aught buck. Don't load any bird shot. We won't need any of that these days. And go light on the gunpowder. The last time I shot some of y'all's shells, my ol' shotgun kicked like a mule, and I think I might've even singed my eyebrows."

"We'll be careful, Papa," Buddy said. "It ain't like we're stupid."

"Nah, neither one of ya'll is stupid. But you're both still fairly little to be loading ammunition on your own. I'm just telling you boys to be careful."

"We can do it by ourselves, Papa."

"I know you can," Buckshot said. "but I might come out in a little while and help y'all."

The two boys seemed satisfied with that answer.

"Hey, Buddy," Dumptruck said. "You know how you got them freckles? Somebody threw dog poop at you through a screen door."

"That's Papa's joke, except that he doesn't say 'poop.' And at least I don't poop my pants like you do."

"I don't poop my pants," Dumptruck replied.

"You don't poop your pants every day."

Dumptruck sat down on the floor and started to cry.

"Stop blubbering, Dumptruck," Papa said. "If you cain't stand the heat, stay out of the kitchen."

"Have you boys finished all your schoolwork today?" Memaw asked. "I know y'all's teachers sent work to do because I heard them say it on the Internet this morning. Have you two done all your work?"

"I ain't done my math yet," Buddy said.

"Well, why not?"

"Didn't much want to."

"Well, you have to. Go back in y'all's room and do your math. If you need help, ask your Papa. He's good at math. He has to do math all the time when he's delivering car batteries."

"What about you, young man?" Becky asked Dumptruck. "Do you still have schoolwork to do?"

"I've got to work on my numbers. And I still need to write about my family," Dumptruck said, shifting his weight from one foot to the other. "Memaw, will I get to have my birthday party at the putt-putt place next week?"

"I'm afraid not. Everybody has to stay home because of the virus."

"So I won't get to turn six?"

"You'll still turn six. It's just that we'll have to eat cake here at the house. It'll be lots of fun. Now you two boys go back to your room and finish your schoolwork. Y'all's teachers will be asking about it when they talk to your classes on the Internet tomorrow."

"Yes, ma'am," the two boys said and then ran toward their room, crashing into one another about halfway down the hall and knocking a picture from their parents' wedding onto the carpet. Becky did not even bother to comment. She just shook her head and returned the photo to its place, tilting her head to assure that it was level, though she had to adjust it again after one of the boys slammed the door to their room shut. Then, with worry on her brow, she returned to the living room to talk with her husband.

"I don't think it's the end times," she said, standing next to Buckshot's chair. "But I do think God is punishing our country."

"For what?"

"For keeping businesses open on Sunday, for not letting the courts have monuments to the Ten Commandments outside of them, for not allowing prayers to our sweet Lord Jesus at high school football games. Things like that."

"I don't know. All I know is that I'm mighty glad we have lots of ammunition. And plenty of provisions, too."

"It's not going to come to the point of having to use your machine gun to protect the toilet paper."

"I'm talking about protecting us, protecting our family. You just never know what will happen."

Buckshot spat a tight amber arc of tobacco juice into the spittoon on the floor and did not miss a drop. This point in time, this strange new era, was the one he had been waiting for all of his life. His wife had constantly questioned him about why he thought he needed to have dozens of guns. Shotguns and pistols and rifles. A semi-automatic with a bump stock that pretty much made it a machine gun. She just didn't understand.

For the last twenty-three years, Buckshot, whose nametag read Larry, had worked for Charge Master Batteries delivering their products to auto part stores and garages all across the Hill Country. The job was not particularly demanding, but it was also not particularly interesting. Every weekday for more than two decades he had driven the same roads, spoken to the same people, and laughed at the same old jokes. And now, he would finally be what he had always wanted to be, a man taking on the world like the gun-slingers of yore, a man whose true purpose had finally become apparent.

Buckshot put on his leather vest and crocodile boots, slid a pistol into the waistband of his jeans, and walked out the front door into the open air. The air was fresh and clean, though it all felt strange. It all felt different. He wondered if he had enough beer. Maybe he did, but if he didn't, he could probably stand to shed a few pounds of belly anyway. But then, maybe he could still buy it somewhere, or at least swap a little toilet paper or some bullets for a case or two. He paced the yard with his nostrils flared and his eyes sharp and vigilant as if he were a ranger on patrol, listening intently, distrustfully, to sounds he had always known, to the sound of leaves rustling on the pecan tree near the sidewalk, to the flags flapping above the porch, and the relentless staccato of the lawn sprinkler pivoting in the distance.

Well, Buckshot thought, no matter what happened, no matter what came his way, he felt truly ready to rise up to his life's greatest challenge, his life's most venerable struggle, whether it be defending his family in the end of days or the fulfillment of some other odd destiny.

Football Cards

★ ★ ★

Charles Hopkins sat on the third row in Miss Tomball's fourth grade class at Moses Austin Elementary School in the little town of Warnell, Texas, wearing a blue and silver sweater with a Dallas Cowboys star on the chest. His black, curly hair was closely shorn, and his caramel-colored skin was smooth and healthy-looking. It was almost Thanksgiving, and the room was decorated with turkeys made from the outlines of the students' hands. Charles had been making turkeys like that every year since he was in kindergarten, and he thought that the activity was for babies, but he wouldn't tell Miss Tomball. He loved her and would maybe even marry her if she could wait until he finished college in twelve years, which was a long time, but it would be worth it. He liked how Miss Tomball didn't wear shirts with apples on them like the other elementary school teachers did. He liked that she wore jeans and rhinestone flipflops and was so, so pretty with her long blond hair and sweet smile. And she always called him "Sugar Pie," which he loved even if it did kind of sound like a name for little kids.

A couple of weeks ago, she had called him over to talk to her during lunch. Charles liked that he was the only one called to the teachers' table, where Miss Tomball told him that a new student would be coming and that he would be Charles's partner. The boy would sit next to Charles, and Charles would need to teach him everything about the class and show him how to be a good citizen. The new kid was coming from another school, and he wouldn't have any friends yet, so the boy would need Charles to

71

show him around. Charles assured Miss Tomball that he would take good care of the new kid for her, and he did.

The new kid's name was Samuel Green. He was pale with a dirty face and wild dark hair. His teeth were yellow, and his breath stank, but he offered Charles a dip of snuff by the back fence during recess his very first day, so Charles didn't complain. Samuel wore the same green corduroy pants every day, though he did change T-shirts every two or three days. He talked kind of slow, and his speech was a bit hard to understand sometimes, but he was not too bad. Samuel was a nice enough guy, Charles thought. He was kind of dirty, and his feet stunk through his shoes, but he was friendly enough.

Either way, Charles liked Samuel and did his best to help him. He explained how to work math problems since Samuel's old school was in a different place in the book, and he showed Samuel how to find text evidence when they had to answer questions in reading class. Charles also told Samuel that the best way to keep out of detention was to always say "yes, ma'am," whether he was in trouble or not. Samuel seemed grateful for all the help, and after a short time sitting next to one another, the two boys considered themselves friends.

This morning the class had just returned from recess. There had been a few flurries of great big snowflakes, which excited all of the students, considering that it was Texas and it normally didn't even snow at Christmas, much less the week before Thanksgiving. When they got back inside the classroom, Samuel was still shivering since he never brought a jacket to school. He told Charles that he had a brand-new Dallas Cowboys team jacket at home, but he could never remember to bring it.

Lunch was only twenty minutes away, and Charles reached into his pocket and rattled his lunch money. Samuel never brought lunch money. He told the lunchroom lady a number, and he got a lunch. There were a few kids like that in Charles's class. Charles just figured their mamas and daddies paid a different way. With only a few minutes left before lunch, Miss Tomball had the students all work with a partner. For the last two weeks, Charles and Samuel had always been partners. Charles was happy to help the new boy, and he was glad that Miss Tomball had called on him to do so.

"I'll be glad when it's time for lunch," Samuel said.

"Me too. It's been a long time since breakfast."

"I didn't have no breakfast this morning."

"Why not?"

Samuel looked away.

"Well, I guess I forgot to eat. Hey, Charles, I want to show you something."

He pulled a stack of bent-up football cards from his back pocket.

"I got the whole Cowboys team. Look at this. I got Aikman. The Moose. Emmitt Smith. Deion Sanders."

"Man, you've got them all."

"I'll give you Sanders and Smith if you want 'em."

"That's okay. I have their cards at home. I wouldn't want to take yours."

"No, take 'em. I want you to have 'em."

He held the rumpled cards toward Charles.

"That's nice of you, but I have them already."

Samuel looked frustrated.

"Take 'em."

"I don't know why you want to give away your stuff. Those are really good cards."

"My daddy told me to tear up the cards of all of the black players and throw them in the trash can."

"Why would he say that?"

"He's in some kind of secret rebel flag club, and they don't like hardly nobody. I think Emmitt Smith is the best player there ever was. I told my daddy that I tore up his card and the cards of all the other black players, but I didn't. I figured I'd give the cards to you since you like the Cowboys too, so at least somebody would have 'em."

Samuel offered Charles a small stack of cards. "These are all the black players I have," he said.

"Well, thank you," Charles replied as he reached out and took them. He placed the cards in his desk. "How about I keep the cards at my house, and you can come over and look at them whenever you want? They'd still be your cards. Would you like that?"

"That would be good. Real good. And my daddy wouldn't have to know that I went to your house. Like I said, Emmitt Smith is my hero. I didn't want to give his card away, but I sure didn't want to tear it up neither."

Charles looked up at the clock on the wall and then put his folder in his desk. When Miss Tomball saw Charles putting away his folder, she would notice that it was time for lunch. But Miss Tomball was helping a couple of girls with their work and now had her back to him, so Charles started to rattle the change in his pocket. It was already two minutes past time to line up. Samuel sat there staring at the clock as well. He seemed to be concentrating on something, and he had a sick expression on his face.

"Lunch time," Miss Tomball called. "Put everything away and get ready to line up."

Samuel gave Charles a slight, sad smile, and the two stood behind their chairs ready to go to lunch.

"We made it, brother," Charles said, reaching out to shake Samuel's hand.

Samuel stood still and looked at him for a moment, and then he slowly stepped forward, smiled an awkward smile, and extended his hand toward Charles.

Baby Head

★ ★ ★

Johnny Benton, in his cowboy hat, starched jeans, and boots with a walking heel, parked his truck alongside the state highway, stepped across a bar ditch, and headed toward the gate of Baby Head Cemetery. The cemetery, which was situated beneath a rugged hill of pink granite and Texas scrub, was all that remained of a settlement that bore that same grim name. The burial yard was surrounded by a chainlink fence, and invariably, it seemed, every time Johnny visited someone had strung doll heads on the gate with baling wire. Most likely, he figured, this was done by high school boys from the nearby town of Warnell when they had nothing better to do on a Saturday night. They seemed like odd totems, those plastic heads, and Johnny Benton thought of them as artificial surrogates for the trophies hung outside the lodges of warriors of bygone times, a physical warning of the danger within.

But there was no danger here. Not now anyway. And though Johnny Benton was unclear on many of the details, he knew that his family was tied to the history of this place and to the lore of its danger and horror, for his great-great aunt, a child of only four years old, was stolen and beheaded by Comanches, who then placed her head on a pike on the stone hill above. The Comanches, Johnny was told, thought this would make the outsiders leave. Instead, the outsiders named the settlement Baby Head, a gruesome reminder of the times, and stayed where they were.

Johnny Benton wondered where Nettie Louise, the little girl, was actually buried. He wondered if a chunk of granite or perhaps a long-gone wooden cross had marked her grave. There was no one to ask. The descendants of the Baby Head community, even the members of his own family, were now scattered throughout the county, and little had been passed down through the generations. There was no community knowledge, no local heritage. And perhaps the old-timers had remained reticent. Perhaps they had nothing they cared, or were even able, to say.

Johnny walked the cemetery silently, stepping around the headstones and contemplating the lives of people who had somehow become nothing more than a name and two dates in an out-of-the-way cemetery along a two-lane road. The oldest graves were of white marble, with bas reliefs of angels, lambs, and crosses upon them. Many of the graves were of children who had not yet reached their second year. The children had names, which was somewhat unusual, since many that young had not. They had simply been called "baby" until it appeared that they would manage to live. The children buried here, Johnny thought, never had the chance to truly live or enjoy life. They never had the chance to fall in love, to have a family, to pass on their values and traditions.

No one had been formally buried in the cemetery for more than half a century. And every settler family Johnny knew of had moved on or died away. The cemetery stayed mowed because Johnny mowed it. The cemetery had no weeds because Johnny sowed herbicide in early March and pulled thistle and crabgrass in the spring and summer. He wondered what would happen after he passed on. He had no children. No wife. No family. He had no one to pass the job on to. He had no one to teach the cemetery's secrets, or at least the secrets that he knew.

Once he had a wife, but he had one no longer. She had left him years ago. Once he had three children, but they all arrived stillborn. His heirs had come stillborn, one after the other, like drowned puppies from her womb, and he and his wife had had no taste to try again after that. They had seen the three arrive dead, one after the other, one hope after the other arriving dead, without life, death wrapped in a placenta, death in the shroud of life, and he and his wife would wager for the miracle no more. They had rejoiced in the gift of life but were given the blow of stillness thrice in a single day, and never would they try again. Never again would they wager on such a cause. They loved each other. That was true. They loved each other ever-more, but they became distrustful, dysfunctional, and they buttressed their love by exchanging the pills of propagation for the pills of prevention, and somehow after four more years the pain of intimate knowledge, the pain of constantly being reminded of the tragedy just by seeing one another's face became more than they could bear, though they never unhinged their lips to speak of it, for there was no expression to speak, no expression they cared to share, for reticence was their only savior, all that could save them from the madness and grief of that thrice-cursed day, and they would drift to different rooms and different beds before drifting to different lives, lives in twain, and banishing themselves from the garden of the pills of infertil-ity and the life they lived together. The tragedy had merged them together and then been their undoing. The act, the only act, the act of love, had become an act of trepidation, the act that could end in another calamity, a day of rough, arduous, dangerous birth that could once again end in lumps of death sprawled upon a white sheet.

Johnny walked toward the back fence of the cemetery and lay down in the grass looking up at the sky. The sky was blue and wide, and the clouds moved quickly, for Waylon County was a place where weather patterns col-lided, and he thought about the clouds and what they looked like, though to him they were nothing but clouds. He did not imagine seeing animals or ships or anything else. The clouds were simply clouds.

The plot where he lay had no headstone, for he had not yet ordered one. This was his grave. He had already bought it. And he had bought the plot next to it in case Deborah changed her mind. Above what would be both of their heads, he had buried the three boys, one next to the other, each in swaddling clothes and lying in a bed of limestone. He had buried each of them himself, with his own pick and shovel. He had chosen not to give them a tombstone, for that would have warranted chiseling their names, Shadrack, Meshack, and Abednego, upon their joint grave. He wished he could have just called them all baby, but these were not the times. The boys' location was unknown to anyone but Johnny and his former wife, though he knew in his heart she had not been to this cemetery in at least eight years, for he doubted her heart could take it.

Johnny lay in his place and looked into the sky. He felt comfort here. Comfortable to be lost with the others, comfortable among the other broken dreams, the other tragic losses, the obsession with a past and no honest hope for a future. He was comfortable to be in a place where all was stagnant, decayed, or gone, where all was in retrograde except the nourished green grass on which he lay. Perhaps Deborah would come back to him. Perhaps she would not. Perhaps it did not matter. It probably did not matter. He doubted it even mattered. Anyhow. He would lay on the grass in Baby Head, and he would not wait on anything or anyone, but then, he would not move on either.

Ivy Lee Jones and the Fisher of Fish
★ ★ ★

"Harlan, I think you love mudcats more than you love me," Ivy Lee Jones said with a finger in either end of a spool of twelve-pound test line.

Harlan was reeling fast, the fishing line zipping through the eyes of his graphite rod and onto his open-face reel. The two of them were standing in the middle of their garage, cat litter to absorb the transmission fluid that occasionally leaked from Ivy Lee's powder blue Buick on the floor between them. Harlan chuckled and kept reeling.

"I'm serious, Harlan," Ivy said.

"I know you are, but you do this every time I get ready to go fishing. And I don't love mudcat more than you. Hell, I don't even fish for mudcat."

"Then bass. You fish for bigmouth bass."

"Hell, Ivy, I love you more than bigmouth bass and mudcat combined."

"That's romantic. Real romantic."

"If you want me to stay, then I'll stay."

"If you want to go, then go. But you know this is Easter morning."

"Now that's a brain game. What's it matter to you? You ain't going to church. Not with me. Not alone. Not at all."

"If I want to, I will."

"You're not going. As soon as Reverend Norwell saw you walk into the doors of the church, he'd call an audible on his sermon and start harping on divorce. And there'd you be having to listen to his righteous bullshit three husbands deep."

Harlan reached out for the fishing line, cut it a couple of feet past his rod tip with a pocketknife, and put the rod on the rack by the livewell. He then reshaped the bill of his ball cap with either hand and smiled a half-cocked smile. His smile accentuated the width of his already wide jaw, which always seemed to be blue in color and in need of a shave. His gray eyes twinkled at Ivy, and then he continued speaking.

"Ivy, I love the Lord just as much as anybody else, but I ain't no fisher of men. I'm a fisher of fish. Men can do whatever the hell they want to do. It ain't none of my affair. The whole deal is between an ol' boy and God. And I reckon I'll talk to God while I'm out on the water. That's better than ol' Norwell's church. Nature is the cathedral of the Lord."

"Well, don't think you can use that line of bull to leave the house every weekend. You're not going to tell me that you're going to the big church on the water or whatever. I'm not buying what you're selling."

Harlan put his arms around her. He was long and thin and wiry, an electrician by trade, and his work dictated his shape like a trowel sculpts a brickmason's hand or sheetrocking gives a drywaller his triceps and lats. Harlan was light and well-proportioned because he had to be. Otherwise he'd fall through an attic. And he was smart. Of course, every electrician had to be smart, or he would be on the fast train to Jesus City.

"Well, Ivy Lee, I reckon I'd better go pick up Sand Bass Steve at his house before first light."

Ivy Lee thought about telling Harlan that he should have married Sand Bass Steve instead of her. She thought about telling him that the two of them would have made a better pair because Steve was always ready to go fishing. And then she would tell him that Steve was always ready to go fishing because he didn't have a job. And then Harlan would probably say something about Steve being on disability, and she would say that the only disability he had was that he drank so much beer he couldn't hold a job. But she didn't go there. She had been married enough times to know that holding her tongue was sometimes the best thing for a marriage.

"I imagine you should go pick him up," Ivy said as flatly as she could.

"Well, baby, I reckon I'd better git then."

He took her in his arms, and she responded in a temporary way, for it felt like a temporary arrangement, and Harlan held her tighter, held her in a way that let her know that he would not be gone long, though he was still going to leave. And although Harlan had told her that he hadn't picked fishing with Sand Bass Steve over her, Ivy still thought otherwise, for if he truly loved her, at this time of morning he would still be in bed with her languishing in love instead of getting ready to go sling a spinner bait in some snake-infested slough.

"All right, Harlan. Be careful."

Harlan gave her a sad, lukewarm smile. Ivy knew that he loved her enough to marry her but not enough to stay home every weekend. She also knew that she would be alright. She always was. At least, Ivy figured, Harlan would be around enough that the two of them would stay in love. And if being in love meant that they drank whiskey and slept together every Saturday night after watching a movie on cable and him getting up to go fishing on Sunday morning, then that was how everything was going to have to be.

One thing Ivy Lee knew was that it was always better to be the angler than the fish. And these days, she had found that it was best to set her drag loose when it came to men. Ivy had no intention to let them bust her line, so she gave her men plenty of slack, plenty of room to buck and pitch and splash once she had them on the hook. She could always wear them down, even the trophy catches, but she had learned through experience not to tighten the drag too much.

To her credit, Ivy truly had been patient and endured Harlan's real, not figurative, fishing all fall when they were still dating. And she had endured the jig and pig season of winter without a cross word between them. She just worked overtime, and that was fine. Working extra not only made money but saved money as well because she could set the thermostat low while she was gone and keep the electricity bill down. Now the spring had come, and the bluebonnets were in bloom. She wished Harlan would be there to drink coffee with her, to enjoy the spring morning with her, to talk about what was in the paper, to laugh about the horoscopes. But he was going fishing again.

"Ivy, you know that you can come with me," Harlan said.

"I know, Harlan. And you could go with me to get your toenails paint-ed," Ivy replied.

"I know. You don't like fishing, but I thought I'd ask anyway."

"That was very sweet of you."

Harlan hopped into his old pickup truck and backed it up to the garage to hitch up his boat, and Ivy guided him toward the tongue of the trailer as he looked into the rearview mirror.

"Left, left," Ivy hollered. "Left. Now the other left."

Once he was lined up, Harlan climbed out of the truck and cranked the tongue of the trailer onto the ball of his hitch and then clasped the chains onto the truck bumper and plugged in the running lights. He then got back into the truck and stomped on the brake.

"Good," Ivy said, giving him two thumbs up.

Harlan switched on the blinker, with Ivy giving him a thumbs up on both sides. Assured that the running lights were working, Harlan went inside, got his duffel bag, and put it in the cab of his truck. He then put his tackle box in one of the compartments of his boat. After everything was loaded, he walked over to Ivy Lee and took her in his arms one more time.

"I love you, baby," he said.

"Almost as much as a bigmouth bass," Ivy replied, and kissed him on the lips.

"I'll be back," he said as he climbed into his truck.

"Be careful out there. If there's lightning, get off the lake."

"Will do. Considering my line of work, I got a healthy respect for elec-tricity. See you this afternoon, baby."

Harlan pulled out of the garage. Ivy Lee Jones smiled a sad smile, waved, and closed the garage door. Maybe she was leaving too much slack in the line. Maybe she should have tightened the drag and reeled a little harder, but that had never worked before, and she doubted it would work now. She loved Harlan, and she figured that he loved her, too. And anyway, life was what life was, and that had to be good enough.

Preaching His Mother's Funeral

★ ★ ★

Reverend Ferrill Crenshaw sat on the side of the bed holding his mother's Bible. Although he knew she was a believer, she had never wanted him to be a preacher. Her own brother had been a youth pastor when he was young, and rumors had circulated about him sleeping with the pianist in the church nursery between Sunday services, though those rumors were not true. Her brother had been driven to the brink of self-annihilation from the humiliation that came with the completely unsubstantiated rumors, but rather than move on to another church and start again, he chose to end his ministry altogether. He took a regular job at an insurance company, and being a kind, honest man, he was well-liked and well-trusted.

Reverend Crenshaw wished his mother had asked that her brother officiate her funeral. Over the years, although he had left the ministry, her brother, his uncle, had always been a churchgoer, and he had officiated the services of a couple of their older, more reclusive relatives at the funeral home there in Warnell. Uncle Hollis, it seemed to the preacher, could deliver a eulogy with an almost supernatural ease. He spoke with compassion, comportment, and a casual reverence that calmed the storms of heart and spirit. He did not speak of streets of gold or gates adorned with pearls. He did not call mourners to the casket to be saved. He did not warn of Hell or brimstone. No. He spoke the words of the Psalmist, Walt Whitman, and William Blake. And he succored those gathered with the comfort of the words in red.

Perhaps it was his uncle's background in the ministry. But then, it could have been his work selling insurance policies. He could speak so candidly about dismemberment, accidental death, and cataclysmic acts of God. He could suggest with kind conviction the security of a twenty-dollar-a-month life insurance policy that would yield a stack of cash rising almost to heaven were a breadwinner to pass. He could speak so easily about such matters. Reverend Crenshaw knew this firsthand, for he had purchased one of those policies to ensure that his wife and children would be taken care of were he to leave this world and enter the afterlife unexpectedly. Enrollment rates rolled off Uncle Hollis' tongue like manna from heaven, and he could speak so matter-of-factly about these preparations for the future.

Preaching the funeral of one's own mother was considered a rite of passage for ministers, though this rite had nothing to do with the seminary or formal education. It was one of the yardsticks by which preachers measured themselves and a topic of preacher lore when they sat together for coffee at the convention. A good preacher could transcend his own personal grief and praise the glory of God. A good preacher could remove himself from the sorrow of his own mother's passing and find a way to glorify the Lord.

But Ferrill Crenshaw wished that he could have been passed over. His uncle would be at the funeral, in the family section, but he himself would have to preach the most difficult funeral of his life. He prayed to God that he would not lose his shit, and then he prayed forgiveness for his obscenity. He would have to do the preaching himself.

Logically, he understood why that was so. His uncle, good man that he was, was still considered a disgraced minister in the eyes of many of those who would be attending the funeral despite the fact that he was completely innocent of wrongdoing. Perception, in this case, mattered more than reality. In the small Texas town where their family had lived since the Republic, memory was long and well-preserved. In a single lifetime, a fallen man could see an expression of learned disapproval course the faces of four generations, starting from the golden age of trikes and bikes and skateboards to the age of canes and walkers and wheeled chairs.

Reverend Crenshaw sometimes wondered if his uncle's sister, his own mother, had started the rumor that ended his uncle's ministry. Perhaps she had been jealous of the attention he received. In a town so small, a preacher has influence and celebrity. Perhaps she derailed him because she herself was almost ignored when the two went somewhere together. Perhaps she thought the church was not the place for him to be. Perhaps she knew the troubles and snares that awaited, the scandals that flared over trifles and misunderstandings. Perhaps she knew the glass through which he would be observed, the glass that burned those below it with the full light of the sun. Perhaps she thought that she was saving him from this.

And now the Reverend Crenshaw was sitting on the edge of his mother's bed holding a King James Bible without blemish, a Bible with no notes in the margins, no underlined verses, no markers to hold chapter and verse. His mother had left no clues in her Bible, no signs of inspiration. She had left a virgin lamb, an *agnus dei* for him to somehow interpret. Reverend Crenshaw always used a person's Bible when writing their eulogy, and his mother's Bible appeared untouched, though surely she had read it in times of sorrow and trouble.

He did not want to tell a preacher's lies, a preacher's charitable lies, a preacher's merciful suspension of the truth at his mother's funeral. He did not want to say that she was a devout Christian woman who read God's word daily. He did not want to say that she was on fire for the Lord, that she provided a Christ-like example for others. When he was a boy, she had made sure that she got him to church, but as soon as the future reverend was able to drive himself, she no longer attended. And she told him that he could choose whether he went to church or not. She told him that he was practically a man now, so it was his decision. And he chose to go.

His mother never spoke about Christ or the Second Coming or life after death. She talked about dinner, about laundry, about whether or not Ferrill had done his homework. She did not curse. She did not covet. She did not drink. And she kept the Lord's commandments, but that was what was expected of anyone. She behaved the way she was supposed to behave, and the Reverend Crenshaw thought that his mother was more easily described as disciplined than devout. She was more conventional than charismatic.

Reverend Crenshaw desperately wanted to meet with his uncle to talk about the matter at hand. If he could get his uncle to preach this funeral, it would take a huge burden from his shoulders. So he called his Uncle Hollis, who immediately invited him to his house. In his uncle's old rock house, he was known as Ferrill, not Reverend Crenshaw, and he sat across a rough wooden table from his uncle, a white-bearded old man in a checkered flannel coat. They said grace, broke bread, and shared a pot of coffee.

"I never thought this day would come," Ferrill said, his hands around the brown clay cup on the table, his mother's Bible beside him.

"I know it. It's hard. You walk around in a fog. In a dream. But it ain't a good dream. But still it is a dream. Except that it's real. And sooner or later you'll come out of the dream. And everything that happened will be unchangeable."

"Would you like to preach my mama's funeral?"

Uncle Hollis leaned back and shook his head.

"Cain't do it," he said. "Wouldn't be right. Your mama said that she wanted you to do it."

"I don't think I can do it."

"I don't think you got a choice."

"There's always a choice."

"But there ain't always a good choice. There ain't always a choice you'll be proud of later. There ain't always a choice you would like to have following you around the rest of your life, following you to your own grave."

"I guess not. But I wish there was."

Uncle Hollis wrinkled his brow.

"But there ain't. Wish in one hand and shit in the other. See which one fills up first."

"You got any cream?"

"For what?"

"My coffee."

"I don't keep cream. And I don't use no sugar."

"I think I figured that out."

Uncle Hollis laughed and stroked his pate.

"I'm glad you figured that out. But you know I'm here to help you. I'll help you write her eulogy if you need me to."

"I appreciate it. It's kind of embarrassing really. A preacher that can't

86

write a eulogy."

"Well, under heavy fire, I reckon there's plenty of expert marksmen that cain't shoot to save their lives. So don't think twice about it. What do you remember about your mama?"

"That she was in charge. She always had to be in charge."

"She was kind of a domineering pain in the ass, I will admit."

"Come on, Uncle Hollis. She's not even in her grave yet."

Uncle Hollis took a draw of coffee.

"Then say she had authority."

"She had that," Ferrill said with a grin.

"Well, let's start working on this eulogy. Daylight's burning. What's marked in her Bible?"

Ferrill looked away. His uncle knew full well that his sister was no church-goer. He knew full well that she had no kind words for the church. He knew that she could very well have been an unbeliever, though she never would have said it. Now Ferrill wondered why he came here. He wondered why he had bothered to come to his uncle's place, for not only was he provided no easy answers, he was presented with ever more difficult questions.

"She didn't mark anything," Ferrill said. "Not even John 3:16."

"Then we cain't take that tack. It'd be easy if you could preach from her Bible. But if she never marked nothing, then there's nothing you can do with it."

Ferrill looked into his coffee. No sugar. No cream. No nothing.

"I loved my mama. Hard as it was, I loved my mama."

"I know you did, boy. But that ain't the right tack for a funeral either. A funeral ain't about your relationship with the deceased, even if the deceased was your mama. That makes a preacher look self-absorbed. And you sure as hell don't need the congregation clucking about that, saying that you didn't care about nobody but yourself and only cared about your own grief. Do what they taught you in seminary. Talk about God. A funeral ain't really about the dearly departed. It's about God."

"Then what should I say about God?" the preacher asked.

Uncle Hollis smiled.

"Hell, preacher, you should say that God has a plan, and that this was

87

part of it."

Ferrill shook a memory from his head. Or at least he tried to. He had been alone with his mother in the hospice room when she died, and he had seen her raise herself straight up in bed like Lazarus from a morphine tomb, stare blankly at him, speak without voice for a few jabbering moments, and then return to her pillow, her mouth contorting, the gurgle and flow of death staining the white sheets. And then it was finished.

It was all so strange and intimate and real. It was animal. Organic. Life. It was life. We are but leaves of grass that spring from the Earth as if from the womb, grow strong and vibrant, and then wilt and die when winter comes. Ferrill did not question any of it. He had buried many people's parents, grandparents, and even children. He understood that his experience was by no means special, but it was his experience, and it was his own blue-eyed mother, the first face he had ever seen, the woman who gave him suck, nourishment, life, that would be lowered into the grave. It was the woman who had put a cool rag on his forehead when he had a fever, the woman who had nursed him when he was a sick boy, the woman who found more work so that he would have food, books, and clothing. He would be preaching her funeral, and though she knew him the best, and he knew her in the way that only a person's child could, from the idolatry of childhood to the understanding of her mortality in his teens to the irrational space of memory that had arrived only yesterday. Her day had come, the day he had dreaded and prayed would never come, though he knew it would, and now it was here.

"I know it, Uncle Hollis. I know God has a plan. And I will talk about my mother's role in the plan. I won't treat it like my own personal Hiroshima. I will praise the Lord for letting her shrug off her mortal coils."

"That's it, son. That's how it's done. Whether it's bullshit or not. That's how it's done."

"You got any cigarettes?"

"Always got cigarettes."

Uncle Hollis reached into his shirt pocket and pulled out a soft pack of unfiltered Camels. He handed one to Ferrill.

"You smoke the strong ones, Uncle," Ferrill said.

"If you're gonna smoke, smoke. And I'm not going to smoke a cigarette with a tampon in it. A damn filter cain't be good for you. It'll give you cancer or some shit."

Ferrill leaned back in the kitchen chair and smoked. He would let that one be. He thumbed through his mother's Bible, stopping at Psalms. He liked Psalms and Proverbs for funerals. They were a good place to go. He would stay out of the epistles. Although many preachers quoted the Apostle Paul at funerals, Ferrill thought the evangelist was too much of a compliance officer, a little too intense for a funeral, and, well, the Book of Revelation should be left to the Louvin Brothers, with their country songs about the Lord and nuclear holocaust.

"Well, Uncle, I hate to smoke and run, but I guess I'd better do just that."

"I appreciate you stopping by. And I'm sorry. We all loved your mama. If I can help you, let me know. I'd preach it if I could, but I cain't."

Ferrill took a final drag, crushed out the ember, and left the butt expired in the old glass ashtray.

"I appreciate it, Uncle. I appreciate you getting me through this. If you weren't here, I imagine I'd feel like folks were whipping me like I was a piñata."

"They'll be judging you."

"Yeah, but judge not lest you be judged."

"I like the sentiment, but I also know that shit sticks to your fur, just like it sticks to mine, and I have a feeling that the shit will be flying. You best wear a raincoat. And duck. The folks at Second Baptist have been throwing shit into a good industrial box fan for years, but dodge it. Don't let it stick. And if it does splatter on you, wipe it off and throw it back at 'em."

"Eye for eye. Tooth for tooth," Ferrill said. "I'm not normally an Old Testament kind of guy, but that is some pretty sound advice. I'm pretty sure nobody would be expecting the preacher to sling it back at them, but that doesn't mean it couldn't happen."

"That's the spirit. The Lord said to turn the other cheek," Uncle Hollis laughed. "But after that, he didn't leave no more directions."

Reverend Crenshaw shook his uncle's hand and walked toward the door.

"Take care of yourself," Uncle Hollis said, and patted him on the shoulder.

Reverend Crenshaw was glad that he had come to see his uncle, and he was glad that he would be the one to preach his mother's funeral. He was glad that his would be the final words spoken before her body was committed to the ground. He would preach an altar call. He would call the unsaved to the casket to commit their lives to the Lord. He would praise God and His glory. He would praise the Lord for giving him the opportunity to testify to his loved ones at his mother's homecoming with the Lord. He would call the congregation to prayer. He would hold the Bible high in the air and praise the Lord's name. And then, when the hole was dug, the funeral finished, and the barbeque of mourning consumed by the family, he would try to make sense of it all. He would wonder if his mother was right, whether his uncle, and he himself, should have ever been preachers at all.

Bubba Lou's Western Sartorium
★ ★ ★

Boleslav Linka stood behind the counter at his tailor shop on South Congress Avenue fiddling with his tape measure and watching the minute hand of the rhinestone-studded wall clock above the street door. Boleslav, who went by Bubba Lou, was born in the little town of Varnsdorf in what was then Czechoslovakia, a textile town where a person could tell what color clothes were being made that day by the color of the river. Bubba Lou's parents, like most people in Varnsdorf, worked in the textile factory, and the family had managed to immigrate to the United States when he was only a boy. Once in the United States, his parents found work at a textile mill in Waylon County, Texas, and though their life was not much better than it had been back home, where they had been teachers before being forced into manual labor due to their political beliefs, in America at least they felt like they were entitled to an opinion.

Bubba Lou had learned about fabric and sewing from his parents, and after a stint in the army, decided to become a western tailor. This, perhaps, came as no surprise to his parents, for all of his childhood he had been fascinated by the Old West, and he had loved to watch Old Shatterhand and Winnetou on state-run television in the apartment block where the family lived in Varnsdorf; and once the family moved to America, Bubba Lou found himself in awe of the singing cowboys, and he learned English from singing their songs. Much of his working vocabulary, in fact, still came from those songs, and he always greeted his patrons with a "Howdy, Buckaroo" in a Texas drawl tinted with a slight Slavic accent. These days he was known as the tailor to the honkytonk stars. He sewed custom-made suits embroidered with G-clefs, horseshoes, and anything else a musical juggernaut might care to have sewn onto his polyester bellbottoms or onto the yoke of his western shirt.

That afternoon Bubba, who was wearing a sharkskin pearl snap with four aces embroidered on either side of his chest, was waiting for T. Texas Tommy, who had reached national prominence after one of his cowboy weepers, a song called "Mama's Cathead Biscuits," reached the top of the charts. And now, after years on the beer joint circuit playing behind chicken wire and barely paying the rent, he was a star up in Nashville, and he had made an appointment with Bubba Lou, the country and western tailor for those who had arrived. Bubba Lou was happy for T. Texas Tommy, and he imagined the old guitar slinger probably still couldn't register how much money he was making after living out of tip jars and eating pinto beans his entire adult life.

The cowbell clanged above the front entrance, and T. Texas Tommy walked in the glass door past bolts of shiny fabric, mannequins dressed for honkytonk success, and autographed pictures of Bubba Lou with just about every major recording artist who had ever graced the boards of the Ryman. Tommy, from what Bubba could tell, was a bit thicker than he had been when he last stopped by the tailor shop about a year ago to look at the suits and dream. Like every other musician passing through Austin, Tommy always stopped by the tailor shop to see who might be there and to think about what kind of suit he himself might buy once he became a star. Tommy grinned, tipped the brim of his Stetson, and then swaggered across the floor and reached out his big right hand to shake Bubba Lou's.

"Howdy, Buckaroo," Bubba said with a grin.

"It's mighty fine to see ya," Tommy said. "How you been, amigo?"

"Happy as a drover in Dodge," Bubba told him, looking through his mother-of-pearl-rimmed glasses up at the dark-haired man who stood about a head taller than him. "I keep hearing them playing your songs on the radio down here, and I read in the *Chronicle* that you have a platinum record now. Congratulations."

"Thank you, Bubba. I been mighty lucky these days. That's why I'm here.

It's time to get me one of them fancy suits like the big stars wear on their album covers."

"Well, you have come to the right place."

Bubba noticed a couple of giant gold rings on Tommy's fingers, one of which featured a gold nugget shaped like Texas and the other a prominent letter "T" studded with diamonds. A year ago, Tommy couldn't have paid for a chicken fried steak dinner, and now here he was in diamonds and gold.

"I got a new album coming out, and I need a good suit to wear on the cover of it, and for some television performances, too. I'm gonna be on the Yeehaw show in a couple of weeks, and I need something that'll make me look skinnier, or at least not as fat."

Bubba took a step back, scratched the side of his pompadour, and tilted his head to get a better look at Tommy's frame.

"Everything was fine until my cathead biscuit song became a hit," Tommy said. "Then everywhere I went somebody was feeding me their mama's biscuits with redeye gravy. Now I can barely zip up my britches."

"Don't you worry. I'll make you look as fit as a fiddle. Please allow me to take your measurements."

Tommy stood still and Bubba crouched to one knee and then gradually rose as he measured the singer up and down. Bubba wrote everything into his notepad.

"So what do you have in mind?" the tailor asked.

"Something like this here," Tommy said, pointing to a mannequin that was wearing a yellow suit with green cactuses embroidered across the chest of the jacket.

"In this color? Or this design? Or both?"

"In that color. If I had a suit like that, my fans could see me from the nosebleeds. They might even be able to see me from a blimp if I was playing at a football stadium or over at the stock car track."

Bubba Lou glanced at the mannequin and then back at Tommy.

"Trust me, Buckaroo. Yellow is not the color you want. Yellow can make a big, strong cowboy look like the large bird on children's television. You do not want to be on stage singing 'Mama's Cathead Biscuits' looking like a giant yellow bird. I would suggest a color that absorbs light. Perhaps you should consider wearing black."

"But there's already an ol' boy who wears all black."

"Your suit could be covered in rhinestone-laden fringes. You would have your own look. And one color for the whole suit is definitely the way to go."

"Are you sure that's what I ought to do?"

"Trust me. I am just a humble tailor, but the stars come to me for a reason. They come to me because I tell them no. I tell them that if they trust me, I will put them in clothes that make them feel like four aces. Now you are a star, and I won't yes, yes, yes just because you are. My job is to make a star shine even brighter, so I am very liberal with the truth."

Bubba stroked his chin and continued.

"One color is always better if a country music cowpoke has got some table muscles. If you are dressed in black with the spotlight dancing on the rhinestones, nobody will even notice that you have put on weight. All they will see is a star on a stage. Do you happen to have ideas about what you want embroidered on your suit?"

"I reckon I'd like to see a map of Texas and at least a T or two."

"That could be done. We could put a big T on each of your front yokes and a map of Texas on your back. I think that would be good."

"What if I still look kinda big once the suit is made?"

"You'll look great. And if you are self-conscious, we could run a stripe down each side to dress up your silhouette."

Tommy adjusted his hat and looked nervously at the tailor.

"Bubba Lou, normally I wouldn't care a lick about a little bit of belly, but up in Nashville, how you look is as important as how you sound. And they say on television an ol' boy looks about twenty pounds heavier."

"Do not worry, Buckaroo. I will sew a cape for your shoulders, and you will look like a dashing pistolero up there on the big stage."

Bubba Lou quickly drew a sketch of the costume and scribbled his notes and the singer's measurements to the right side of the drawing. He then showed the page to Tommy.

"Dadgum. That looks real nice," Tommy said, holding the notepad in his hands.

"And you'll want some anaconda boots to go with your jet-black suit, of course."

"Done got some," Tommy said, glancing up at the rhinestone clock.

"Is your schedule tight?" Bubba asked.

"It is. And it's been kinda hard to adjust to that to tell you the truth. I used to have more time than money, and now I got more money than time. I kindly had to shoehorn in my visit to your shop today. We got a show up in Dallas later on tonight."

"Well, I have everything I need to make your suit, so don't worry about that."

"I sure appreciate it, Bubba, and I hate to leave good company, but I reckon the boys and me had better get on the road. I imagine they're all chomping at the bit."

"Well, stop and get some kolaches in West on your way up to Dallas."

"We always do. I'll bring you some next time we're back this way."

"That would be mighty fine."

Tommy reached into his back pocket, pulled out his wallet, and handed Bubba Lou a large stack of hundred-dollar bills like it was something he did all the time.

"Thank you, Buckaroo. I'll give you a call when your suit's ready. Once you have that new suit, you'll be riding even taller in the saddle."

Tommy swaggered past racks of polyester cowboy suits in every single color of the rainbow and walked to the front door.

"Happy trails to you, T. Texas Tommy," Bubba Lou said. "Until we meet again."

"Until we meet again, amigo."

And then Tommy smiled, tipped his hat, and left with the clang of a cowbell.

The Closet Agnostic
★ ★ ★

"Honey, I'm worried about you," Memaw Davis said while putting on her apron. "I'm worried that you're going to Hell because you don't go to church."

"Mama, I'm pretty sure that whether or not a person goes to Hell doesn't hinge on their church attendance record."

"Well, I wouldn't take any chances, and, honey, I'm getting old. Too old. I probably don't have too many years left here on this Earth, and, Rhonda, I want to see you in Glory. I want to greet my daughter at the gates of Heaven."

Rhonda stood there in the kitchen making sweet tea. She loved her mama and tried to be respectful, which meant that sometimes she just had to hold her tongue. And this was one of those times. She wondered how people in Heaven knew when their relatives arrived. Did someone inform them? Was there a newspaper in Heaven that covered the new arrivals as well as reported on who had gone to roast weenies with Beelzebub, something like a birth announcement or perhaps an obituary? Or did the citizens of Heaven just stand around by the gate waiting for people who might not ever arrive? Rhonda figured there would surely be some kind of announcement. If there wasn't, it would all be kind of sad.

But what was truly sad, Rhonda thought, was that she wasn't so sure she believed in Heaven, or even God for that matter. She had been raised in the church and dunked in the cool water of redemption, yet still she struggled with faith. Around the age of eleven, it must have been, she had determined that she didn't know whether there was a God or not, and it scared her. It scared her to not believe.

When she was a girl, her mother and father had waited patiently for her to decide that it was time to give her life to the Lord. They watched her closely every altar call, though she never left the pew until one Sunday she reached the epiphany that every minnow in the bucket would eventually be hooked, so she figured it would be better to take the barb sooner rather than later, so she walked down the aisle to tell the preacher she wanted to be baptized, though she was sharp enough, even as an eleven-year-old, to leave out the fact that she didn't actually believe in God.

Believing was the right thing to do, but still she couldn't believe. God, to the best of her knowledge, had never appeared to her, had never shown a sign, and all of the Bible stories seemed nice, but she figured they were all just that, stories. So, for the past thirty years, she had pretended to believe in God, His Son, and the supporting cast of characters. What shame it would bring her family if anyone knew that she was an agnostic, or if she was honest with herself, an atheist who couldn't come to terms with calling herself one.

In her secret, guarded heart, she simply thought of herself as a closet agnostic. She would bow her head to pray at Christmas dinner. She would say amen at the prayer's end, after her mother had asked the Lord to bless this food to the nourishment of their bodies, and so on and so forth, but it was simply an act, a performance she put on to keep from disappointing her mother, to keep from breaking her heart.

Rhonda took the pot of sweet tea off the burner and then started cutting carrots. Her mother, known by most everyone as Memaw, snapped peas on the counter while Rhonda's husband, Bud, and her daughter, Sabrina, sat at the kitchen table and watched. Normally, Rhonda would ask Sabrina, who had just turned thirteen, to help as well, but the kitchen in her mother's little frame house was small and Sabrina, who was all elbows and knees, would only be in the way. So Sabrina and Bud just sat at the table watching the ladies make lunch.

"Mama," Rhonda said. "I think all you have to do to go to Heaven is be baptized and say you believe in John 3:16. I think those are the only requirements."

"Well, not everybody thinks that way," Memaw replied while reaching a sun-spotted hand into a plastic bag for a handful of peas to snap. "That would be real hard to explain to the church mission committee, the deacons, or even the preacher. They all have to go to church, so you should have to go, too. There's no free ride to Heaven. You should already know that. Next week is Easter. I want y'all to go to church with me."

"I'll bring Sabrina to hunt Easter eggs at your house after church, but I don't think we can make it to the service."

"Then on Mother's Day. You should come on Mother's Day to make your mother happy."

"But I'm a mother, too, and it's my day, too. I don't want to spend it at church."

"Do it to make your mother happy."

"Ok then," Rhonda said, turning to her own daughter. "Sabrina, we're going to church on Mother's Day."

"But I don't want to go to church."

"Well, you're going. We're all going."

Memaw put the snap peas in a skillet on the stove, wiped the fog from her bifocals with a cup towel, and headed to the back of the house to the bathroom. Once she had left the kitchen, Bud adjusted the brim of his Waylon County Feed and Seed cap, scratched his stubbled jaw, and looked up from the table and over at his wife.

"Hell, Rhonda, she's your mama. Not mine. I ain't going to church."

"We're all going. If I have to go, then everybody has to go."

"Don't look at me," Sabrina said, her diction impaired by her braces. "I don't want to go either."

"We're all going on Mother's Day," Rhonda said. "Do it for your mother."

"Well, my mother doesn't want to go. Do you, Mama? You don't want to go. So it's not like I'm doing it for you."

"You're doing it for me because I'm doing it for your memaw. Just do what I ask, and that'll make it a lot easier on all of us."

"Going to church isn't easier on all of us," Sabrina said, swishing her jet-black hair. "They make you fill out a visitor's card and then bug you for six months trying to get you to go to church."

"Then put a fake name on the card."

"But everybody knows me. It's a small town."

"Just go to church for your mama. And your grandmother, too."

Bud spat tobacco juice into the empty ranch-style bean can that was sitting on the kitchen table.

"Well, Rhonda, I reckon I'll probably have the flu on Mother's Day," he said.

"Brown bottle flu, maybe," Rhonda said. "And you wouldn't be the only one afflicted with it at church that morning, I'm sure. You could sit in the back pew with all the secret drunks who bathe themselves in aftershave hoping the preacher won't be able to smell them."

Memaw came back from the bathroom, where apparently she could hear everything.

"I'm praying for you, Bud," Memaw said. "If you are struggling with alcohol, I'll put you on my prayer request list and share it with my prayer team up at church."

"See, Mama," Sabrina said. "They all know who we are. Memaw tells them about everything we do and asks them to pray about it. That's not praying. That's gossiping in the name of the Lord."

Rhonda wondered if Sabrina, her daughter, was a closet agnostic, too. But she could never ask, for it could expose her own lack of belief. Were anyone to ever find out her secret, the ensuing wildfire of gossip could cause entire congregations to know that she didn't believe in God. She could imagine Reverend Norwell and the forty thousand members of his megachurch praying for her salvation on network television. What a nightmare that would be, she thought. She could imagine the church service going into syndication. When the show aired again in reruns, would the prayers for her soul that were offered in the original program now count as new prayers? Or would only the original live performance of prayer count as prayer? Rhonda really did not know, though she hoped that the syndicated prayers would improve her spiritual condition.

After putting a meatloaf into the oven and setting the timer at half an hour, Rhonda found that she was already starting to dread the idea of going to Second Baptist Church to attend the Mother's Day services. She could already picture the scenario. She would bring her mama a corsage she bought at the Hoggly Woggly the night before and would likely be wearing one that Bud had bought on clearance at the Texalube earlier that morning. Rhonda would enter the church, and people would look at her like Lazarus arisen from the tomb. She had not been to church in ages, and she could imagine how the tongues would wag. And they would look at Bud, who would likely be red-faced and hungover, and Sabrina, who had dyed her hair raven black and would undoubtably be dressed like a mope-rock singer. There would be plenty to talk about, and Rhonda dreaded having committed to go.

After a while, the food was all ready. They would have meatloaf, snap peas, mashed potatoes, carrots, and Memaw's homemade Mexican cornbread. Rhonda put silverware on the table, and her mother poured everyone a glass of sweet tea. Bud turned off the television in the living room, which was playing an old John Wayne movie, and Sabrina got everyone a paper napkin. Then the family all sat down at the table.

"Rhonda, would you please bless the food?" Memaw asked.

"But Mama, you always do that," Rhonda replied.

"Yes, but I am an old woman now, and I think it's time to pass on the honor."

Rhonda didn't know what to say or do. Her husband, her daughter, and her mother all just looked at her. Sitting there at the table, she reached out her hands and took those of her daughter and her mother. Her husband, across the table, took their hands as well. And so Rhonda began.

"Our Heavenly Father," she said, and then sat silent in a total loss for words.

The Lost Mine of El Noveno Hoyo
★ ★ ★

Andrew Dorantes pulled gently at the point of his Cervantes beard while staring intently at a map of New Spain drawn by Zebulon Pike in 1807. "Spanish towns of consequence" were denoted by a small icon of a mission, and "Old Towns evacuated" were marked by a circle with a short line on top making the symbols resemble tiny wedding rings. In areas that Dorantes knew to be plains, Lieutenant Pike had noted the location of "Immense Herds of wild Horses." Andrew, who was an antiquarian bookseller by trade, raised his magnifying glass, an object that once belonged to Don Bernardo de Miranda, the lieutenant-general of the Texas province, and closely examined the location of one of the small wedding rings. Above the symbol were the words "Santa Barbarita" next to a crooked river called the Río de los Dragos, the River of Dragons, a fitting appellation for a waterway filled with enormous alligator gar.

The Spanish ruins of Santa Barbarita, which lay next to the river Andrew knew to have been renamed the "Blazeby" thirty years after the map was drawn, were situated in a sparsely populated corner of Waylon County. According to eighteenth century church records, the presidio and its adjoining mission were built in Lipan Apache territory, and, as the name Santa Barbarita suggests, the settlement was primarily a mining concern. In the 1770s, Native Americans massacred the friars and every other Spaniard in the area, and the viceroy chose to leave the presidio and mission abandoned. Although scallywags and adventurers of all sorts searched the ruins of Santa Barbarita and its surrounding area for the next several decades, no one, to Andrew Dorantes' knowledge, had ever discovered anything.

Then, in 1831, a young American named Gad Brooks, who was traveling with Jim Bowie and his band of fortune hunters in search of the San Saba mines, became lost and wandered the wilderness until he arrived at the ruins of Santa Barbarita, which were then inhabited by Apaches wearing human fingers, hands, and even feet on their necklaces. The indigenous people, despite their rather grim choice of ornamentation, proved to be a friendly lot, and the young soldier lived among them for seven moons. Brooks then set out for San Antonio supposedly to return to his family but instead tried to recruit men to form a small army to take over the rich silver mine as well as locate a Spanish coffer the Apaches had buried near the banks of the Río de los Dragos. No one believed Brooks' tale, and were it not for the single letter dated 1833, which happened to be located in Andrew Dorantes' filing cabinet, no record of the young scoundrel's exploits would even exist. Andrew, though he was hardly a treasure hunter, had always been fascinated by the convergence of the past and the present, by the seed of truth from which bloomed the wild bouquet of every legend.

Andrew himself was a direct descendant of Andrés Dorantes de Carranza, who explored Texas with Cabeza de Vaca in the sixteenth century and fathered a son who would be named the treasurer of Veracruz. The next several generations of the Dorantes family worked in the service of the treasury and most likely played an administrative role in this mining concern in New Spain. Although Andrew did not care for conquest nor did he lust for fortune, he did care about history's obsolescent moments. Sitting behind his Spanish colonial desk surrounded by shelves of leatherbound volumes, he decided that he himself would quietly search for the lost San Barbarita mine and the buried coffer. While he leaned back in his pleasantly ergonomic office chair contemplating the potential whereabouts of the lost mine and the strongbox, a knock came at the massive, carved wooden door of his office.

"Come in," he called.

The colossal door, which once hung in a Mexican church, creaked slightly, and piercing rays of light entered the dark, almost monastic chamber that was illuminated by a wrought iron candelabra situated beside Andrew's burnished colonial desk. The door opened wide, and Laura, his wife, forever beautiful in a sundress, silhouetted herself at a flattering angle in the threshold.

"Are you hungry, Daddy Bear?" she asked.

Andrew thought for a moment, as if human concerns such as sustenance did not affect him, and then he spoke. He adjusted the ruff collar around his neck and squinted in the direction of his wife like a person who has just left a movie theater on a summer afternoon, or perhaps an inhabitant of a cavern who had just left the cool, damp darkness for the bright, blazing heat above the Earth's surface.

"Yes, I am hungry."

"That's good because lunch is ready."

Andrew blew out the tall beeswax candles and crossed the threshold behind his wife. The living room was bathed in light that shone through its many windows and refracted off the tile floor. Straightline furniture in primary colors filled the room, and a modern steel sculpture stood on the coffee table beneath a colorful mobile designed by an artist clearly influenced by Miró. Andrew's two young children, Ricky and Amelia, rushed from their playroom to greet him.

"Daddy Bear has risen from his cave," Laura laughed.

Laura always was and always would be a schoolteacher, though she was now staying at home until both of her children reached school age. Amelia, the younger, was now three, so it would be two more years before Laura would return to the classroom. In the interim, she was writing and illustrating books about Daddy Bear, who wore a ruff collar and had a pointy little beard. She had no intention of publishing her funny little books, but it did make her children happy to see characters based on themselves and their parents going on wild adventures.

At the children's request, today's lunch was peanut butter and honey sandwiches and apple slices. Andrew would have preferred a hearty caldo with fresh tortillas, but he was not the type of rooster that had to rule the roost. He just felt fortunate that his family could all eat lunch together every day, and he was grateful that his online enterprise, Colonial Parchment Books, made enough money to keep the family comfortable.

"What have y'all been doing?" Andrew asked the children.

"*Hemos estado jugando en el* backyard," Ricky said. "We were swinging."

"Daddy," Amelia laughed, pointing at his neck. "Daddy, the honey is dripping."

Andrew looked down to see the honey on his ruff collar. He would have to take it off and spray some Out-Damn-Spot stain remover onto it. And that was his last clean collar, too.

"Do you have any packages that need mailing today?" Laura asked.

"I have a couple of packages to send to a museum in Arizona, but I'll take care of that myself today."

"Daddy Bear is completely leaving the cave during the daylight hours. That is unusual."

"I must foster an air of unpredictability. I hear women like that."

Laura smiled. Her chestnut eyes sparkled.

"Actually, Andrew, I'm fine with predictability these days. We can leave unpredictability to the couples on the telenovelas."

"Then you will probably be disappointed to know that after I finish at the post office, I'm going golfing."

"You are clearly fostering an air of unpredictability. You don't even like golf, and you haven't been golfing since the chamber of commerce had its charity scramble or whatever they call it."

"Informally it's known as the Warnell Hack and Cuss. But you're right. That was the last time I went golfing."

"Who's joining you?"

"I'll be playing *solito*."

"Really?"

"Absolutely."

Andrew reached into his pocket and produced a fat gold watch. He checked the time.

"I'll head out later this afternoon. First, I have a little research to do."

Andrew pardoned himself, quickly washed his plate in the sink, and left it on the drying rack. He then gave each of his children a kiss on the forehead and his wife a kiss on the lips.

"Okay, *mis ositos*, I'll see y'all soon," he said.

Andrew sprayed his ruff collar and placed it in the laundry basket before returning to the colossal oak door and entering his library. He lit five candles with a single match and blew it out just as the flame was about to reach his index finger and thumb. He then took Gad Brooks' letter, which he stored inside an acid-free protective sleeve, from his filing cabinet and placed it on his desk. The letter, which was on browned parchment and written in now-fading ink, was dated April 12, 1833, with the words Coahuila y Tejas written below the date. Brooks wrote of rapidly declining health, and as far as Andrew Dorantes could tell, likely had cholera, which explained why he vanished from the public record so abruptly. In this letter to his brother, he wrote of an Apache named "Cuatro Manos," who wore two human hands on his necklace, showing him a Spanish strongbox filled with silver before burying it on "a small, unassuming hillock beyond the presidio walls."

Andrew Dorantes believed he knew the likely direction in which the hillock Gad Brooks was describing would be located, for not only had he visited Santa Barbarita on four different elementary school field trips in his childhood, he was a local business owner, even if the business was online, and he participated in the annual charity scramble. The Waylon County Municipal Nine Hole Golf Course abutted the ruins' western wall, and though there was a sign saying "Do Not Enter" next to a pile of rubble, golfers whose balls had flown deep in the rough and into the fortress ruins routinely stepped past the sign and used a nine iron to get the lift needed to clear the wall of this unusual obstructive feature in hopes of reaching the green beyond the mesquite trees and prairie grass. The golf course was on land that was previously part of the Spanish presidio and mission complex, and Andrew always wondered why the land was not included in the state historical area.

The land was likely cursed, Andrew surmised, considering that a bevy of priests had been massacred on what was now the golf course, and at least one eighteenth-century skirmish between angry Apaches and occupying Spanish troops had transpired in the general vicinity. The ghosts of the Lipan elders and the Spanish soldiers surely were exacting their revenge in the form of triple bogies and botched mulligans. No player in the history of the Waylon County Municipal Nine Hole Golf Course had ever reached par. In fact, twenty strokes over seemed to be par for the course. The land was also infested with western diamondback rattlesnakes, causing many golfers to break from traditional sartorial norms and wear chaps, jeans, and high-shafted cowboy boots instead of polyester pants and studded saddle shoes. Andrew thought the incredible rattlesnake presence could also be the work of the spirits, but then, it was probably the result of the rattlesnakes hunting the mice that dined upon the spilled popcorn from the little tubs served by the sexy church girl who worked in the concession stand outside the clubhouse.

Clubhouse, Andrew thought, was a funny word in this case, considering that the clubhouse was a single wide trailer with rowdy, boisterous varmints living under the floor. But Andrew paid the clubhouse little attention, for he didn't think the coffer would be found beneath it anyway. The ground was too flat.

Upon deciding that it was time to leave, Andrew changed into his slate gray "Colonial Parchment Books" golf shirt, put on a pair of heavily starched jeans and tall, tooled cowboy boots made in his parents' workshop, and went to the garage. He found his golf clubs, which he had not used in months, and put them into the back of his truck. He then verified the addresses on the packages of rare books he was sending to the museum in Arizona and placed them on the bench seat beside him and headed toward the post office.

There was no line at the squat little brick post office, and he walked right up to the counter to Darcy, the clerk. Darcy, whose hair could best be described as a tall copper perm, tended to sigh whenever Andrew entered the post office. Andrew did not take this personally because he was always mailing unusual packages that required customs slips and return receipts. He sent registered letters. He sent packages to countries she did not know existed. Andrew figured that in Darcy's mind, he was a lot of trouble. Sometimes she even had to call the manager, Mr. McNutt, from the back to help her figure everything out. But Andrew liked Darcy, and he was pretty sure Darcy liked him, even if he did seem to exasperate her.

"Hello, there," Darcy said. "Where are you sending these packages today?

China?"

"Both of these will be going to Arizona. Registered mail."

"Okey dokey. We'll get you fixed up in a jiffy."

Andrew handed Darcy the shipping label he had printed at home. She then slapped a registered label on each package. He paid with a card and was handed his receipt.

"Well, that was easy as pie," Darcy said. "Have a nice one."

"You too. See you next time."

Andrew hopped in his truck and drove to the Waylon County Municipal Nine Hole Golf Course. He had a folder on the front seat with a color print of the Pike map and a copy of Gad Brooks' letter. He wished that he had a copy of the 1758 Spanish map and the ecclesiastical records, but all such records were lost in the fateful raid that expedited the Franciscan priests to the pearly gates and ended with anything that was not made of stone being burned to ashes. To the best of Andrew's knowledge, the area was not surveyed again until 1807, and then in 1824, when Mexico gained independence, and again in 1836, when Texas became independent, though the 1824 and 1836 maps provided no further insight into where the silver could possibly have been than Pike's 1807 version. The 1824 map, which was in Spanish, showed slightly more detail than the other two, but it provided no clues to the whereabouts of the shaft.

Andrew took his golf clubs, which were in a green bag that resembled a kilt, out of the bed of his truck. Since golf was invented in Scotland, he liked the idea of having a bag that seemed Scottish. He hooked the bag to his little two-wheeled cart and headed in the direction of the clubhouse. At first he felt a little self-conscious. He did not hit balls, much less golf to any real extent, so he wondered how well he would fare. He walked into the single-wide clubhouse, with its wood paneling and pictures of Pebble Beach, Augusta, and Saint Andrew's decorating the walls. He paid his green fee and then stepped out the door headed to the first tee box.

Standing there at the blue tees, he was glad that the course was mostly empty. He had been known to shank his first drive, and he did not want to brain some poor fellow minding his own business on the next fairway. The only golfers he could see were on a cart in the distance, out on what he figured to be the fourth hole. The golfers were dressed in camouflage shirts and hats, and they both wore jeans and cowboy boots. While such outfits would not be up to snuff on a big city course, that was the standard in Waylon County. If a ball went into the rough, there was always a good chance of being bit by a diamondback, which took the idea of a sudden death playoff to a new level. In Waylon County, no one was too interested in a sudden death playoff, so a lot of folks golfed in the same clothes they hunted in, which, of course, included boots that went up high enough to make any rattlesnake that cared to strike eat leather.

Andrew pulled out his driver and swished it around a bit. He could see clearly from the tee box that the hillock in Gad Brooks' letter was not in the first fairway. Andrew teed up his ball, wiggled his hips, and then boogered his drive, which zinged past a rock squirrel's head, careened off a chunk of limestone, and landed in a stand of prickly pear. Andrew pulled his cart into the rough and smacked the ball out of the cactus patch and onto the fairway with a seven iron, the club he used the vast majority of the time. He then proceeded to hack up prodigious divots with his lucky seven, though he always stuck the clumps of grass back into the ground for etiquette's sake.

Although he was playing alone, he let a foursome of bankers in mauve polos, polyester driving pants, and golf shoes pass him in their custom-made golf carts. He nodded and smiled. They waved as they passed. While he was waiting for them to finish on the second green, Andrew looked all around him. There were no hillocks to be found. He also looked over to the Blazeby River, which ran beside the course and past the abandoned presidio. He could see no hills on the other side. As he hacked and chopped along with his clubs, he did not see anything that resembled Gad Brooks' description. Could the hill have eroded that much in less than two hundred years? And even if he did find it, had someone quietly excavated the hill, taken the treasure, and managed to keep their tale-teller closed? He doubted that. Surely someone would have said something. There would at least have been a legend of some sort.

Finally, after the bankers had finished and the sun was setting low, Andrew reached the ninth hole. And then he saw it. The green. The hillock

110

that Gad Brooks had written about had to be the ninth green. How on Earth would he be able to casually find out if the green, which was visible from the clubhouse, was the location of the lost treasure Cuatro Manos showed the young adventurer? Andrew decided that he would finish the round and then park his truck on a nearby side road and come back and investigate once the course was cleared.

Andrew finished with a triple bogey, which was not his worst hole of the day, though it didn't matter to him either way because he wasn't even carrying a scorecard. Golf, to Andrew, was an excuse to enjoy the good weather and get some light exercise. It was hardly a competition sport. It was, in Andrew's mind, more of a pastime, like throwing horseshoes or playing dominoes.

After removing his ball from the ninth hole, Andrew got in his truck and drove to a quiet dirt road and parked. Once the sun was down, he returned to the golf course. Night had come. Stars were pulsing in the Texas sky. Andrew took his golf bag over to the ninth hole and pulled a metal detector from it. He then walked around the green with the metal detector waiting for a beep. Any beep. Just a beep. He walked all along the hillock, upon land that over the course of centuries had been claimed by more than six nations, and then the metal detector beeped hysterically over the hole. Could the treasure be directly below the ninth hole?

Although he could hardly use the club well in regulation play, Andrew was an absolute master when it came to swinging a pitching wedge in any other pursuit than golf. So Andrew took out his pitching wedge and began to hack at the green in the moonlight. Divots flew into the air landing on the fairway and occasionally as far away as the rough. However, he quickly changed to the sharpshooter he had hidden in his golf bag and drove it into the ground. He soon discovered that the ground was not as rocky as he had anticipated it to be, and so he was able to dig at a rapid clip. With the dirt flying and his eyes peeled, he began to question whether he had actually been right, that this was the right place, that he wasn't making a giant, yawning hole on the ninth green for nothing.

Then, after an hour of digging, Andrew was shocked, relieved, and exhilarated when his shovel slammed into what appeared to be a wall of the filled-in shaft. He could hardly believe what he had found, and a few cautious shovelfuls later, to his strange, dreamlike delight, he uncovered the small Spanish strongbox at the lip of the concealed mine. A rush of euphoria coursed through him, and upon regaining his analytical faculties, Andrew dug around the perimeter of the box, hunched over the hole, and then took the coffer, with its ornate hasp and beautifully crafted corner brackets, into his hands, and placed it beside him on the turf of the green before filling in the gaping maw he had made of the ninth hole. Maybe the greensmen would think that prairie dogs had dug the hole, Andrew laughed to himself. He thought about his strange fortune, about the sheer improbability of him finding the lost treasure of *el noveno hoyo*, the treasure of the ninth hole.

Once he had patched in the green, which looked a bit like one of Amelia's art projects, and shoved the flag into the ground like a conquistador, he picked up the small metal strongbox and placed it on the bench seat beside him in his pickup truck. He would not mention a word about his discovery until he knew exactly what it was, and when he felt the time was right, he would contact the state historical and archaeological societies so that new pages could be added to the chronicles of time, and the treasure he had found could take its rightful place in the Museum of the Banners of Texas. In the interim, Andrew would keep the box hidden in his library until he had completed his research.

After starting his engine, the bookman drove contentedly towards his home with a set of golf clubs in his truck bed and a Spanish colonial strongbox on the bench seat beside him. He chuckled at the fact that, despite being an abysmal golfer, he had managed to score, historically speaking, something akin to a hole-in-one. Still, he thought, another search awaited, for he had one more hole to contend with, a hole for which he would have to find a baroque wrought iron key.

The Kolache Contest
★ ★ ★

Byron Herblight was an avid advocate of festivals. He enjoyed the East Texas Yamboree largely due to its catchy name and his status as a vegetarian with a yen for yams. He also enjoyed the Texas Onion Fest celebrating the venerable 1015 onion, and he, of course, enjoyed Oktoberfest in Limburg, the little German town in his native Waylon County, where he invariably dined upon an enormous pretzel and quaffed a frothy Limburger beer.

But today he was at the Krasna Lipa Kolache Festival, which included a baking competition for kolaches in six different categories, those being apple, apricot, peach, poppy seed, prune, and sausage. There was apparently much controversy about the inclusion of the sausage product, for ground pork in a gut casing enshrouded in dough could hardly be called, in good conscience, a kolache. Nonetheless, the sausage kolache was judged as a kolache, though most of the locals obstinately, and perhaps rightly, called it a "*klobásník*," which, if translated directly, meant something like a "little sausage." Apparently, a small contingent of out-of-towners elected to the city council was responsible for this sausage kolache business.

Byron, with his thick ponytail, pince-nez glasses, and Woodstock footwear, walked on the Saints Cyril and Methodius church lawn inspecting booths of kolaches, garlands, crocheted doilies, homemade pickles, Czexan bumper stickers, and traditional Moravian costumes. The Texas Fold 'Em Polka Band was playing "Roll Out the Barrels" in Czech, though Byron had no idea what they were singing. The musicians were all wearing white

113

T-shirts with the band's name on the front as well as bright red suspenders, and each one was wearing a different kind of hat. The tuba player, in a Waylon County Volunteer Fire Department helmet, honked out the bass line. The accordion man, in a straw cowboy hat with a buzzard feather plume, was grinding out the melody, and the rather diminutive drummer, donning a purple stovepipe with a "Pivo for Breakfast" pin on it, made sure the polka remained a polka.

As Byron stood there watching the band, people took curious glances at him, but he did not mind. He was different. He had always been different. Yet he found the fact that he was unusual easiest to bear when he was an outsider. People will often look curiously at someone new and different in their own surroundings, so this behavior seemed normal to him. But in his hometown of Warnell, people had always looked at him curiously, strangely, cautiously, and that unnerved him, for he was at home. So he had always tried his best to be somewhere other than Warnell, and he had largely succeeded.

Walking along, Byron saw a beautiful blonde with Renaissance braids standing behind a booth selling raffle tickets. She was wearing a red apron with the words Kolache Kween across the front, and Byron, finding the trick with the K's amusing, stopped to tell the young lady.

"I like your apron," he said.

"That's the dumbest pickup line I ever heard," a wooly-bearded guy in a pearl snap shirt said as he passed by.

The young woman smiled.

"Don't mind him. We dated in the eighth grade. He's still mad that I broke up with him. And thank you. I'm glad you like my apron. I'm Sunny Patek."

Byron was a bit surprised. He really had only wanted to acknowledge the clever phonetic trick on her apron, and now this young lady, who had flowers in her hair and a third eye tattooed above her wrist, was actually holding a conversation with him. She was quite beautiful, and he was a bit startled that she told him more than simply "Thank you."

"I'm Byron. Byron Herblight."

"Nice to meet you, Byron. Where are you from?" she asked.

"Warnell, but I live in Austin."

"Wow. Austin. That's cool."

Byron smiled. Everyone seemed to think Austin was cool. And he supposed it was. It was the only place he knew of that had commercial enterprises with names like "Biscuits and Groovy," and where one could find cosmic cowboys in ten-gallon hats and Roman sandals playing sitars and didgeridoos in honkytonks that smelled of patchouli, proletarian beer, and clove cigarettes. It was, quite frankly, Byron's kind of town. And at least in Austin, only the tourists gawked at him. Still, he could not deduce this beautiful woman's intentions. Maybe she was just being polite or perhaps she wanted him to buy raffle tickets. The winner of the raffle, Byron had read, would receive a year's supply of kolaches and a double-barrel shotgun. Considering that Byron had no desire to dine upon such a prodigious number of pastries nor be a bearer of such arms, he hoped that she was just being polite.

"Have you been to the kolache festival before?" Sunny asked.

"This is my first time. How about you?"

"I've been every year for as long as I can remember."

"So you've been coming here your entire life?"

"I have. I was even Miss Kolache when I was seventeen."

"That's outstanding. What was it like being Miss Kolache?"

Sunny pursed her lips in reflection.

"Well, they gave me a silk banner and a rhinestone crown, and I had to smile holding a plate of kolaches for a good solid hour while they took pictures for the newspapers and the Tex-Czech calendar. I had the biggest hair you've ever seen, too. You can't be Miss Kolache without having big hair. To tell you the truth, being Miss Kolache was not exactly my thing, and I never really even planned on running for it, but I'm still glad to have had the experience."

"Then how did you end up on the ballot?"

"After the FFA nominated me, my mom and grandmother badgered me until I agreed to run for the crown. Both of them won it when they were young, so they wanted me to run, too. They act like we are some kind of kolache beauty dynasty. Honestly, I'm more interested in music and art than hairspray and makeup and all of that. So the crown doesn't really fit. But I have no regrets. All I really want out of life is the chance to enjoy lots of different experiences, and that was an experience."

Byron smiled. He and Sunny Patek were clearly riding the same cosmic wave.

"I understand," Byron replied. "All I am really looking for is the chance to enjoy the sheer randomness of existence."

"You should go watch the kolache-eating contest," Sunny said, "or enter it."

"How do you enter it?" Byron asked, his fingers twisting the scruff of his wispy beard.

"All you have to do is pay your entry fee to the man at the next booth over there. Just talk to the guy in the 'Kolaches are for Lovers' T-shirt."

Since Byron was somewhat famished, he thought he would enter. He had, after all, forgotten to eat breakfast that morning due to his excitement about attending the kolache festival, and, he figured, having not already dined could very well put him at a competitive advantage.

"I think I'll give it a whirl," Byron said.

"Well, I wish you good luck," Sunny replied.

Byron grinned, nodded his head, and walked over to the next booth to enter the competition. Truth be told, Byron was not a lover of competitions, for he believed in the good of all humanity as a community and found no value in the proverbial pissing contest, but, still, he felt obliged to follow the advice of this reluctant beauty queen, this former Miss Kolache, this former holder of the title of titles at this civic event held in honor of disc-like pastries filled with fruit and cream.

The man at the next booth, for a mere ten greenbacks, registered Byron for the competition, which would begin in twenty minutes. Byron would be competing in the men's thirteen to a hundred-and-ten-year-old division. With his proof of registration in hand, Byron sauntered over to the podium where the other eleven competitors were already assembled. There was a skinny kid with a bowl haircut at the end of the table, a fat kid in an "Uncle Igor's Sausage Emporium" T-shirt next to him, and a couple of Stink Creek football players in their black and white jerseys next to them. A couple of older men in cowboy hats were in the middle, apparently telling one another jokes in Czech, and a guy with a golf visor and spiky hair sat next to them. After the man with the spiky hair came four heavyset men wearing matching 'Kolache Konquistador' T-shirts. Byron took the last seat on the end. A moment later, a woman set a plate of ten kolaches in front of him. The competition was about to begin.

"My money is on Ernesto," Byron heard a young man in the audience, who was wearing a Waylon County Feed and Seed cap, half-whisper to the curly-haired woman standing next to him.

"Five bucks says his brother, Federico, will beat him," the woman replied. "Federico won the Barbeque Blowout in Bigfoot Wallace County last year. He was wiping his mouth clean after his tenth chopped beef sandwich before anyone else could even scarf down sandwich number six."

As the contest was about to begin, Kolache Festival royalty from the past and present assembled on the back of the podium. Byron could see Sunny, and presumably her mother and grandmother, beside her. The current Kolache Kourt in their tiaras and Moravian dresses stood together and smiled at one another excitedly. About that time, the band leader, in red suspenders and a porkpie hat, stepped onto the stage and took the microphone.

"Ladies and gentleman, *vítáme vás*! Welcome to the eighty-fifth annual Krasna Lipa Kolache Eating Contest. The rules are simple. The first person to eat ten kolaches is declared the winner. However, the competition will continue until every contestant has finished his kolaches. I'll count to three in Czech, and say, 'Go.' Contestants, please put your hands on your heads."

Byron looked next to him and saw that the other contestants had put their hands just behind their ears. This appeared to provide a tactical advantage over putting one's hands directly on top of one's head, which would perhaps cost a contestant a split second when reaching for the first kolache.

"*Raz! Dva! Tři!* Go!" called out the band leader.

The man next to Byron began squishing kolaches together in order to eat them two at a time. The skinny boy at the opposite end had his face in his plate using what was commonly known as the canine strategy. The others seemed to be using the swallow and stuff technique, that is, as soon as they could swallow one kolache, they had the next one ready to stuff into their mouths.

Byron started out with an apricot kolache. He found the filling delicious, and he could not remember when he last had such a delicious pastry. He followed the apricot with an apple kolache, and it seemed to him that the baker must have used a Gala apple, or perhaps a Fuji, to make such a fine baked good. After the apple kolache, he ate a peach kolache, which was surely made from Fredericksburg peaches, and if not, perhaps peaches from Parker County. Then he tried the poppy seed, which he did not finish, thinking it was probably an acquired taste, and proceeded to eat a prune kolache, which he found somewhat tart, but tasty.

While Byron was wiping his mouth with a napkin after finishing the prune kolache, a roar came from the crowd. Had he won? Surely not. He still had five and a half kolaches to go. Maybe he had won the competition for politest diner. He was, after all, using his napkin, and he felt that his table manners were impeccable.

Then the current Miss Kolache, who had remarkably white teeth, held Ernesto's hand in the air. He had won, as predicted by the man in the Waylon County Feed and Seed cap. The other contestants continued to shove kolaches into their mouths with incredible urgency, Byron noticed, so he quickened his pace. First, he finished the poppy seed kolache he had left to the side, for his mother had taught him never to waste food. Then he started on the second apricot kolache. He truly liked the consistency of the filling, and he wondered how the baker had made it so perfectly delightful.

The crowd cheered again when the man named Federico finished, and he gave a high five to his brother who had taken first place. Then the boy in the sausage shirt finished, followed by the two men in cowboy hats and then the other two gentlemen in Kolache Konquistador shirts. The football players finished at the same time, and they stood up from the table and gave one another a rather complicated handshake that Byron had never seen before. At this point, the only contestants still eating were Byron, the skinny kid with the bowl haircut, and the guy in the golf visor. Byron decided that he would need to quicken his pace so as not to be the last one on stage. Then the man in the golf visor wiped his chin and jumped up from the table. One of the more buxom members of the Kolache Kourt ran up and took him into an intimate embrace.

Now only Byron and the kid with the bowl haircut remained. The kid, who must have been thirteen or fourteen, was starting to turn a light shade of green, and Byron wondered if the pubescent lad would be disqualified if he puked his pastries. The announcer had not mentioned anything about vomiting when he presented the rules, so Byron was left to wonder.

Byron ate his second poppy seed and proceeded to eat his second apple kolache, still trying to decide if the baker had employed Galas or Fujis. And then he dined upon the peach kolache, which he had now decided had Fredericksburg peaches for the filling. The skinny kid, unsteady with nausea, pumped his fist in what appeared to be a Pyrrhic victory, leaving all eyes on Byron. At this point, Byron imagined, if the kid could refrain from upchucking for eight seconds, the judges would surely consider it a ride. Byron, now alone on the stage, smiled a shy smile and thoughtfully nibbled on the final prune kolache.

"You can do it!" a young boy with buck teeth hollered.

"Two more bites," an elderly woman in a Moravian costume called.

Byron finished the final kolache, wiped his mouth with his napkin, and took an elegant bow. A few people clapped, and then the crowd dispersed, with many people heading in the direction of the beer tents. Byron, stepping down from the stage, saw that Sunny Patek was waiting there for him.

"You can't just stop and smell the kolaches," Sunny said with a laugh.

"I thought that's what life was all about," Byron replied.

And then Sunny reached into her Kolache Kween apron and produced a business card that read "Scarlet Begonias Mobile Florist," which had a picture of a Volkswagen van covered in flowers above her name, number, and e-mail address. Taking the business card into the palm of his hand, Byron was both surprised and elated. Perhaps Sunny was not really interested in selling him scarlet begonias or forget-me-nots. Perhaps she was interested in him in a more substantial way. Perhaps she was the kind of woman who could love a man who was essentially a *klobásník* in a world of little round pastries. And Byron, though he had been the last to finish his plate of fruit and seed kolaches, at this beautiful moment in time, truly felt like a winner.

He Drank His Coffee Black

★ ★ ★

The old man sat in the café drinking black coffee. He was tall and lean in bootcut jeans and a button-down Oxford shirt. In the past, he had worn boots with a riding heel but now wore black tennis shoes to add sureness to his step. His winter felt hung on the ear of the chair next to him. He came to this café most days, and the waitresses could usually predict his orders. Black coffee was the constant, as well as the Ranchman's Breakfast, though his lunch orders changed occasionally, except for Tuesdays, when he ordered the special, chicken fried steak, green beans, and mashed potatoes.

"Anything else for you this morning?" Tammy asked. Tammy Smith had been well-loved at the Wailin' Biscuit Café for two decades now. She was quick with a compliment and quicker with the coffee, tea, and Dr. Pepper. She was blond-headed with a fine body, which the men invariably noticed, yet she had a kind disposition that even earned decent tips from the wives if she happened to bring the check while their husbands were in the bathroom.

"I might like to try one of those cinnamon rolls," the old man said.

"They're as sweet as your heart."

The old man smiled. He smiled softly sometimes, but he rarely spoke. He had worked in New Mexico, at the laboratory at Los Alamos, and had been present at the first wild flash of apocalypse in the Jornada del Muerto, the Wasteland of Death. Unlike most of the other scientists, he had not reacted with grim silence nor had he wept in the realization of what the blinding

121

flash portended. He had laughed. He had laughed hard and unhinged, though he never knew why. He had often laughed in situations when he did not know what to do or say. But this was different. It was not like anything he had ever experienced or had to cope with before, which made him burrow ever deeper within himself. After that strange, awkward laugh, that laugh that went unheard beneath the roar of the atomic explosion, he did not even seek the kinship or counsel of his fellow scientists. He did not seek solace in the understanding of people who had lived what he had lived. But still, the potential of his creation, of what his group had created, made him proud, for they had done what they had been tasked to do. They had made the abstraction of physical science abundantly concrete. They had turned theory into action. They had done something that could change the world as they knew it.

And then the news came three weeks later. The project he had worked on, where he had contributed to the design of the neutron initiator, was responsible for atomizing a city. And then, three days after that, another city. He had helped build a bomb that left but shadows on the ground where people once stood. He had helped build a bomb that caused incredible human suffering. He had worn a white badge, a badge of open clearance, a badge of undeniable culpability. He could not say that he had simply washed the glassware or served as a guard or a secretary. He had used his intellect and creativity to help build a device used to vaporize a quarter million human beings and the generations that would have followed, the vast multiplication of children and grandchildren and great-grandchildren. Centuries of future life extending into infinity were decimated from existence or potential existence because of his work. Upon receipt of the news that a city had been flashed out of existence, he no longer laughed when he was nervous. He rarely laughed at all, and for many years he could barely muster a smile.

He had never said the words "neutron initiator" to anyone outside the Los Alamos gate, and he was glad that he had managed to remain unknown. Other scientists had become famous, were found on the covers of news magazines and on television, but luckily, he had managed to avoid all of that. He had managed to remain an ordinary man.

"Could I talk you out of another napkin?" the old man asked.

"Absolutely," Tammy said, pulling one out of her apron pocket and placing it on the table next to his fork. "Well, what sort of mischief are you up to today?"

"Oh. Not much. I need to go to the Hoggly Woggly to get some dog food and a loaf of bread. Heard it might sleet later. Don't want to drive if the roads are slick."

"I don't blame you. You have to be careful out there."

All of those years ago, the old man had crossed the threshold of the hacienda at 109 East Palace in Santa Fe, had walked through the shade of the street entrance into the brightness of a courtyard that framed the wide blue sky above. He had walked through that courtyard toward the simple, common door with its bronze knob and hinges, that simple, ordinary door that led to assignments and organizational structures that would change him and humanity for all eternity. He signed his name, received his white badge and identity, and was sworn to silence, a silence he never in his life disavowed.

Though he preferred the now-defunct Plaza Bar, where Natives and cowboys and workers of all types relieved their thirst, in the months before the first atomic test he often sat for drinks at La Fonda with his friends Oppie and Einstein, who, like him, answered to a different name outside of the laboratory and talked only of common life on Bathtub Row. He had drunk and dined with greatness, had been among them, had been one of them, and now here he sat in a café in Texas drinking black coffee and speaking only about ice storms, church potlucks, and the like.

These days, in his advanced age, he allowed himself to laugh, though not often, for his laughter at the exploding sun in the white sand desert bore hard on him. He had always felt that he never deserved to laugh again for what he had done, for what he had helped create, if create was the right word for something that reaped such destruction.

"You need a warm-up?" Tammy asked, coffee pot in hand.

"Yes, ma'am. Please."

"Well, what kind of dog you got?"

"Got two of 'em. I think they're both part skunk though."

123

And then he chuckled. Tammy cocked her head and smiled with curiosity, her surprise perhaps evident to anyone paying attention. The old man smiled back, though somewhat sadly, and then the smile diluted from his face.

If he approached it all honestly, if he could somehow defeat his defense mechanisms, perhaps the dark weight would lift, but even decades later when he returned to that courtyard on East Palace and sat in a turquoise metal chair looking at the ceramic rabbits and ornate tiles and Mexican mirrors for sale at the tourist shop, when he looked at the shellacked ristras of red chile peppers hanging from the rough beams of the stucco porches ready for a postcard photo, he could see that times had changed, and space as well, though neither fundamentally. And even though time and space had been slightly altered, they had not changed beyond recognition, not like Hiroshima or his heart.

"Good cinnamon roll," the old man said.

"Sweet as a mama's love," Tammy replied.

"Yes, ma'am. Very sweet."

The old man took a slow drink of his coffee.

"You need anything else, hon?" Tammy asked.

"No ma'am. I reckon it's time for me to head down the road."

The old man paid, put his hat on his head, and walked past tables of families eating their breakfasts. There were grandparents with gray hair, nervous young parents with children in highchairs, a teenage boy stealing glances at the girl in the corner booth. He passed their tables, and with his jaw set and his eyes looking ever forward, the old man who always drank his coffee black walked out the café's front door and into the street, his shadow stretching before him in the late morning light.

Remove the Hardness from My Heart, but Deliver Me from Evil
★ ★ ★

"Remove the hardness from my heart, but deliver me from evil," Red prayed among the mesquite scrub and Spanish bayonet. He stood there alone at the edge of the Roemer Escarpment, above the stratified karst that pitched to the prairie floor below.

He carried a twelve-gauge over-and-under, which he used for quail hunting, though there were no longer any quail to be found, for pesticides and fire ants had dwindled their numbers. Still he carried the shotgun, though it was open season for nothing.

He had considered placing the barrels in his mouth and curtaining his consciousness, entering the great nowhere of vacuity and nothingness before his body tumbled down the escarpment, slammed on the rocks, and hurtled rough to the bottom, sprawled and splintered and shattered. But he saw no point. He would not play out his pain in such a final way. He had been staying in his girlfriend's trailer, where she lived with her parents, for the last nine months. He was only seventeen, too young to be living with his girlfriend, but her parents understood his situation and gave him their couch, though after a few weeks, they yielded, and let him sleep in their daughter's room, with their golden-haired pride one year his senior. It was easier anyway, for they had grown tired of stepping lightly past the quilt-covered couch to the kitchen on their way to work.

Red's father had asked him to come home, but he refused. He would not return to that house, not with his father's wife there, for she had given his truck to her brother fresh from the county jail so he could get to work, or so she said. And Red's father had done nothing, for his wife was young, and he was old, and he would not wager on losing her flesh at any cost. Yet Red had paid for most of the truck himself, had roofed houses to buy it. He had carried shingles up ladders and worked on roofs in the summer heat for day labor wages for a truck whose note was carried in his daddy's name to be given to a man who had spent that season watching television at the county jail.

Red walked through the thorns of honey mesquite and past the long-spined cactus-pear across the prairie grass. The whipping wind blew hot, and mesquite beans rattled on the trees like a den of diamondback serpents. Red's girlfriend, Tina, had gone to the movie theater on the state highway with her parents, and he had been invited but was embarrassed, for he had little money, and he did not want them paying his way. So he walked the escarpment, the place where the plates met, where differences collided and grated against one another, like the difference between forgiveness and acquiescence to evil.

He could move back home and try to stomach that woman's lies, he thought, though he worried about the gradual theft of identity that could come with uncontested lies being repeated so often that even the listener started to profess their veracity, that even the one hearing found himself defending the most blatant of falsehoods until he lost who he was and everything he valued.

No. Red could never go home, for he knew how easily this could happen. He knew because it had happened to his own father. He had lost respect for the man who had once been his hero, his champion, his lodestar. It was a brutal revelation to learn that his father was only a man, nothing more than a man. Mortal. All too mortal. Some said that Red was wise for his age. An old soul, a quiet woman who served as a missionary in a distant land once told him. But he did not think so. He thought that he was only observant and had the ability to learn from other people's mistakes rather than have to live them for himself. And his father had made a lifetime of mistakes in a short span of years.

Through money and lies, his father's wife supported criminals and parasites, the members of her family, and his father was complicit in his silence. But Red did not want to be a part of it. He did not even want to bear witness to the corruption. He did not want to go home. He prayed the Lord to take the hardness from his heart, to take the hardness forged like the iron nails of Christ away from him, but he did not feel the manna of assurance in his heart that he would be delivered, and so he walked the escarpment with a shotgun in his hand, a youth upon a barren heath with too much on his mind.

On Independence Day
★ ★ ★

Freebee Tomball crouched in the back of his brother's pickup whiteknuckling the lip of the tailgate with his left hand and firing a Roman candle at the truck speeding toward them with his right. The night was dark on that Hill Country road, and Freebee liked the sound the shooting stars made when they bore out of the cardboard tube, the same sound he figured a long-gun would make if a long-gun could be fired underwater. The first bright green balls shot high, missing the truck and curving toward the shoulder before fading to darkness.

"Damn you, Freebee," Sonny, his brother, hollered out the window of the truck.

The truck behind them was filled with the entire Stink Creek Skunks six-man football team, all eight of them, and the boys, all wearing black and white T-shirts, started waving their fists, and by the time Freebee had fired his sixth shooting star, which hit the truck's windshield with a thud and then bounced off the hood, two boys standing in the back of the Stink Creek truck started firing Roman candles over the cab of their truck toward Freebee's position behind the tailgate.

Freebee ducked, and so did Short Stack Jenkins, who was kneeling beside him. Hardluck Stevens and Bubba James, who were sitting next to Sonny on the bench seat, were giving the Stink Creek team the one-finger salute out the back window.

Freebee's buddy, Rooster Brown, who played offensive tackle for the Skunks, hung out the side window of the Stink Creek truck aiming his candle high in an attempt to lob a red star into the bed of Sonny's pickup truck.

"Poke your head out," Rooster yelled.

"Like hell I will," Freebee hollered back, raising his head above the tailgate so Rooster could hear him, a fiery green ball whistling past his ear by the time "hell" passed his lips.

About that time, the trucks jumped the highway and rolled down a grated gravel road toward Lake Henry Warnell, the half-washed-up little reservoir everybody drove out to if they wanted to try to talk their girlfriend out of her panties or gig a frog or two.

"Hell," Rooster hollered after jumping out of the truck at the boat launch. "You damn near busted the windshield."

"You almost got me in the head," Freebee said.

"Almost don't count."

"Hell it don't."

"Almost counts in horseshoes and hand grenades. I was shooting Roman candles."

They both laughed and slapped one another on the back. Freebee was proud to be out at the lake with everyone. He had just turned sixteen, and his parents had allowed him to go out with the older guys for the first time. He considered the Fourth of July his Independence Day.

Rooster handed Freebee a bottle of Wild Turkey. Freebee took a long draw, shook his head violently, and made a sour face.

"Hell, boy, you drank so much Turkey you got feathers caught in your throat," Rooster said.

"Just taking a little sip to wet my whistle," Freebee replied, his stomach queasy, but not letting on.

Sonny's headlights and the tips of a couple of cowboy cigarettes were the only lights to be found other than the million pinholes of stars on the black velvet dome of sky. Franklin Key, whose daddy owned a car dealership, started shooting fancy, high-grade fireworks over the lake. Each one looked like a little mortar, like they use in the army, and the explosions were as loud as a shotgun but looked like glowing dandelion thistles in the sky or even the big ball in the Dallas skyline.

Somebody shot a screaming road racer into a circle of boys drinking beer, and they jumped like they had the hot foot. Fireworks shot high, and little gray puffs of smoke glided across the sky, the smell of gunpowder strong and pungent, a smell that thrilled Freebee's nostrils, for it reminded him of hunting whitetail deer with black powder rifles with his daddy.

Tricephus played on a stereo singing a song about mudding in his four-wheel drive. A couple of pretty girls who came in a ragtop jeep started talking to Freebee while he stood near his brother's truck. The girls had big, well-tended hair and were wearing tight tank tops that accented the gravitational defiance of their titties and the flatness of their bellies. They were the only girls at the lake, and Freebee was surprised that they chose to talk to him when there was a famous football team right there beside him.

The girls' eyes suddenly got big, and when Freebee looked over his shoulder, he could see his brother sitting in the cab of his truck with a lighted string of Black Cats in his hand. Sonny casually flicked the string in Freebee's direction, but the firecrackers hit the inside of the window, which was open about as much as it would be to hold a tray at the Sonic Drive-In, and then they bounced back into Sonny's lap.

Smoke billowed from the open windows as the cab lit up in increments, Sonny rattling with the pop of a hundred firecrackers exploding on the crotch of his jeans and on the belly of his PBR T-shirt. His face glowed like a jack-o-lantern with each small explosion. After Sonny had been rattled like a Tommy-gunned snitch in a gangster movie, the last pop popped and everyone laughed except Freebee, who, despite the fact that his brother had tried to embarrass him in front of those girls and felt that he got what he deserved, also knew that Sonny would not hesitate to kick his ass in front of God and everybody if he started laughing, too. They were brothers, and thicker than water, even if they did try to bust one another's nuts on occasion.

Pretty soon, one of the girls, who had "Texas Prison Rodeo Sweetheart" silkscreened across the front of her tank top, was dry-humping Freebee in the back of his brother's pickup while the two of them made out. When their session got heated, she raised the tailgate so that the casual observer would not easily see them in the bed of the truck.

131

The girl, who said her name was Nancy, climbed on top of him in the back of the pickup. He had never been in a situation like this before, and he was in awe as she rubbed up against him in the light of the summer stars and the burst of the car dealer's son's fireworks, which made his first night of independence truly seem like a holiday, or a trip to Six Flags, even if the closest he had ever been to Six Flags was the Waylon County fair.

He wondered if one of the older guys would throw a string of firecrackers into the bed of the truck to interrupt them, but no one did, and he did not know why. Maybe they were too busy getting drunk. Maybe they were too busy shooting fireworks or watching the bursts of hot color over the lake. He did not know. But now he was a man, a man who drank whiskey and made out with women. He was a man, an independent man, on Independence Day.

But he wondered. He wondered if his parents would be waiting up for him and his brother. He wondered if the girl he called Sweetheart would now demand that he be her boyfriend. He wondered if his independence was really independence or simply a transition into a lifetime sentence, a lifetime sentence serving the family he could have very well started in the bed of his brother's truck. He thought about all of that as he gave Sweetheart a final sloppy kiss while the Black Cats popped and the road whistles streaked across the gravel.

And he continued to think about all of that as he rode in the bed of his brother's truck with the wind whipping through his bilevel on the way back home. He thought about independence, about his first day of being free, and then he crouched down behind the cab to light his last Roman candle before quickly crawling toward the tailgate to shoot it between the headlights of the Stink Creek truck, which was following behind them. Freebee fired his Roman candle into the Hill Country darkness, the glowing green and red balls volleying across the sky like lazy shooting stars, and him thinking about nothing but the matter at hand.

Under the Banner of Willie Nelson
★ ★ ★

Prairie Dog Brown was standing in the Bermuda grass outside the county courthouse when Shotgun Willie started riding Trigger across the first verse of "Whiskey River." Prairie Dog had saved up three months' worth the profits from selling flags on the side of the highway for this very moment. There was nothing, in his long-held opinion, better than hearing Willie thump on his guitar like he was spurring his pony and then start singing "Whiskey River, take my mind" above the rowdy encouragement of a friendly, hell-raising crowd.

Over the years Prairie Dog had seen Uncle Willie play in Dripping Springs, Bee Cave, and even up in Cowtown, but never had he seen him play here in Warnell. But then, nobody had, considering this was the first time the Red Headed Stranger had ever appeared in Prairie Dog's hometown. Willie, good man that he was, was playing a benefit concert for the Waylon County Courthouse, which had been flooded when a bank of toilets overflowed on Memorial Day weekend, and the water had traveled its inevitable path to the basement to accumulate, ruining or at least waterlogging a whole century's worth the birth certificates, hitching licenses, and death certificates. The concert would offset renovation costs as well as provide an endowment to keep the county courthouse afloat.

Prairie Dog felt bad for the town and for all the folks whose paperwork was in the basement and got messed up, but he was still glad to see Uncle Willie, in his braids and bandanna, riding Trigger across the honkytonk plains above the courthouse steps, which were covered by the big wooden stage where Willie and his band now performed. Behind them, to Prairie Dog's delight, the roadies had draped a giant Texas flag, which Prairie Dog figured must have been even bigger than the thirty-by-sixty-foot versions flown above big city car lots. He himself had never sold one even close to that big, and he reckoned he could have bought a fistful of tickets from the profits of one of those.

Standing there on the courthouse lawn, Prairie Dog felt mighty proud to be a native of Warnell, where the biggest flag he had ever seen was now flying behind the greatest musician in the world, and he was thankful that his little side business selling flags near the shoulder of the state highway had enabled him to buy a ticket to the concert. Normally he used the money he made to buy fishing lures and bullets, or when times were leaner, to pay the water bill, but times were not so lean right now and this was something special. It wasn't every day that Willie Nelson came and played just up the road from your house.

Looking around, Prairie Dog reckoned that about half the county had saved their buffalo nickels to attend this concert, and he saw all sorts of folks he knew, including some he had even sold flags to. To his left he saw Buckshot McGee, to whom he had sold about half a dozen Come and Take Its, a couple of Stars and Bars, a Don't Tread on Me, a Texas flag, a Christian flag, Old Glory, and even one of those red flags like Santa Anna flew before the Battle of the Alamo. Buckshot was certainly one of his best customers, and his purchases had provided a great deal of the funding for Prairie Dog's ticket to see the Red Headed Stranger.

Prairie Dog also saw Francis Willingham while he was standing in the beer line. Francis had not bought nearly as many flags as Buckshot, but still he had purchased flags. Prairie Dog remembered selling Francis a Rainbow flag, a Hammer and Sickle, and a Maple Leaf. None of these were flags that Prairie Dog normally sold, but he kept them in stock just in case. An ol' boy could hardly predict who would happen along that empty stretch of highway and decide to buy a flag or two.

Willie started into his mid-show medley, beginning with "Funny How Time Slips Away," and Prairie Dog was happier than a possum in a dumpster. A Willie show, in Prairie Dog's estimation, was better for the soul

134

than going to church, though he would never say that to his wife. Prairie Dog had, of course, been washed in the blood and dunked in the river, but still he found it hard to deny the fact that a Willie concert was a hell of a lot more uplifting than a preacher threatening him with brimstone and Beelzebub, and having to sit and listen to miserable, off-key renditions of "Holy, Holy, Holy." A Willie show, like church, was a ritual, and Prairie Dog could count on certain elements every time. The man in the red bandanna would always open with "Whiskey River," would normally play the "Crazy How the Night Life Slips Away" medley somewhere in the middle, and end with "Will the Circle Be Unbroken" and a couple of other gospel songs. And the show, unlike church, was never interrupted by the offertory since admission was always paid on the front end.

The day was hot, somewhere in the neighborhood of a buck-oh-five, and though Prairie Dog was not drowning in a whiskey river, he was certainly stumbling around after chugging down a bucketload of barley pop. Normally, he didn't drink so much that the earth began to buckle, but Prairie Dog's wife, Maureen, had decided not to join him for the show today. Without his wife there to help regulate his intake, Prairie Dog had found himself running neck and neck with ol' Cooter Brown to see who could get more shit-faced.

Maureen was Prairie Dog's first, and thankfully, only wife, and he was glad of that. She was nice, so nice that the ladies at church always tried to give her the jobs they did not want for the Sunday potlucks, and Maureen just smiled and took them without an unkind word. And though Prairie Dog's wife didn't want to go to a concert so close to home, she encouraged him to go and said she'd pick him up afterwards, so he reckoned he was pretty lucky. Even if Prairie Dog was drunker than Cooter Brown, to whom, for the record, he was not related, Maureen would just shake her head and tell him to get in the car. Having read somewhere that one of Uncle Willie's wives had sewn him into a sheet and beaten him with a broom handle when he passed out drunk one time, Prairie Dog reckoned he was mighty fortunate to have Maureen. She was, by most accounts, at least somewhat understanding.

Willie and his band played a song about a little Texas town and then started into "Amazing Grace." Prairie Dog began to sing along, and when he looked around, he saw that the other folks were singing too. There were women in tube tops, cutoffs, and cowboy boots. There were bikers in leather. College kids wearing letters he didn't know. Ol' boys in summer straws and pearl snaps. Hippies in sandals and beads. And even a couple of guys in bright red MAGA hats, and still others in camouflage bibs. Everyone was singing along regardless of the flags they usually flew. At this moment, they all rallied beneath the banner of Willie Nelson. In the sweet, skunky air of twilight, they rallied beneath the giant Texas flag, a flag that had somehow been transformed into a banner of peace and harmony and goodwill. Uncle Willie began singing "Will the Circle Be Unbroken" and everyone sang along, smiling at one another as he ended the show, smiling as he played "I Saw the Light." And Prairie Dog surely hoped that everyone did. He finished his last beer, threw the plastic cup into a trash can, and headed toward the gate in the fluorescent glow at concert's end truly glad that he came, truly glad to have seen the Red Headed Stranger ride his old palomino across the courthouse square, truly glad to have been one with all of humanity beneath the ever-waving flag of a honkytonk messiah.

Swim Party
★ ★ ★

When the engine arrived, the young boy was lying on his back beside the pool with frantic adults stumbling from margaritas and longnecks circled around him and children in dripping bathing suits shrieking on the other side of the yard where a fairly sober, quick-thinking aunt had corralled them. Sterling H. Cash, in bunker suit bottoms, a white T-shirt, and his fire helmet, approached with a medical kit in his left hand.

A heavyset man in Hawaiian-print shorts and an older woman in a one-piece bathing suit stepped aside so the firemen could access the child. Sterling appraised the situation and then quickly dropped to his knees.

"Son, can you hear me? Can you hear me?" he asked, shaking the little boy's foot.

"His name's Judd," a woman said.

"Judd, can you hear me?" the fireman asked once again.

The little boy looked to be about four years old. He was brown-headed and round, with a childish little belly and baby-fat on his limbs. His skin was gray. Sterling put his ear to the kid's mouth and nose but could not hear breathing. He checked the pulse. Nothing. He suspected that some-one had broken one of the boy's ribs trying to apply CPR, but he hoped not. The whole scene was a clusterfuck.

He hated these scenarios. Always the same. Adults drinking. Children swimming and running around the pool. Nobody paying attention. The little boy was dead. Probably had been for ten minutes. Brain damage if

137

he lived. Never the same. Nobody the same either way. Everything would change. Everything. Every life would change one way or another. For every damn one of them. Adults relaxing on a Saturday afternoon shooting the shit never thinking Death would rap on the door. And Lord help the children.

Sterling took the kid's chin, tilted back his head, and made sure that the windpipe was clear. He then put his mouth over what seemed like half of the kid's face and blew. The boy's chest expanded with each breath. Sterling then began to work on the child's heart with the heel of his palm, and though his compressions were quick and accurate, the kid was still not responding. After thirty compressions, he gave two more breaths and started the compressions again.

The kid's name was Judd. He knew the boy's name. He wished he didn't know his name, but he did. He continued the compressions. He worked and worked. The children were crying in the yard. The parents stood drunk around him. He gave the child two more breaths. The kid's lips had turned blue, foam upon them. Sterling would keep working, keep trying, but he had answered enough of these calls to know the boy was dead.

He would continue in order to make these people feel better. The boy was gone. Dead. Not coming back. But Sterling would continue to push fast on the heart, blow on the intervals, and start again. He had now been working for who knows how long, and the kid had not responded. And Sterling still hadn't heard an ambulance. Where the hell were they? Answering a call on the state highway? Sitting in the Wailin' Biscuit Café drinking the free iced tea for first responders?

Well, they weren't first today. They almost never were first. Sterling wondered if they planned it that way. He was working on the little kid, and at this point he had might as well be beating on a sack of potatoes because there was nothing he could do. The boy was dead, but still he would put on a show. He'd put on a show so the family would believe that he and his crew had done everything they could to save the boy's life. But they could not have saved his life. He was dead. Long dead now. Sterling raised up and let Strombo, the engineer, have a go at it. Strombo worked and worked, but he could not get the child to breathe. Strombo began to cry. He cried

138

openly. He needed help. Real help. But Strombo kept on.

Sterling should have never asked Strombo to try to work on the kid. He should not have dealt that to his brother. Strombo had kids, and these situations were much worse for people with kids. They would think about their own. He should have thought about that, but he hadn't.

Sterling knew about half of the people standing around him. In a small town like Warnell, that was normal. This group had been a party crowd in high school. They hauled kegs out into the country in the backs of pickup trucks and threw parties at the lake and in open fields and sometimes in barns. Sterling remembered keg parties where everyone sat around drinking beer on the tailgates of trucks raising hell until deep in the night.

He had graduated in the same class as a couple of these people. One of them was a gymnast, a male gymnast, who was now working in sales. He used to do tumbling passes after a few beers, which always livened up a party. Today he was too drunk to walk across the yard, much less do a tumbling pass.

"What do you think, Sterling?" the former gymnast said, his face red and filled with concern.

Sterling's eyes darted to the left, and then they returned their full gaze on the man.

"I don't know," he said.

The boy's mama shrieked and dropped a longneck onto the concrete that lined the pool, the bottle shattering into shards and splinters. A heavyset man walked over to see the fireman's progress and filleted his foot on a piece of broken glass, the blood coming fast because of the alcohol. Sterling muttered to himself about what a dumbass the man was to step onto the broken glass considering that everyone had heard it, and it had caused a big commotion. Blood was now all over the side of the pool, diluting itself in the puddle left from when they had dragged the little kid from the water. Sterling stepped over to where the dumbass was and took the man's foot into his hand. At least he hadn't hit a damn artery. Sterling pulled the shard out of the man's foot and bandaged him up with gauze and tape from his medical kit.

"Do you need to go to the hospital?" Sterling asked.

139

"Nah. Nah, I'm fine," the man told him.

It was all a complete damn mess, Sterling thought. He'd be glad when the ambulance got there.

By now Strombo was exhausted from trying to resuscitate the kid. Sterling tried again. He ran two fingers inside the boy's mouth to clear anything that might be in the windpipe, and he tried to save him. Maybe he really could save this kid. Maybe he lacked faith. Maybe the boy would come around, like his old sputtering lawnmower after what seemed like the thousandth time he pulled the cord. Still, there was nothing. No pulse. No heartbeat. No breath. No nothing.

"Can you save him? Can you save him?" the mother asked.

Sterling looked away.

"I'm only a man. I tried, but I'm only a man," he told her.

And then he covered Judd's body with a raggedy beach towel hoping that the ambulance would arrive soon. He moved across the yard away from the dead child. The wailing was too much to bear.

Land and Sky

★ ★ ★

"Boyd, I done made the decision," Ezekiel Hays said with a cold one in his hand.

Mr. Hays leaned back in his hardwood chair and took a long look across the sprawling acres of Texas Hill Country before him. A huge, centuries-old oak tree stood in the distance, and patches of prickly pear cactus dotted the land at intervals. In the foreground, just past the porch where he was sitting, stood a limestone smokehouse and a little tool shed. He took a slow slug of Lone Star and then scratched his ample belly.

"Now what decision is that, Mr. Hays?" Boyd finally asked, adjusting the bill of his Texalube cap.

"I'm going to start making me some art."

Boyd tilted his head at an odd angle and looked directly at the old rancher.

"I know it probably sounds like another one of my wild hairs," Mr. Hays continued, "but I've been thinking about this for a good long while. I'm gonna take my blow torch and start welding old junk together to make it into something new. I seen it done on television. They showed how Picasso took a bicycle seat and some handlebars, welded 'em together with the seat facing down and the handlebars facing up, and the next thing you know he had a bull's head hanging on the wall. I guaran-damn-tee you I can do that, too."

"But wouldn't you still want to have the bicycle for riding up the road when you got on another one of your health kicks?" Boyd asked, leaning

141

against a column of the wooden porch.

"Now, Boyd. You know full well I ain't talking about parting out the bicycle. I'm talking about other junk. The bicycle was just an example. We've got rusty dykes, broken saw blades, Glidden wire, a couple of busted ploughs, most of an old Edsel, and all sorts of junk."

"Well, that sounds like a real good use for a lot of the stuff piled up around here. And that old rust-bucket of an Edsel ain't nothing but a rattlesnake condominium at this point. Considering there's no lack of material to work with, I imagine you'll be making great big statues before you know it."

"I don't know about that," Mr. Hays said, taking another draw of beer. "I reckon I'll start out small. I'll do little pieces that can go on the wall or stand on the table, and later, once I feel like I'm pretty good at it, I'll do great big pieces like they put in front of the banks in Dallas and Houston."

"No offense, Mr. Hays, but aren't the sculptures they stick in front of banks usually kinda ugly?" Boyd asked.

"I will admit that some of those pieces ain't exactly beautiful in my opinion, but beauty, as a wiseman once said, is in the eye of the beer-holder. Now there's pieces that some folks might consider the dadgum pinnacle of artistic endeavor that I think are ugly as homemade sin, but what do I know? I'm not the one they asked to put a big ol' hunk of metal in front of a bank or a library or in an open field way out there in West Texas, where they got them weird lights glowing at night."

Boyd stood and listened with his sinewy hands resting on his narrow hips.

"Now, I know what you're thinking," Mr. Hays continued, his belly protruding slightly from beneath his pumpkin-colored polo shirt. "You're thinking that I'm too old a dog for this particular trick."

"Actually, that's not what I'm thinking at all. I'm mostly thinking about breakfast, though I do think it's good that you've decided to try something new."

"You know, at first I didn't figure I oughta pursue this since I honestly don't know nothing about art. But then I got to thinking about kindergarten. In kindergarten, kids get a bunch of paint on their hands and swirl it around on paper however they get the notion. It makes 'em happy. It makes 'em take their pictures home and give 'em to their mamas. And their mamas put 'em on the icebox. Those kids don't know nothing about art, but art makes them happy. And it'll make me happy, too. I reckon happiness comes from the process. Happiness comes from creating."

Mr. Hays took a final pull from his beer and placed the empty bottle on the little barnwood table beside him.

"You worked hard for many, many years, and you still work hard, and you deserve your fair share of happiness," Boyd said. "I think you should try your hand at making some art and see what happens. You hungry?"

"I'm hungry enough to be twins."

"Then I reckon I'll bring us both a bowl of posole."

"I love posole for breakfast," Mr. Hays said. "That sounds mighty good."

Boyd went inside and ladled them up a bowl of posole each and brought it out to the porch. Mr. Hays relished each mouthful. The posole was good and red and filled the stomach.

"We're pretty lucky out here," Mr. Hays said. "Here we are chewing the fat on a porch overlooking acres and acres. We got oak trees and prairie grass. Deer running around. It's nice out here. And if we want to whip us up some art, we got the space to do it. And we also got peace. Think about them artists in New York living four to an apartment. They don't have enough room to make a ship in a bottle, much less a Cadillac Stonehenge. And they probably have to hear a bunch of bozos laying on the car horns while they're trying to create some art."

Boyd stood and listened with a raised spoon in one hand and his bowl cradled in the other.

"You're right. We're lucky out here," Boyd said. "But that's not what folks've always thought. Now even the folks in New York are starting to think about the beauty of land and sky, and they're sticking their work in fields and on plains, where the land and sky become part of the art, or maybe the art becomes part of the landscape. I reckon it all depends on how you look at it."

"I hadn't thought about that," Mr. Hays said before slurping a spoonful of posole, "but I sure think it's an interesting idea to chew on."

After Boyd finished his breakfast, he walked back inside and put his bowl and spoon in the dishwasher.

"Well, a philosopher's work is never done," he said. "I'd better go check on the cattle."

"I imagine they'll be glad to see you," Mr. Hays told him. "You know, Boyd, I hired you on as a philosopher, and I must say you are doing a fine job of philosophizing and watching after cattle. And, as ol' Freddy Nietzsche more or less said, an ol' boy who works more than a third of his day is a slave, and I do make it a point not to keep you in chains."

"I appreciate that. Well, I reckon I better get moving. Daylight's burning."

"See you in a little while," Mr. Hays told him.

"Adios," Boyd said.

Boyd stepped off the porch and climbed into Mr. Hays' old two-toned pickup truck and drove down the rutted dirt road in the direction of the giant oak tree. With as many acres as the Hays Ranch contained, checking the cattle could be somewhat of a chore, but that was part of the job, and Mr. Hays knew it suited Boyd just fine.

From his vantage point on the porch, Mr. Hays could see the cloud of dust trailing the old pickup down the dirt road until it disappeared over by the creek, where many of the cattle were likely congregated. These days, Mr. Hays kept a small herd of longhorns, which was good for his taxes since he could claim an ag exemption. He didn't actually need the money, but he also didn't want to hand any over to the government for no good reason. His family, after all, had managed its money well over the generations, and, based on his current spending habits, Mr. Hays had enough money to live another hundred lifetimes or more. He had millions of dollars in the bank but still thought it wasteful to spend money that didn't need to be spent. In fact, he would not go so far as to buy a new truck considering that the old one he had driven for the last two decades still ran just fine.

After putting away his dishes, Mr. Hays grabbed another beer and went out to the old gray barn. He got a thin welding rod, started up his welding machine, pulled down his helmet, and got to work. The arc of heat burned blue as he melded the metal. Slag dripped and splattered. Sparks flew. Red hot metal cooled and retreated to black. Soon piles of junk were starting to stand upright, as if they had taken on intellect, as if they had taken on language and sophistication. There were tall sculptures, some as tall as a man even. There were piles that became barrel-shaped, that took on the look of Mexican cactus. There were men and animals and pieces that did not suggest anything that Mr. Hays had seen before. To accommodate the rapidly growing collection, he laid a couple of old doors on top of saw-horses and covered them with smaller works, works that would later hang on walls perhaps or stand upright somewhere or another, or at least that is how he imagined it.

He walked around the barn looking at what felt like an exhibition. He was proud, proud of what he had done. And he was surprised. Here he was, an old man, and only now had he found what felt like his calling. He could have been doing this all of his life. It seemed so strange. It felt so natural. He had worked. Yes, he had worked. He had run cattle. He had inoculated. He had gelded. He had fixed gates. He had planted crops. He had worked hard to keep the family place running, to keep it successful. It was his duty and his heritage.

Yet this felt different. He did not do it out of duty, out of honor, out of any sense of loyalty to anyone else. But it did not feel selfish. It just felt like a need. Making these things made his mind feel good, and he could almost feel the different parts of his brain dancing around as he worked. It made him feel happy in a way he could not describe. Ever since his wife had died, he had felt empty. He had felt an almost hopeless restlessness. He was not a churchman, but life these days reminded him of the Book of Ecclesiastes, all of that dust in the wind business, all of that futility. But now he was creating. He was creating despite all of that. Maybe everything really was futile, but at least he would occupy his time with the positive force of cre-ation. He would make sculptures that made him happy. He would plant a sculpture garden near the house, and he would watch it grow and grow as he created more and more pieces. All of this excited him to no end.

"What do you think?" he asked Boyd when the young man joined him in the barn that afternoon.

"I like it. I like it all. What are you going to do with it?"

"Display it. Put pieces in odd places to shock folks and surprise 'em."

"I reckon that might make it harder to mow."

"You're probably right. But we could put out little gravel pads for each of the big pieces. That would make it easier to mow around them. Now, honestly, and don't tell me no windy to save my feelings, what do you think about all of this stuff? I want you to look at it all and critique it."

"I ain't no art critic."

"Well, you know something about art. You went to college, didn't you?"

"Yessir. And I took Art Appreciation. Got a B in the class, too. If that qualifies me to be an art critic, then I guess I'll start critiquing."

The old man pulled a package of plug tobacco out of his back pocket and bit off a chew.

"So what do you think?" Mr. Hays asked with a nervous grin.

"I like this tall figure with the trowel for a chest and wire cutters for a body. It's like a rustic Giacometti."

"What do you think about this one?" Mr. Hays asked, pointing to a valentine-style heart he had made out of horseshoes.

"I don't think a real art critic would necessarily be interested in that piece, but the workmanship is nice."

"Why wouldn't an art critic like it?"

"I reckon art critics would consider it… Well, it's hard to say."

"Well, say it."

"They'd probably call it kitsch."

"Kitsch? Why would they call it kitsch?"

"Well, you know, hearts are never a good idea."

"Why not?"

"It's kind of a tired shape. There's nothing original to it."

"But you said that other piece was like Ghirardelli or whatever it was."

"Yes, it's like his work, but it's not derivative. It's clear that it's not derivative because it doesn't look like you're too familiar with Giacometti."

"What about this piece?" Mr. Hays said, pointing to an owl with wings made from an old circular saw blade he had cut in half.

"Kitsch as well."

"What is the difference between kitsch and high-fallutin'?"

"A feeling. A feeling that separates high art from kitsch. It's kind of hard to express. There are certain shapes, certain attitudes that separate the two."

"What about that ol' boy from France that displayed a dadgum commode? What was that?"

"High art."

"But it's a commode. What makes it different from any other commode?"

"How he displayed it. He put it in a gallery."

"Then I'm going to build a gallery right here in the middle of this ranch. And I'll put everything I make inside it. That'll keep us from having to split hairs and decide what is art and what is kitsch."

"I didn't mean to get you riled up with all my critiquing."

"You didn't get me riled up. It's just that I've lived my whole life on this land, and there are some things I don't know much about. It all kind of surprises me, I guess. Some ol' boy can stick handlebars on a bicycle seat and he's a genius. Some other ol' boy can make a heart out of horseshoes or a fat little metal owl and he's not."

"Mr. Hays, you're sharp as they come in my books."

"I ain't looking for you to tell me I'm the sharpest screw in the box to make me feel better. I never claimed to be a genius, and for good reason. I'm just having trouble understanding what is art and what is not."

Mr. Hays picked up the standing figure with the trowel and carried it outside the barn. He walked off into an open field, put it on the ground, and then sat down a few feet away. Boyd sat down beside him.

"I like that a lot," Boyd said. "A lone figure in an open landscape."

"I like it, too. But you ain't just humoring me, are you?"

"I'm shooting you straight, Mr. Hays."

"You know, this has all got me to thinking. It ain't just about creating. It's about somebody else enjoying what you create as well."

"Even if it's just a ranch hand you call a philosopher?"

"Especially if it's a young ranch hand who is indeed a philosopher. Tomorrow I think I'll try this again. I think I'll whip up another mess of art."

Boyd smiled. The two men sat beside one another as the sun glowed warm and orange on the western horizon. Birds chattered in the trees, and a young doe appeared in the distance. The metal figure cast its shadow across the ground before it. Mr. Hays was happy and strangely proud.

Skunk Scent

★ ★ ★

Emily Allcorn pulled off the side of the state highway and slipped a pair of rubber gloves over her thin, manicured hands. She then placed a pink surgical mask over her face, climbed out of her pickup, and slammed the door. After lowering the tailgate, she reached into the bed of her truck and took out an "EMILY ALLCORN for RAILROAD COMMISSIONER" sign. This was the third time she had come to plant signs near the cattle guard at Mr. Smithson's place, and she hoped it would be the last, for this election anyway.

Mr. Smithson, whom she had known most of her life, was her best friend's father, and he had happily given her permission to place the signs on his land. The first time she had planted signs here, someone had yanked them out of the ground, torn them each in half, and left them on the side of the road. Hoping that this was an isolated incident, Emily had quietly replaced the signs and moved on. Then, last week, someone had taken her signs altogether. What flustered Emily the most was that, although she was a Waylon County native, people were still swiping or destroying her campaign signs.

Emily, of course, understood that winning Waylon County, which was not densely populated, would probably have little impact on the state-wide results, but she was nonetheless determined to win it for the sake of pride. She had attended school from kindergarten to twelfth grade here, had even been on the Warnell Wardogs drill team, and had worked at the local Hoggly Woggly to help her family. Since starting her campaign, Emily had already held town hall meetings as far west as El Paso, as far south as

149

Brownsville, and as far east as Texarkana, but it still bothered her that her signs were being vandalized or stolen in her home county.

Emily now lived in Austin, though she traveled back home whenever she could in order to see her mother, who was starting to slow down a little. Emily herself was now thirty-five. She was still pretty, perhaps prettier than she had been in high school, with dark curly hair, olive skin, and bright hazel eyes. Austin had influenced her sensibilities and her fashion, and it was not uncommon for her to arrive at the law firm where she worked wearing a bohemian smock dress, bangles, and Buddhist prayer beads.

Her opponent, the scion of an oil dynasty headquartered out of Odessa, said that she was not in touch with Texas values. He said that she was not in touch with farmers and ranchers and good country folk, this man who traveled in the family jet and had never had to risk floating a check or live off of beans and cornbread to make it until payday. Yes, his family owned a ranch where they raised angus and longhorns, but he was merely lord of the manor. He did not actually work there. He passed his time going on big game hunts, where he had his picture taken next to bears and antelope and rhinoceroses that he had been led to so that he could shoot them. He posted the pictures on social media and laughed at his detractors. And even though he had insulted pretty much everyone but himself on television last week, he was still leading Emily by more than ten points according to the most recent poll.

Emily, in contrast to her opponent, was raised in a trailer near Lake Henry Warnell and was the first person in her family to go to college. Her daddy, who worked at a filling station, hunted to keep his children fed in the winter, not to flaunt death and boast. And Emily had hunted with him when she was a girl, had used skunk scent on her boots just like her daddy to mask her scent when they were stalking deer on public land in Bigfoot Wallace County. And now Emily was going to show these people that said she was out of touch with her fellow Texans a thing or two.

In the back of her truck, in a five-gallon bucket, she had a one-ounce vial of skunk scent sealed inside two zip-lock bags. She opened the zip-locks and pulled out the skunk scent, unscrewing the lid and using the dropper to place a couple of beads of eau de polecat on her election sign, shaking the sign from side to side to ensure that the scent ran and spread. She did the same with the other sign she planned to display along the fenceline. Now any fool wanting to tear down her signs would first have to contend with her country values. She was hardly out of touch. And whatever clod decided to undermine her campaign would soon have a clear understanding of the ingenuity she had gained from her upbringing.

About that time, an old man on a four-wheeler came barreling down the caliche road toward the cattle guard. This man was her best friend's daddy, and he had a 1911 Colt strapped to his hip and was wearing a golf visor with the words "Padre Island" emblazoned across the front. He rolled up to the cattle guard and applied the hand brake.

"Well, if it ain't Emily Allcorn," he said. "When I left the shack to fetch the bills and junk from my mailbox, I was hardly expecting to come face to face with greatness."

Emily laughed and blushed.

"I don't think you've exactly come face to face with greatness, Mr. Smithson," she said, taking off her pink surgical mask.

"Well, you're great to me. I'm proud of you. Running for railroad commissioner. I'm not real sure how much you know about railroads, but I do know you'll be a quick study once you're in office. When Penny told me you wanted to put campaign signs on our land, I was happy to oblige."

"And I thank you. But, you know, if people don't stop pulling my signs, I may have a hard time getting into office."

"They yanked 'em again?"

"Yes, sir. But I put up new ones. And I put a dose of skunk scent on each one."

"That'll fix their wagons."

"That is my hope."

"So what do you know about the railroad?"

"Not much. But it doesn't really matter. The Railroad Commission doesn't oversee the railroad anymore. It's over oil and gas."

"Then why is it called the Railroad Commission?"

"So the fat cats can keep everything under their hats."

"That doesn't sound too dadgum forthright to me."

"No, sir. It doesn't to me either. That's why I'm running."

"Well, good luck on being elected a Railroad Commissioner, even though that ain't what it really regulates."

"Thank you. I appreciate it."

Mr. Smithson dismounted from his four-wheeler and walked over to the mailbox to get his mail.

"Junk and bills. Just like I thought it would be. At least I got some fresh air."

"Is the air still fresh?"

"Other than that skunk smell when the wind blows. But I don't mind. That's the smell of success. Good luck, Emily Allcorn," the old man said. "I reckon I'll go out and vote this time, and you know I'll vote for you."

"Thank you, Mr. Smithson."

The old man got back on his four-wheeler and headed home down the caliche road. Emily Allcorn put her skunk scent dropper and plastic gloves in the five-gallon bucket in the bed of her truck, secured the lid, and jumped back into the cab, where she then stowed her surgical mask in the glovebox. About that time, a strong wind blew through the mesquites from the direction of the Smithson place. Emily smiled as she rolled up her window, started the truck, and drove toward the horizon. She had plenty more signs to plant and enough skunk scent to cover them all. Victory, she believed, was hers. She could truly smell it.

The Most Famous Person
in the Room
★ ★ ★

Clyde Reeves sat on a barstool holding a twelve-string Spanish plugged into a tweed amp, his mouth against a microphone that smelled of stale cigarettes, flat beer, and halitosis. Once a month the man that owned the Old Coyote Bar let him play for drinks and tips, which Clyde figured was a far sight better than a good kick in the ass. In Fort Worth and Austin, he actually got paid, but the sweet little stacks of guaranteed greenbacks came with two swift kicks, those being the cost of a tank of gas and a stiff back, for he always slept in the bed of his pickup when he played away from home.

Clyde had salt in his beard, and he wore a Waylon County Feed and Seed hat everywhere he played. It was his trademark, if an unknown singer could have a trademark. Being unknown did not frustrate him though. He knew there was even an advantage to it. He could continue to write song after song without having his work poisoned by praise or criticism. And he certainly did not have to worry about fame diluting his intensity or concerns about sales causing him to look the wrong direction. He could be a voice in the wilderness, if the Old Coyote could be called the wilderness.

And then, were he ever to become famous, he would have a half dozen albums' worth the songs already written, and he would buy a thousand acres of land in the middle of the Old Republic and disappear. He and his wife and children would live in a ranch house far from any paved road,

153

and they would continue to be the people they had always been, though he and his wife would shitcan their day jobs, and the family would no longer have to live paycheck to paycheck. If Clyde became famous, he would insulate his family from the world around them. They would live untouched by glamor or rumor or ego, and though there was truly little chance that fame would come his way, he felt that it was always helpful to have a plan, for a person's fortune could change in a wildcatter's minute. But until that change occurred, Clyde would keep on checking dipsticks at the Texalube and strumming a few cowboy laments whenever he could.

Yes, he would always play music, for that is what kept him above the tulips, but sometimes he would only play other men's songs. Some nights he needed to climb into other people's skins. He would try on their tunes, dance in their hides. On those nights he would summon the spirits, invite the Lost Highway into his marrow, invite the spirit of Woody Guthrie to enter him, the freight train baritone of the Man in Black to bring him solace, even if Clyde's voice sometimes cracked and his fingers struck blunt on the strings.

The truth was that he didn't want to wear his own skin for a while. He wanted to live in the skin of another. He wanted to be someone better. His own songs had surfeited his soul, eased his heart when he wrote them like confessions to a bleary-eyed god who accepted them, and though He did not absolve any sins, still granted Clyde the catharsis he needed to keep living. The songs helped Clyde survive.

In Austin, Fort Worth, and such places, he would play his own songs. He would splay his heart in the barroom, reveal himself raw and naked to strangers, for the intimacy did not matter. He could reveal himself and never be seen again. He could open his soul, and the discomfort of being known too well would never come, for the euphoria of performing would still be pumping through his heart when he left town. At home the songs and their revelations of the past would dog and follow him.

Sometimes when he was playing out of town, or even on his porch, he did not want to play his own songs. He lived these songs when he played them, and he did not want to live them again. So he would play the songs written by others, not the songs written in his own gall and tears and blood.

Tonight he played the songs of the old ones, songs of the dead. He played the chords as if the movements of his fingers constituted a ceremony, a spell to raise the old ones from the grave. A couple of pretty girls sat down to listen in the glow of the Lone Star light, but Clyde closed his eyes to shut out the distraction. Their beauty could cause his mind to wander, and a family man could never be too careful. Still, it was always good to be the most famous person in the beer joint, Clyde figured, even if his name had only once made the paper, and that was on the police blotter. Yes, it was always good to be the most famous person in the room. It somehow balmed the sting. And at least he could play away his life in a bar, no matter what a dive it might be, and be heard.

Clyde played the old songs, and the drinking men nodded. Two dollars fell into his tip jar. Someone placed a beer beside his stool. He considered playing one of his own but then looked across the room and saw men he'd known since childhood, a woman he had once known by moonlight, and then he couldn't. He could not splay his soul in this room. So he strummed his guitar, looked to the ceiling, and prayed that someday the spirit of one of the old ones would enter his heart and mind amid the drunken hollers and clanging of bottles, and he would finally be found, and finally be set free.

Six-Man Football

★ ★ ★

The Fiddler Creek High School Band, making their first playoff appearance, honked out the Star-Spangled Banner the best they could. The horns, which were, for the most part, playing together, displayed all the musicality of geese being chased by a hound dog, while the three drummers, one of whom was a rather energetic young man with a snare drum, appeared to be playing three different songs altogether.

Burly Bill Baxter, Fiddler Creek's head football coach, gritted his teeth and hoped that the band's performance was in no way an omen that his team, the Fiddler Creek Fire Ants, would underperform during the Texas regional six-man quarterfinal football match against the Laubensbach Live Oaks. After the anthem reached its merciful end, smatters of clapping came from the bleachers, which were filled with men dressed in camouflage overalls and women covered in blankets and quilts. Fiddler Creek's three cheerleaders, two of whom were sisters, began chanting and waving on the sideline.

Burly Bill had rarely cracked a smile the entire season. Fiddler Creek had squeaked past formidable teams such as the Stink Creek Skunks, their local rival, and there were teams even more formidable awaiting them. Were they to win tonight, and they would win tonight, for Burly Bill would will them to win, they would face highly-ranked teams such as the Abbott Panthers, the Windthorst Trojans, and the Happy Cowboys. There were also the Nazareth Swifts, the Spur Bulldogs, and the Marfa Shorthorns to consider.

To Burly Bill, everything was personal. If a boy fumbled, he blamed himself for not emphasizing how to carry the football. If a boy missed a tackle, he became angry with himself for not running enough drills the previous week. If the team lost, he went home and punished himself by banging his head against the closet door over and over again. If the team won, he would sit and watch video over and over again to see how the team could improve. Nothing short of the state championship was ever good enough.

However, he came by this honestly. Burly Bill was raised out in Midland, where football was all that mattered, and he had played high school ball there. He had even been an all-state linebacker, but he did not have the size, so he played Division II in college. All of his life, he had dreamed of playing professional football, of playing for the Dallas Cowboys, and then, no matter how he tried, no matter how many hours he spent in the gym, no matter how many sprints he ran, how much weight he could bench press or squat, he could not offset the fact that he was simply not big enough. He played hard and was a ferocious linebacker in college, and a professional scout had even come to watch him, though nothing ever became of it. He gave everything he had every day, and still he was no closer to his dream.

When he finished college, he went to the Cowboys' training camp as a walk-on. He was fierce. He was focused. And he was strong. He was good, one of the defensive coaches told him. It was clear that he ate gunpowder for breakfast, but he still needed more lead in his backside. From the age of sixteen, he had always had to duck the threshold when he walked into a room, but he was still too small to play on the big stage. So he took a high school coaching job in a small town. He didn't know anything about six-man football when he took the position, and he figured that he would only coach it for a couple of years and move to a larger division, but he had not moved on. He had come to like the players, the game, and the community.

Although he would settle for nothing less than the state championship for his team, the reasoning behind that had changed. In his first two years of coaching, he still firmly held the belief that football was all that mattered. But somewhere along the line, he discovered that it really wasn't all about football. It was about teaching kids to set goals and strive for excellence. It was about grit, determination, and the relentless pursuit of one's dreams.

Coach Baxter had good teams, strong teams, teams with heart, but none of the boys ever got the chance to play in college. Colleges didn't really look at six-man teams much, and only one six-man player in the last handful of decades had ever managed to succeed in the pros. But Bill saw these boys go out and get jobs in town. He noticed that they were always on time, that they were respectful, that they were disciplined. He noticed that they were transforming into good adults, that they had become good people. He knew that the discipline they learned by playing football and the will to always do their best every single down, whether it be in practice or a game, played a part in that. And so every day Coach Baxter did his best to serve these kids and this community. He wanted to give them his best just as the boys gave him theirs. He wanted the players, their parents, and the community to be proud. He understood that it was only football, but he also understood that for many of these boys, these would be the days they truly remembered. These would be the days they told their grandchildren about. And so he worked tirelessly for them, did his best to help them succeed.

The captains ran out on the field for the coin toss. On the sideline, the players jogged in place, butted helmets like young rams, and loosened up before the game. The two teams' captains stood in the center of the field and shook hands. A referee flipped the coin, and Laubensbach, who called heads, would receive the kick. Cheers erupted all around the stadium.

A boy named Hall stood next to Coach Baxter. He was a head taller than the other boys, and he was tough and he was strong. And though he was one of the best players in the region, not a single scout had come to see him play. Still, the crowd was calling his name and hollering his number. Hall buttoned his chinstrap and cracked his knuckles.

"This is the best day of my life," he told the coach.

Burly Bill smiled and patted the boy on the back. And then Hall ran like a mighty warrior out onto the field while the trumpets played his fanfare.

Playing the "New World" Symphony
★ ★ ★

Ellen Kreutzmeyer sat in a hardback chair with a cello between her knees. She played in the Central Texas Symphony and was a celebrated musician in her part of the Hill Country, though still she made her living issuing license plates at the Waylon County Courthouse. Almost half a lifetime ago, as a high school senior, Ellen accepted an offer to study at a conservatory in New York, the announcement of which made the front page of the *Waylon County Messenger*, though once she reached the city, she found herself pregnant before the first snow even fell, and she came back home to Texas alone at the end of her second semester to give birth to a child that would have no real father.

Her dreams, she thought, would only be deferred for a short time, and once her daughter, Theodora, was in kindergarten, Ellen began working her way through college, and she managed to graduate with a degree in Music from a small university in West Texas. And though she had the opportunity to play with professional orchestras, she could not afford the cost of a babysitter on such a meager salary. So she worked at the courthouse, where she made enough money to get by and could leave work early enough to pick her daughter up from school. And every evening, out of what could perhaps be described as a physical need, she practiced the cello after her daughter had eaten, completed her homework, and gone to take her shower.

Her daughter, Theodora was fourteen now, and had dreams of becoming a graphic novelist, and so she spent her time locked in her room writing and illustrating stories she would let no one see. And with Thea, as her mother called her, being at a temperamental age, Ellen did not insist on seeing any of her projects. To pay for Thea's art classes, Ellen taught a couple of private lessons a week, though her young students, who had been sentenced to music school by parental decree, were uninspired at best.

This week Ellen had made the front page of the paper again while practicing with members of the South Moravia Civic Philharmonic, who were currently in Waylon County to join the Texas musicians in a performance of Dvořák's "New World" Symphony at Saints Cyril and Methodius Catholic Church. In the photograph, Ellen was pictured playing next to Dalibor Řezník, whose surname she could not pronounce, though she tried her best. Although she was musical and had a good ear, that initial consonant was too much for her tongue.

Dalibor, who was now sitting in the same place as he had been in the photograph, was tall and lean with a mop of sandy-brown hair. This evening he was wearing his standard uniform, American jeans, Italian drivers, and a black T-shirt, and the Texas women had been looking at him and whispering to one another ever since he had arrived, a fact that was not lost on Ellen. Dalibor haled from the town of Uhersky Brod, the hometown of Jan Amos Komensky, the great Czech educator who turned down the opportunity to serve as the president of Harvard in the seventeenth century, an unusual fact that Dalibor always liked to share with the people he met in the United States.

The orchestra was rehearsing the third movement of Dvořák's Ninth, the movement based on Longfellow's "Song of Hiawatha," and Ellen occasionally glanced at Dalibor while they played, intoxicated by the way her cello merged with his, intoxicated by how the two instruments seemed to make love with one another, how they shared the same intimate tone, how they resonated together, Ellen ever-cognizant of the slide of Dalibor's bow, completely lost in the way she and Dalibor played as one, completely lost as the music they made traveled into the infinity of space, where it would remain forever entwined.

For the first time in a long time, Ellen felt self-conscious. She had been a single mother for a long time. She knew her body was thicker than it used to be, her pretty cinnamon hair now streaked with silver, her eyes lined with more worry than joy. She had not had much time for men nor even been interested in them in many years. Yet this man interested her. For the first time in ten years perhaps, a man truly interested her. It surprised her frankly, but she would not act upon it. She was simply surprised that she felt that way.

She understood quite well how ridiculous and unrealistic it would be to initiate a relationship with a man who lived on another continent, who probably had a wife and family there, or, if he didn't, would likely have no interest in getting involved with a single mother and subjecting himself to everything such a relationship would entail. A man like Dalibor could have any woman he wanted, and he would likely choose someone young, beautiful, and carefree, not a single mother with bills to pay and a child to support.

After rehearsal ended, the room broke into a din of activity, with people moving chairs, putting away their instruments, and talking loudly. Dalibor gently placed his cello into its case and carefully fastened the latches. Ellen packed her instrument as well and was about to get up and leave when she turned to Dalibor and began to speak.

"I just love Dvorak's Ninth," she said. "It's such a great symphony."

"Yes, I think so, too," he said.

"It's so exciting to play. It's got so much energy."

"I like playing it, too. I like it because it sounds so American."

"To me, it sounds European."

They both laughed. Ellen liked the way Dalibor tilted his head back when he laughed. She liked how his laugh inhabited the middle ground between restraint and abandon.

"I was thinking about going to get something to eat," Ellen said, glancing over Dalibor's shoulder at the two old schoolteachers who played the oboe. "You wanna join me?"

"I have food in my room, but that sounds nice. I could go with you."

Ellen hoped Dalibor thought she was just being friendly, that the invitation was merely an expression of kinship, a cordiality that comes with playing the same instrument, reading the same sheet music, responding to the same movements of the baton.

"Do you like Mexican food?" she asked.

"I like it. It is a little spicy, but I like it."

"We could get something else," Ellen said, though she wondered what. Other than the filling station at the edge of town, there was little else open in Krasna Lipa, Texas, on a Monday night.

"Mexican food is good," Dalibor said. "Thank you for inviting me."

The two cellists walked toward the door nodding and smiling and saying goodnight as they passed the basses and then the horn players. Ellen, with her eyes fixed on the exit sign, could not help but wonder if the others thought her a whore even though she had been alone for more than a decade. But then, some had probably considered her a whore since she came back from New York, since she had a child out of wedlock, since she had not been ashamed enough of her sin to move to another town, or even another state, and start again.

The two musicians left the rehearsal hall, which was simply a clapboard assembly building behind Saints Cyril and Methodius, the oldest church in Krasna Lipa, and had gone to Jalisco Joe's, which served the best food in town. Thea, Ellen figured, would be happy to have the time alone and would be happy that her mother would not be there to tell her to go to bed, and she and her daughter would not have to engage in the usual dialogue, which always seemed to end in both of them being frustrated and angry. Ellen would send Thea a text saying she would be a little late, and everything would be fine.

Ellen and Dalibor sat at the table in the far corner away from the window. A young waitress with dark hair and eyes like a doe brought a bowl of chips and a small stone molcajete of salsa. Dalibor ordered a Mexican longneck with a lime, and Ellen ordered unsweet iced tea. Dalibor, who appeared to be rather hungry, ate a few chips he had dipped in salsa, and though he coughed on occasion, Ellen did not acknowledge it. She did not want to embarrass him, and besides, serrano peppers were hot if a person wasn't used to them.

Alone with an attractive man for the first time in years, Ellen became nervous and spoke very little at first. She figured she couldn't talk about the same old stupid topics she normally discussed with her family and friends. She could not talk about television shows, sales at the grocery store, or the local high school sports teams. She imagined that Dalibor normally talked about books and music and architecture when he met someone for dinner. She imagined that he did not talk about bills and work and football like other men did.

Dalibor crunched a chip and took a long draw from his beer.

"Nice place," he said, looking at the ponchos and sombreros that hung on the concrete wall of what was once a Dairy Queen.

"It's the best we've got," Ellen replied. "It's not like some place in Prague, but we like it."

"I like it, too."

"Do you really?"

"I do."

"That surprises me. Really?"

"Yes. Of course. Why wouldn't I like it?"

"I don't know. I thought it might not meet your, you know, standard. It might not be sophisticated enough. There aren't spires and sculptures and such."

Dalibor laughed.

"I come from a small town, too," he said. "I raise chickens in my garden. You have no reason to worry."

"Well, I didn't want to disappoint you."

The waitress arrived at the table. She smiled at Dalibor as she set their food in front of them.

"Hot plate," she said. "Be careful."

Dalibor had ordered green enchiladas with borracho beans and rice. Ellen had ordered two chalupas with a side of guacamole.

"Is this your first time in America?" Ellen asked.

"No. I was here for two years when I was younger."

"Were you here to play music?"

"No. I wish I could say that. I was waxing floors at night. I was on a crew with two Poles and a Russian. We cleaned grocery stores. I thought I would come to America and learn English better. But instead I learned

165

better Russian. The Russian man was a history professor in his country. He made more money cleaning grocery stores in the black than teaching history at home."

"In the black?"

"Illegally. We did not have work permits. But we made good money."

"Well, then, why did you go back to the Czech Republic?"

"I was tired. I worked all night and slept in the day. And I watched television, which helped my English. But mostly I was tired. I had no family. No real friends. No one I could trust. I had to watch for the police. This was all in Alabama."

"But now you're a professional musician."

"I have a job. I work in construction. What about you?"

"I work at the county courthouse."

"Are you a lawyer?"

"I'm a clerk. I issue license plates."

"That is good."

"I don't know about that, but it's a job at least."

Dalibor cut his enchiladas with a knife and fork.

"This is really delicious," he said. "And thank you for suggesting the drunken beans. I like them more than the mashed beans."

"You're welcome. Do you get bored?"

"Bored?"

"At work. Do you get bored at work?"

"Oh yes. It is boring work, and it is tiring, but it is fine. It makes the music sweeter when I can play it."

"I hate my job."

"Then why don't you quit?"

Ellen hesitated for a moment, and then she spoke.

"I've got a daughter."

"How old is she?"

"Fourteen."

"Fourteen? You don't look old enough to have a fourteen-year-old daughter."

"Thank you. Even if you're just being nice. Do you have a family back home?"

"I have two daughters. They both live with my ex-girlfriend in Prague. The girls are five and seven."

"Prague. It sounds so wonderful. I've never been to Europe. I always wanted to go."

"You should someday."

"I doubt I'll ever be able to."

"Life gives surprises. I did not have money to come here now. But the ministry of culture provided a grant for our group to come to Texas. And here I am."

"Yes, but you know Prague."

"I love Prague, but I could never live there. Too many people. Too many tourists going there only for drinking. But when I go to Prague, I go to the high city and visit the churchyard where Dvořák is buried. I pray at his grave. For me, the 'New World' Symphony is very personal. I can hear his frustration, and I can hear his wonder, his fascination with the music and the cultures of America. So many things were beautiful, but the life in America was hard for him. And the life here was hard for me, too, when I was cleaning floors at night."

"So you've been to Dvorak's grave?"

"Many times. I feel related to him. You see, my surname is Řezník, which means butcher, and his father was a butcher. Though Dvořák came from the proletariat, he became a great artist. I do not pretend to be a great artist, but I feel a kinship to Dvořák."

Dalibor smiled softly and touched Ellen's hand lightly.

"Sorry if I talk too much," he said. "I normally do not talk at all. At work I only work. I have nothing to say, but still I am happy in my country. Life is good there. It is always nice to walk down the street for a beer with one's friends, to play the old folk songs with one's friends in the pub. It is nice to walk in the woods, to pick mushrooms in the fall, to go skiing in the winter."

"I'd like that, too," Ellen said. "These days, life is the same every single day. But I'm lucky because I play music. Music takes me somewhere else. It makes everything go away."

167

"That is what music is for."

"Sometimes I just want everything to go away."

Dalibor finished his beer. When the check came, he reached for it.

"I invited you," Ellen said.

"I understand. But I am paying. You can pay next time."

Ellen smiled.

"Well, thank you."

"But for now, we should go. You have a daughter at home."

"Yes, and I placed a to-go order for her, and you just paid for it. I didn't mean for you to do that."

"I am happy I could. It is fine."

The two musicians stood up and walked out to Ellen's car. Ellen then drove across town and dropped Dalibor off at his room near the old stone church, near the rehearsal hall, near the place, Ellen felt, they first made love.

"I will see you tomorrow," Dalibor said as he unfastened his seat belt. "Thank you for this evening."

"Thank you. Yes, I'll see you tomorrow."

"I'm looking forward to it. I love this symphony. It sounds so American," Dalibor said, and then he opened the door.

Shooting Practice
★ ★ ★

Rufe Coe and his son Darrell stood outside the abandoned old house on Grandpappy Coe's last twelve acres with shotguns in their hands. Rufe, his graying red beard just reaching the shelf of his belly, slung his double-barrel Browning over his shoulder, his olive green "Make America Great Again" hat shading his eyes from the pale afternoon sun. Darrell, whose beard was shorter and better tended, was wearing a black shirt with the words "Limburg Brewery" silkscreened across the front in German gothic lettering. He checked his safety with his thumb as he stepped onto the porch's decaying boards.

The two men entered the old house, the door of which was swung wide open, and began to walk around. The wooden floor creaked and groaned with each step, and a useless, broken-down couch and an upright piano were all that was left in the living room. Anything that could easily be carted off or was of any value had been taken from the house years ago.

"You know," Darrell said. "I always wanted to shoot up a piano like they do in the cowboy movies. Never done it before."

"Then shoot it up, boy. Old thing looks beat to death anyway. And hell, the land's already under contract, so you might as well do it while you still can. A couple of soft-ass Californians will own it all in a couple of weeks. I sure do wish we could afford to keep your grandpappy's place, but we cain't. I know he's probably rolling in his grave about all this, but there ain't nothin' we can do at this point."

Darrell turned toward the piano with a theatrical grimace. He then began talking, and though his accent sounded Texan enough, he used one that was even thicker.

"Listen here, piany-man. I don't want to hear any of that Yankee music you're playing. Play 'Dixie,' son. Play 'Dixie.' So you don't want to play 'Dixie'? Then I'll play a little music for you."

Darrell fired three shots from his Remington semi-automatic into the piano. Fire flew from his barrel, and the percussion was enough to ring both his and his father's ears. With each shot, the piano jangled to life for a moment and then returned to silence.

"That was fun as hell," Darrell said.

The two men walked to the back of the house through piles of rusted junk and garbage.

"Don't get snakebit," Rufe told Darrell, stepping around a pile of rotting clothes.

Next to where the stove must have stood, Darrell saw a dusty wooden crate filled with record albums. Some of them were in crumbling paper sleeves with words like Vocalion, Decca, and Paramount on them. Darrell pulled one out of the crate.

"What the hell kind of records are these?" he asked.

"Them are old records like they don't make no more. Your grandpappy used to have some like that. Ain't but one song on each side. These probably belonged to one of them black people that used to live here. Used to pick cotton back before the land gave out, though they were gone long before that."

"When was the last time anybody lived here?"

"They were the last folks to live in this house, and I reckon they left just after the war. After the son got killed. They moved up to Detroit somebody told me. Or maybe Chicago. I never met any of 'em. I heard that they left real fast, though nobody ever told me the reason."

Darrell squatted down to his heels and flipped through the box. He picked up a record with a blue label and the word "Vocalion" on it.

"This one here says 'Terraplane Blues.' I reckon it must have belonged to them black folks like you said, Pops. Well, where'd them black folks come from?"

"Your great-aunt told me that they were the grandchildren of a slave our family used to own. Slave's name was Lewis. Everybody loved Lewis, she said. She said he was a real good man. She knew him when she was small."

Darrell tried to pick up the box of records.

"Damn, this box is heavy. It's a helluva lot heavier than I thought it would be."

"What are you going to do with them records? I wouldn't put those dirty sons of bitches in my garage much less in my house."

"Seeing they ain't worth nothing, I figured we could throw 'em like skeet. They's a helluva lot cheaper than clay pigeons. But then, I reckon free is cheaper than anything."

Darrell grunted and picked up the box.

"Use your knees or you're gonna hurt your back," Rufe said.

"Nice advice after I already picked 'em up."

Darrell carried the box past the junk piles, through the living room, and off the porch. He set the box on the tailgate of his old green pickup, which was parked on the dirt road not far away. He then took his last box and a half of twelve-gauge shells from behind the bench seat of his truck.

"Age before beauty," Darrell said. "I'll let you shoot first."

"How do you wanna play?"

"A dollar a hit."

"Then we both have to agree that it was a good throw."

"Of course we do. I wouldn't screw my old man."

"I know you wouldn't, but there's got to be rules."

"Fair enough. And I'll only load two shells each round so that I don't have more shots than you."

"All right. I'll throw you ten, and then you throw me ten."

Rufe stood on the ground facing out toward the field. Darrell stood in the back of his truck with the first record in his hand.

"This one here is by Son House. Who the hell has a name like Son? That's like my name was Son Coe. That don't make no sense. Damn song is called 'Clarksdale Moan.' I'd rather hear his old lady moan. You ready?"

"Pull."

Darrell flung the record as far as he could. Rufe fired twice, but he missed, and the brittle old record smashed to pieces when it hit the ground.

"Damn. When you hit one, it's gonna explode like the dadgum Death Star in the Star Wars movie."

"That'll be good."

"This one is called 'Poor Me' by somebody called Charley Patton. Well, Charley, you'll be thinking poor me in just a minute."

"Pull."

Darrell threw the record high, and it hung up and spun for a while. Rufe shot it at the beginning of its descent, shattering it into countless pieces. Darrell laughed.

"Damn. You blew that one to hell."

Darrell slung eight more records. His daddy hit five of those. He owed the old man six dollars at this point.

"My time to get in your pocket, Pops," Darrell said.

"You better not miss. I done got six. And every throw wasn't great."

"You should have said something."

"Didn't matter enough."

"It'll matter if I hit seven and whip you."

"Nah, it won't."

"My ass it won't. If I win, you'll be talking about how you let me win because you felt sorry for me. If I lose, you'll be crowing to everybody up at Aldo's Domino Hall about how you outshot me."

Darrell jumped out of the back of the pickup, grabbed his gun from the truck bed, and stood where his father had stood.

His father then climbed into the back of the truck.

"Here come the 'Terraplane Blues,'" Rufe said. "Might be the hydroplane blues for you."

"How's that? There ain't no water."

"You might wet your britches when you see you cain't beat me."

Rufe tried to loosen up his throwing arm.

"You sure you can throw 'em, Pops?"

"I ain't no candy-ass. I just need to warm up a little so I don't throw out my rotator cup."

Rufe stretched his elbow and his shoulder for a minute or so.

"You ready, boy?" he asked.

"I was born that way."

"Then holler when you want me to throw it."

"Pull."

Rufe flung the ten-inch record as far as he could. It caught air and traveled outward, like a quail almost, and Darrell fired twice, the wad of the first shot flying high and wide, and the second shot hitting the old record, sending brittle fragments of shellac in all directions.

"Good shot," Rufe laughed.

"Thank you."

Rufe threw another one, but Darrell missed. And then he missed the next three.

"Hell, boy, if you don't hit the next five you will owe me money. You're gonna have to pull off a damn miracle to break even at this point."

Darrell loaded two shells into his shotgun.

"That's enough running commentary. Why don't you throw a damn record?"

"Then let me know when you're ready."

"Pull."

Rufe twisted his body like a discus thrower and flung the next record. Darrell hit it the moment it crossed his line of sight.

"Four more to break even," Rufe said.

Darrell shot the next three, but not on the first shot. The first shot seemed to give him his orientation, like he was a fighter that relied on his jab to set up the hard right.

"You're shooting pretty good," Rufe said. "You shoot so good that you oughta be out there fighting the Taliban. You'd show those caveman bastards. Ok. Last record for this round. This one says Blind Lemon Jefferson. Lemon ain't no name. Who would name a child Lemon?"

"Hell if I know," Darrell said.

He pulled back the receiver on his shotgun, a gust of pale gray smoke flooding out of the barrel. He loaded two shells from the box on the tailgate and aimed out toward the field.

"Pull."

Rufe threw the disc as hard as he could throw it. Darrell drew a bead on it, and he fired twice when the record was about to hit the ground. It was hard to tell whether he hit the record and it exploded, or if it hit the ground and shattered.

"I'll give it to you," Rufe said.

"Give it to me, hell. I made that shot."

"It was pretty hard to tell, but I'll give you that contested shot and call it even."

"So I reckon you'll be telling everybody you won."

"Hell no, I wouldn't do that. But I'll tell you what. Why don't we shoot some more so that we can declare a winner?"

"That would be the fair thing to do, but unfortunately there ain't but one more shell in the box."

"Then let's go buy some more shells."

"We'll have to wait until next week when I get paid for them old farm tools I sold. I'm out of funny money. I can pay the bills and get everybody fed, and that's all. At least it was fun shooting skeet like that. And we still have a few records left that we ain't thrown yet."

"Well, I ain't got but two dollars and a plug nickel on me, so I reckon we'll have to shoot 'em next time. At least we still have a couple of weeks before we lose the property."

Darrell picked up the old crate, which was much lighter than before, and put it in the living room of the old house next to the shot-up piano. He touched a single ivory key on the piano, but it did not make a sound. And then he headed back to the truck so that he could get his old man home by suppertime.

Cowboy Hats
★ ★ ★

"Ain't no reason to be gun-shy," Frank said, turning the channel on the TV to watch an old movie about Custer's Last Stand. "You might as well just marry her."

"This is a big decision," Isaac said, "and not one I can afford to take lightly. I can't decide on a whim. This could be the most important decision I make in my entire life."

On television, Italians dressed like Indians rode their war ponies down a grassy knoll, their braids flapping behind them as they whooped and hollered like doorbusters on Black Friday in their charge across the jumbo screen. Frank pointed his remote control toward the Italians as if he were trying to unhorse them, though all he actually did was force them to whoop in their indoor voices with a few quick taps of his thumb.

"Well, you got a good job up at the post office and you done bought a nice big house on a VA loan," Frank said. "You're in real good condition to enter the world of marital bliss."

"But what if she's not the right one?" Isaac asked, his elbows on his knees as he sat on the Naugahyde couch across from Frank's easy chair.

"Listen here, boy. Women are a lot like cowboy hats. Sometimes you gotta try on several before you get the right fit. So don't get yourself up in a lather worrying about whether or not she's the right one. If it works, it works. If it doesn't, it doesn't. And if it doesn't work, then go out and keep trying to find the one that's right for you."

Isaac adjusted the collar of his sea-green polo shirt.

"Now Uncle Frank," he said, "you know I'm not the kind of man who has to try on every hat in the store. That just doesn't suit my disposition."

Frank reached over from his big leather recliner and got a handful of barbeque-flavored popcorn from the bowl on the coffee table.

"For me, the third time was a charm," Frank said, crunching on popcorn, some of which had now gathered on the shelf at the top of his belly, where he sometimes rested his beer. "Ivy Lee is the best wife I ever had. She don't fuss. She don't fight. She don't bear false witness. And she knows when to be quiet."

"She knows when to be quiet?"

"I don't mean that in the barefoot, pregnant, stay-in-the-kitchen-and-cook sort of way. What I mean is that some things ain't meant to be said out loud, and she understands that. And I reckon I do, too, which makes us go together like brisket and tater salad. Took me three tries, but she's the best thing that ever happened to me."

"Well, Uncle Frank, I don't think I need three metaphorical hats."

"You never know. It ain't like you're aiming for calamity, but still it strikes. And I got this other theory. I think that there are two kinds of women, just like there are two kinds of hats. There's women who are like summer straws and women who are like winter felts, and a man has to figure out which kind suits him best. A serious young fellow like you could probably use a nice, breezy summer straw to lighten him up. And an old scamp like me? I need a good, reliable winter felt, which is exactly what I've got in Ivy Lee."

Isaac stroked his smooth chin in a state of reflection.

"With all due respect, Uncle Frank, I think human nature is a little more complicated than that," he said. "And, you know, now that you got me thinking about hats, I always did wonder why there weren't spring and fall cowboy hats, but that's not the point of our conversation. We're talking about something serious. We're talking about the prospect of marriage. We're talking about a lifetime commitment."

"Well, since you brought it up, I'll tell you a little bit about western headwear," Frank said and then paused to swish some sweet tea around in his mouth in an attempt to dislodge a popcorn kernel that was stuck between his teeth. "First of all, it's important to understand that a cowboy hat is all about function. It ain't about fashion. There ain't no spring collection or fall collection like they got on that catwalk station Ivy Lee's always watching. When it comes to choosing which kind of hat to stick on your noggin, it's all based on the weather. Some of the ladies up at the church house will say that you shouldn't wear a straw hat or white britches after Labor Day, but that doesn't make a lick of sense to me. In my opinion, if an ol' boy is out there punching dogies, which lid he sticks on his melon should be based on how hot it is outside. And when it comes to finding a wife, it's kinda the same but different. It's all about deciding what best fits your personal constitution."

"Well, constitutionally speaking, once I decide to get married, I want to be with the same woman for the rest of my life," Isaac said. "I don't want someone who is easy come, easy go."

"Then you'd better get a winter felt. It'll be a little stifling in the summer of your life, but you'll be glad to have it in the winter. Is Arlene like a winter felt?"

"She kind of is. She's a little bit formal, and from what I can tell, I think she could handle any storm that comes her way."

"That's good."

"Arlene is a fine woman in my opinion. She goes to church, her eyes don't follow other men, and she keeps a promise."

"Them's all good traits."

"And I'll admit she's not exciting like the girls out in Austin, but she's real nice. And she's fun in a quiet sort of way. She's the kind of girl that likes to make nachos and play board games on a Friday night."

"Well," Uncle Frank said while picking his teeth, "are you good with that?"

"I think so. The only reason I ever went out to the Old Coyote or over to the dancehall in Laubensbach on a Friday night was to try and find a girl, and well, I ended up finding the girl of my dreams at an ice cream social up at church, and I haven't been to a beer joint or even the dancehall ever since."

"Sounds like you've talked yourself into marrying her."

"I guess I have. She's the best girl I ever met."

"Well, if the hat fits, wear it."

About that time, a bunch of Italians in loincloths reached General Custer, whose hair resembled that of a professional wrestler. The Italians, who were still hollering and hooting in their indoor voices, filled Custer full of arrows while he flailed around firing his Colt pistol before raising his saber and posing for the painting that now decorates many a barroom wall.

"You know, I'm a one-woman man, and Arlene and I aren't the kind to change with the season. This afternoon I'll drive to San Antone and buy her a ring, and then I'll get down on my knees with my hat in my hand and ask her to marry me."

And before Custer could fire his final shot, the station broke for a commercial.

"I think you're making a real good decision," Frank said while mashing the volume button with his thumb when the movie started back up, the battle on the grassy knoll now sounding as if it was happening there in the middle of the living room. Frank and Isaac sat watching intently, as if they didn't know how the story would end. "That's a real good decision for sure, boy. I reckon you'll be as happy as a buzzard on a gut wagon. I reckon you'll be about as happy as a man can be."

And then, on Frank's jumbo screen, a screeching Italian in grease paint and feathers stood holding a platinum mullet.

Clutch Reynolds

★ ★ ★

Elsie and Thomas Green had no children. They had been married for twelve years and had made constant love the first three, foregoing food, sleep, television, and even visits with kith and kin to spend their unworked hours together in a cocoon of conjugal bliss, in the feather bed of love and intimacy. And though they had dreamed of multiplying, the seed of life had never quickened in Elsie's womb, and the lovemaking that had kept them in an ethereal daze came at a more staggered pace over the next five years, and in the last four, their intimacy had become little more than a kiss on the cheek after work.

Both were the only child, the only hope for their family lines to pass into the future, which was uncommon for their time and space and generation, but it was true. Their mothers, both of whom were patient and kind, still prayed, still sowed the spiritual soil with mustard seed, though nothing seemed to grow in this vast unyielding land. And Elsie and Thomas, though they had received pressure through innuendo and implication, had never been asked directly about not having children. They had only heard about this baby shower and that child's birthday party, but never had they been questioned by either of their families.

Thomas was now thirty-eight and Elsie thirty-four. Thomas wondered why nothing had worked. He wondered why they were still childless, why nothing had yet happened. They were healthy and amorous and strong, after all, and their efforts had not been haphazard. Their efforts had been concerted, albeit implied and unvoiced, and they should have surely had a child by now.

Last week Elsie went to the doctor for a checkup, and the doctor had told her that she was in perfect health, and then she went to the woman doctor, who told her that everything was fine, in good condition. She told Thomas that much, though he did not respond. But he had listened. He had listened to every word. Elsie now set the table and made both of their plates, his slab of meatloaf larger than her slice, his mashed potatoes a mountain next to her hillock, his pile of beans wider than hers. Thomas took his fork and started eating. Long ago had they stopped saying grace.

"Baby, do you like it?" Elsie asked.

"It's good. Why?"

"Because you didn't say anything. If you don't say anything, it's usually because you don't like supper."

"It's good. I love your beans. And your jalapeño cornbread. I figured you done knew that by now."

"I don't figure anything."

"It's good. Real good, baby."

"What do you think about children?"

Thomas lowered his fork.

"You mean havin' 'em?" he asked.

"Having them. Having children."

"I'd like that, but it don't look like somethin' that's gonna happen for us."

"Maybe it could."

"Well, I've been hopin' a long time, and ain't nothin' happened. Maybe you're not built for havin' babies."

"Well, the doctor told me that I'm healthy, that everything's fine. Thomas, this is hard to say, and I can't believe I'm saying it, but it looks like our little problem could be your sperm count. Thomas, honey, would you like for me to set up an appointment?"

Those words filled the room like the first punch in a fight, a punch that could not be taken back, a punch that would lead to a flurry of other punches, a punch that provided an opening for a storm of brutal, savage punches, wild punches thrown without regard to where they would land, a rage that could not be controlled.

180

"An appointment?"

"An appointment to help me get pregnant."

"I don't want that."

"You don't want children?"

"I don't want to go to no doctor. I don't want to sit in a waitin' room with people lookin' at me and wonderin' what's wrong with me. I don't want anybody thinkin' I'm shootin' blanks, because I'm not. There's nothin' wrong."

"We've been trying to have a child for years. There's got to be something going on."

"There ain't nothin' going on. You can take that to the bank."

Thomas returned to his dinner, which he finished in three swallows and washed down with a drink of iced tea.

"That was real good meatloaf, baby," he said.

Then he got up from the table and walked into the living room and picked up the sports page to see the Major League baseball standings, though he knew full well that his team, the Texas Rangers, were several games out of first, even in that weak division. Still, he raised the paper up over his face and leaned back on the couch in his socks. Elsie cleared the plates and then stood in front of him with her left hand rubbing her temple.

"You can't hide behind the sports page."

"Rangers are nine games out. Unless they catch fire, it looks like they'll be watching the playoffs on television like the rest of us."

"We have to talk about this. We've never talked about it. We've never had a single conversation. I just figured it would happen. At some point, over time, it would happen. But it hasn't. And time is running short. I'll be thirty-five this year. If we're going to have a baby, we are going to have to have it now."

"Well, I'm not going to no damn doctor if that's what you're thinkin'. That ain't happenin'."

"I'll say it again. If we're going to have a baby, we need to have it now."

Thomas put down his newspaper.

"Shit," he muttered.

"We have to do something. I've kept quiet for years, but I can't anymore.

181

We'll break our parents' hearts if we don't have a baby, if we don't give them a grandchild. And if we don't have a baby now, I don't know what our chances are after that."

Thomas looked away. He was a big man, a strong man, with thick hands, sculpted shoulders, and a square jaw. He looked like a prize fighter in his corner as he sat with his elbows across his knees. He looked at his wife as if she was the opponent in the opposite corner. He did not want to have this conversation. If they never talked about it, maybe it would go away. Maybe they would somehow forget about it. Maybe they would find a way to sleep past it and no one would ever notice. But everyone had noticed. No one had ever said a word directly to them, but it was clear that everyone had noticed. He and Elsie had no children. Their rivers had not converged to flow ever-forward into the future.

"Well, I guess I ain't Clutch Reynolds. I ain't some no-account that goes around knockin' girls up all over town and not takin' responsibility. He's got four children by three different women."

"It's unfair, isn't it?"

"Yeah. It's unfair. Real unfair. Some folks try for years to have a baby. They save money and think about how they're gonna raise their kid. And then you get some ol' boy like Clutch Reynolds who doesn't even care. He's like a tornado. He uproots trees and messes things up and lets someone else sort it out after he's gone. You'd think he was the Wichita Falls tornado."

"So what do you want to do?"

"What do you mean?"

"What do you want to do? Do you want to go to a fertility doctor?"

"I'm not doin' that."

"Then how do you want to have a baby?"

"I reckon you have a pretty good idea."

"We've been doing that for years. And we don't have any babies. Right now I dream about babies every night. All I can think about is babies. I'm crazy about babies. I can't think of anything else. And we haven't, well, you know, in a couple of months."

Thomas took a drink of sweet tea.

"Well, let's go to the dance out at Laubensbach tonight, and we can see from there. We can go on a date and see what happens."

Elsie smiled. She swept her stringy blond hair away from her face and off her neck.

"Normally you don't want to go anywhere on a Friday night. You just want to watch TV and go to bed."

"I guess I got a second wind."

"Then let's go. That would be fun. Surprising but fun."

Thomas nodded and smiled grimly before going to their bathroom and taking a shower. He shaved as well, something he never did on a Friday. He normally shaved Thursday night before bed and then again on Sunday night so that he would be ready for work Monday morning. But this evening he would shave. He would treat Elsie nice. He always had. Always would. And he'd always figured that she was infertile because she had never been pregnant as far as he knew. She had never missed a period, never lost a baby, never had anything like that happen. And now she had gone to the doctor, and the root cause of the problem seemed to be Thomas himself. He did not know how to handle this. He felt castrated. Emasculated. Like a goddam gelding but without the freedom. All he did was work and sleep. He should at least be able to have children. Surely he was that potent. But he wondered if he was. He wondered if he was shooting toy rounds. He wondered if it even mattered. He knew that nothing really mattered.

He knew that everything was for naught, that every story ended the same. He knew that everyone was born, that everyone lived, and that everyone died. Some would dispute him and claim variables, but the story did not change. It never changed. The details could change but the end was always the same. But he would try to put the next story in motion. He would try for the story of his family not to end with him, not to end with him and Elsie.

He put on his boots, jeans, button-down western shirt, and the straw hat his mama and daddy had given him for his birthday. Then, once Thomas was dressed and out of the way, Elsie stripped to her panties and bra and put on her jeans and a Mexican top. She looked nice in her black panties and bra. She still looked firm and desirable. She still had contours that pained him with want, a flat stomach with a freckle to the right just below her navel, tits that still pointed to the sky.

Once they were both dressed, Thomas let Elsie's little poodle dog, Minnie Pearl, out so she could pee. Minnie Pearl sniffed the fenceline, did her business, and then trotted through the back door before returning to her place in the middle of the couch. Thomas went to the refrigerator, opened a beer, and finished it in two long swigs so he wouldn't look too thirsty when they arrived at the dancehall.

After tossing the bottle in the trashcan, Thomas turned off the lights, other than a lamp for Minnie Pearl, walked Elsie outside, and closed the door behind them before helping his wife into the truck. Thomas then climbed in the driver's side and turned the key. The engine cranked, and Billy Joe Shaver started singing "Live Forever" on the stereo.

Thomas put the truck in gear and headed out to Laubensbach. Although tourists had found Waylon County, especially the little Texas-German town of Limburg, Laubensbach was still generally unknown. Suburban bikers with middle-age crises didn't converge on the place like they did on other Texas dancehalls, which made Thomas happy, though he knew sooner or later *Texas Traveler* magazine would put them on the map, and that would be the end of Laubensbach being what it was and becoming what he didn't want it to be.

Thomas drove his truck along the state highway and turned off on the county road to Laubensbach and parked in the field outside of what they called town, which was a post office that doubled as a general store and the dancehall. He slid out of his seat and stepped around the truck to help Elsie out of the cab. She took his hand as she stepped on the running board and down to the dry, rutted ground. The two of them walked over to the dancehall, where Thomas had to pay more than he would have liked to get in, but the band, which they had seen for free a couple of years earlier, was now a well-known touring act.

The dancehall was long and gray, with wooden shutters that had been opened to let air in the tall, wide windows. They found a spot at a long, rough table with bench seats, where they sat opposite one another. A couple with two teenage girls and a young boy in a cowboy hat sat at the other end of the table. The band was good. They played honkytonk music.

184

Waltzes and shuffles. Western swing. Cowboy polka. The singer, for whom the band was named, was reading the crowd. The band had played a slow one, but only a handful of couples had danced, so the singer raised the tempo. Elsie and Thomas sat and drank a beer apiece, Elsie having ordered a Dos Equis and Thomas a Lone Star. A couple of young men in starched shirts, jeans, and hats with brims just above their eyes asked the two sisters at the other end of the table to dance. The girls' daddy grinned and locked eyes with both of the young bucks. They smiled respectfully and held out a hand for each of the girls.

The dance hall was starting to fill up. Thomas and Elsie said hello to the people they knew, friends of their parents mostly, though they said howdy to a few people from the rock quarry where Thomas worked as well. There were also plenty of younger people out that night, mostly girls with long hair in tight jeans and low tops and boys wearing summer straws and pearl snaps. When the place was almost full, Thomas saw Clutch Reynolds enter the dancehall. Clutch was wearing a black motorcycle jacket, even in this heat, and he scanned the room before walking over to the bar to get a beer. Thomas had played football with Clutch. They had graduated in the same class. They had both been on the championship team.

Thomas had played on the offensive line, and though he was big, he was not quite big enough to be a lineman. In small towns, there weren't as many players as they had in the cities, so a smaller player could wind up on the line. Hell, Thomas had even heard of a six-man team that had a girl who was their star kicker. Pretty much anything was possible out in the country. Clutch had been a great player, the only one recruited for college, though he quit his freshman year. But now he had a regular job like every-body else, a job that paid a lot less than classmates he had looked down on when he was in school, and he was bitter and sometimes mean.

But he was big, and he was strong. And Thomas got to wondering if this could be the answer to his problem. He wondered if this would solve it. Yes, Clutch was an asshole. He had always been an asshole. He was one of those people who had been told that he was better than other people, so he somehow thought that gave him license to treat others poorly, to treat others like they were below him. Were Clutch not an asshole, he could have easily gotten a good job. Everyone was eager to hire the local football hero, but it is hard to hire a hero that everyone thinks is an asshole. But he had good genes. He was big, and he ran a fast forty yards, and he was fairly smart. If Elsie had Clutch's child, Thomas and Elsie could raise the child right. The child would be strong and smart and talented. And what would Clutch care? He was probably spreading seed across four counties. He had children all over the place. He probably had children that he had no idea existed.

This could work, Thomas told himself. He didn't like it, but this humiliation would be better than the humiliation of sitting in a waiting room in a fertility doctor's office with everyone knowing that he was shooting blanks. He would just need to talk Elsie into it. And then Clutch. With Clutch being the asshole that he was, Thomas didn't think it would be a problem on his end.

"Elsie," Thomas said, leaning across the rough wooden table to his wife. "Baby, I've got to ask you somethin'. I know you want a baby, and this is hard to say, but I've got an idea."

"What is it, Thomas?"

"Why don't we ask somebody to help us. We could find somebody to get you pregnant, and at least your bloodline would carry on."

"Honey, I couldn't do that. That would be adultery. I'm married. We're married, and I'm with you, and I love you. I can't believe you would even say something like that. It's indecent. Do you not love me?"

"I love you so much that I would be willing to let another man hold you for just a little while so that you could have the baby. After that, the baby would be ours, and we would love it. I would love that baby as if it were my own flesh and blood."

"So what are you thinking?"

"About asking Clutch."

"He's not a very nice person."

"But he has good genes."

"I don't know if I could do that. And even if it seemed reasonable, how do you know he would even be willing?"

"You're a beautiful woman. Single, married, or engaged, he's the kind of ol' boy who'll sleep with any beautiful woman he can get into his bed."

"I can't do it. I just can't do it. It wouldn't be right."

The fiddle struck a familiar tune, and the dancefloor filled with people. Elsie watched Clutch Reynolds, who was standing in a corner alone surveying the room with a beer in his hand. Thomas went and bought a couple of more beers and placed them in the middle of the table. He could see that Elsie was thinking about the proposition. He hated the whole idea, but it was the best idea he had. He was not going to be humiliated in a doctor's office.

"I don't want to have Clutch Reynolds' baby," Elsie said. "I don't love Clutch Reynolds. I never did, and I never will. I am not going to breed with him like I was a Holstein cow. I can't do that. I love you, and I want to have your child. I would rather we died old and quiet and childless than to give myself to another man, if even for an evening. Thomas, I need you to go to the doctor. Will you do that for me?"

Thomas was disarmed by her words, and his face must have shown it. He had brought his wife here because he loved her. He had brought her here hoping that somehow he could give her the one thing she wanted the most, the fulfillment of her life as a woman. But she loved him more than her body longed for a child. Thomas reached across the table and took her hand. He took his beautiful wife to the dancefloor. He kissed her as they danced upon the sawdust in that open dancehall, a gentle breeze drifting through the windows. They danced until the band played "Can the Circle Be Unbroken" at the end of the night. Then they, like the other lovers, left hand in hand, walking into the star-speckled darkness toward their truck, passing hundred-year-old oaks on their way.

"I'll do it," Thomas said, helping Elsie into the pickup. "I'll go to the doctor."

He climbed in on his side and started the truck. Elsie kissed him gently on the neck while he rubbed her thigh and smiled. And then he drove them down the county road in the direction of their home.

The Ugly Baby
★ ★ ★

At birth, the child looked like a prize tomato. He was red and plump to the point of shining, or perhaps even bursting, and his eyes and nose and mouth seemed to stretch across the entire surface of his face. His name was Jay Byrd Brown, though his grandfather knew beyond a doubt that the child would never be known by that name. He would be called Tomater Head or Beefsteak or some other such moniker. Grandpa Brown was no fool, and he knew that a boy who looked like an overripe tomato would never be called by his given name, just as Grandpa Brown, who had always been called Prairie Dog due to his uncanny resemblance to a certain burrowing rodent, had never been called Coy Ray.

After giving the child a general appraisal in a manner similar to that in which a casual tourist might survey the produce at a vegetable stand along the roadside, Grandpa Brown inspected the child more closely, and once he had counted twenty digits, he took a thoughtful gander at the hair upon the child's noggin. Prairie Dog, if he had not known better, would have sworn that the tuft of jet-black hair upon the child's crown as well as the carpet of soft-looking fur that spanned between the child's hairline and eyebrows had been superglued in place.

The jet-black tuft, he thought, looked like something one might see atop a television puppet's crown and could almost be described as cute. However, the carpet of fur on the child's forehead reminded him of a low-budget werewolf movie, which, of course, troubled the first-time grandfather. And though Prairie Dog knew full well that the baby fur would probably go away soon enough, he still found it disturbing. Who in Sam Hill's name has fur on his forehead? Prairie Dog wondered. And what if the fur on that boy's head stayed there forever? Would he be known around town as the Tomato-Headed Wolfboy, or perhaps something even more original? Surely the fur would go away, but if it didn't, would one of the child's parents have to shave his forehead every morning until he got big enough to shave himself? Prairie Dog had lots of questions, but he decided not to ask them, and he also had some statements he probably could have made, too, but he would keep those under his hat as well, for he had been raised to say nothing in the event that he had nothing nice to say.

Pigtails, his daughter-in-law, sat up in a hospital bed with an angelic look on her face rocking Tomater Head in her arms. She beamed down upon him with love in her eyes, like Mary perhaps looked at the Good God Almighty lying in His trough. Prairie Dog had liked Pigtails, who was a sweet little blonde with light blue eyes, honey-colored skin, and exceptional manners, ever since the first time his son Jesse brought her home for supper in high school. Now Jesse, who had chestnut hair and a long, ovular head that led to him becoming known as Goose Egg, or Goose for short, by the good citizens of Waylon County, stood at the bedstead beside his darling wife, and he, too, gazed upon their firstborn like the child was an incredible miracle sent special delivery from the main distribution center up in Heaven.

There in the hospital room, with its beeps and dings and piney smell that caused him to raise his head and sniff the air, Prairie Dog looked in his periphery at his wife, Maureen, who was talking about the advantages of breastfeeding over formula, with Pigtails nodding and smiling along. Maureen had shiny red hair and a sweet disposition, and Prairie Dog had fallen for her and found himself engaged and subsequently married almost faster than the preacher could tie his tie. Memaw Brown, as Maureen had suddenly become known, was smarter than she ever let on, and the newly minted Grandpa Brown felt that his wife sometimes made decisions or plans and then led him to believe that everything had been his idea, like the time they went to South Padre Island for vacation not long after an oil spill.

On the other side of the room stood Pigtails' parents, Bean Pole and

Betty. They were nice folks, and Bean Pole, who was tall and lean and looked like an extra from a movie about the Great Depression, gave him a hard, questioning look, though Prairie Dog did not know what the look meant. Bean Pole ran a hand through his dark hair and scratched the back of his head out of nervous habit. Betty, who was short and portly, though remarkably spry, held her arm around Bean Pole's waist and smiled nervously upon her new grandbaby, the nervousness perhaps stemming from her being an introvert, or whatever it's called, in a room full of people.

Prairie Dog hoped that no one could read his mind, for he had never been a good poker player. Whatever cards he had in his hand he always seemed to broadcast across the table. So he picked up a copy of the *Waylon County Messenger* from Pigtails' tray table and held it in front of his face like he was reading, though he knew that he probably looked stupid, so he put the newspaper back where he found it. He felt guilty for thinking that his first grandboy was the ugliest child he had ever seen, for love supposedly transcended ugly, but it had not so far.

Prairie Dog glanced over at Maureen, who was smiling a pleasant, diplomatic smile, and he was curious to know her candid opinion, though he would not ask for it here. He and his wife had been together for three decades, and still he could not always tell what she was thinking. When his son was born, he had also thought him to be the ugliest child he had ever seen. His son, after all, had been born with an enormous noggin that resembled a goose or, if he was honest, perhaps even an ostrich egg, and to make matters worse, the boy had had an allergic reaction to the eye drops in the hospital, which made him strike a fair resemblance to a cartoon sailor with an affinity for spinach. From the very beginning, Prairie Dog had felt fairly certain that his son's face would never grace the front of a baby food jar, but he reckoned he could live with that. Still, his wife had simply called the child a beautiful miracle, despite his puffy eyes, oddly shaped head, and, as Prairie Dog was soon to discover, vile-smelling diapers.

And today, on what should have been one of his life's finest days, Prairie Dog felt terrible about the unwanted thoughts that were now running around between his ears, but there was little he could do about it, for, in all honesty, his grandson really did look like a mutant beefsteak tomato at the county fair, though Prairie Dog hoped and prayed that the boy would grow out of it like his own son had gone from being as ugly as homemade soap to at least being as average-looking as the store brand at the Hoggly Woggly. Leaning against a bare white wall, Prairie Dog glanced at the other family members, and from what he could tell, no one seemed repelled, disgusted, or even disingenuous about being repelled or disgusted.

At this point, Prairie Dog began to wonder whether or not Tomater Head was actually Goose's boy but then kicked that foolish idea out of the beer joint of his mind. Pigtails was a sweet girl and always had been. She had never been one to break the Lord's Commandments. She did not lie, steal, or take the Lord's name in vain, and she certainly didn't covet her neighbor's mule. The plump red baby probably took after Betty's side and was clearly of a champion variety. Pigtails, after all, was as sweet as pumpkin pie, and ugly baby or not, Grandpa Brown was glad that she was married to his son. She and Jesse had been sweethearts since the ninth grade and had eased gently into marriage a couple of years after high school, and Prairie Dog was proud of the happy, responsible young couple and the way they conducted their lives.

After a long while, Pigtails glanced up from the baby she was cradling in her arms. She looked up at the relatives assembled there in the hospital room as if she had just awoken from a beautiful dream and found them there with her.

"Little Jay Byrd sure is sweet," she said. "He is a tiny miracle from God Himself, but I must say he is the ugliest baby I ever saw."

Prairie Dog felt a wave of relief course through his body.

"He'll grow out of it, honey," Betty said.

"I wasn't the prettiest baby there ever was coming straight out of the chute," Goose Egg said.

"Jesse got more and more handsome as the days passed by," Memaw Brown said. "I'm sure little Jay Byrd will do the same."

"He will," Bean Pole said, adjusting a dip of snuff with his tongue and staring out the window.

Prairie Dog smiled and looked down upon his grandchild, the first of surely many who would carry his family into a shiny, beautiful future, who would carry the values of honesty, integrity, and goodness with them long after Prairie Dog himself was gone. He thought about this, about the wonderful potential of the tiny person wrapped in a blanket before him, and it filled his heart with joy.

"That little feller is most surely a miracle," he said.

And Prairie Dog, who had only today become known as Grandpa Brown, truly believed it.

Barbeque
★ ★ ★

The helicopter landed in the stubble field next to Kreutzmeyer's Barbeque on the state highway. The rotors whirred and spun and stirred up dirt, birthing dust devils and tumbling tumbleweeds across the blacktop and under the Glidden wire fence across the road. The pilot, who had trained at Fort Wolters near Mineral Wells, found the landing easy. During training, he had had no trouble landing in the stage fields of North Texas, fields with names like Cam Rhan, Da Nang, and Qui Nhon, names to match staging grounds in Vietnam, names he would later associate with flak, with hot LZs, with door gunner after door gunner peppered and wasted, with boys in ODs turned rust with dried blood. The pilot, Chuck Harris, landed the chopper and turned off the engine.

"Sit tight, boss," he hollered to the man in the fawn-colored western suit behind him.

Chuck had no problem ordering the multimillionaire to stay put. He had no problem telling his boss, the boss of a thousand roughnecks, to stay in his seat. His boss, Cedric Richland, would be better off for listening to those who knew. He would be better off waiting until the rotors of his big yellow helicopter stopped turning. Chuck remembered landing on an incline in friendly territory and a GI running with his head too high taking a rotor at a forty-five-degree angle, taking his death for no good reason in a safe place not far from Saigon. Chuck would not allow his boss to make the same mistake. He would not let him out of the helicopter until the rotor stopped, not even on flat ground.

Cedric Richland, the man in the fawn-colored suit, had decided to take his guest from the Northeast to the best barbeque joint in all of Waylon County, which happened to be the best barbeque joint in all of Texas. His guest, a Boston banker in pinstripes, sat patiently in his seatbelt waiting for instructions. He just smiled a cordial smile and looked at the world around him.

"Hell, Chuck, the damn rotor is almost stopped," Cedric said.

"I can see that, boss. But almost stopped and stopped are two different things. I sure don't want to have to call Mrs. Richland and tell her that your gourd and your hat got split in half by a prop. That ain't what I hired on for. I'll fly you to Hell or Houston if you need me to, and I will get you back home, but I ain't about to let you run into a live prop. That ain't gonna happen."

The rotor hummed to a standstill, and then the three men began to exit the helicopter as the dust was starting to settle, while children across the field stood and gawked. Cedric, who had been holding his high-end silver-belly Stetson in his lap, placed it on his head once he hit the ground. The visitor from Boston jumped out of the chopper and then looked down at his wingtips, the left of which now had an extremely visible scuff on the toe.

"We'll get that buffed out for you," Chuck said. "Ain't no thing to it."

The men walked across the furrows toward the restaurant, where the client from Boston was the first to the wrought-iron pit outside the front door. A short, thick young man in a black Kreutzmeyer Barbeque T-shirt was tending the pit, which was about the size of a fifty-gallon drum. Brisket and sausage and ribs rested on the grate above the coal.

"What would you like?" the kid asked.

The man from Boston, whose name was Peter O'Clery, turned to Cedric with an inquisitive look.

"Hell, I'd get the ribs," Cedric said, "and I'd get some brisket, too. But then, they make their own damn sausage. I'd get all three, the Holy Trinity of meat. Try some of everything, and we can ask for a dog bag if you can't eat it all."

"I'll do it then."

"Cliff, can you give both of us a nice rack of ribs, some marbled brisket, and some of that oak-smoked sausage?"

The young man took his tongs and dropped slabs of meat and sausage on the butcher paper on each of their trays.

"Chuck, get what you want," Cedric said. "Any man that can take me into the sky and land me safely where I want to go eats on me. What are you gonna eat?"

"I'll just have some brisket," Chuck said.

"Sure you don't want anything else?" Cedric asked. "It's on me."

"You ain't got to do that."

"Oil's at a damn hundred dollars a barrel. I'm wiping my ass with twenties. Get what you want."

"Cliff, I'll just have some of that brisket. Yeah, just like that. About where your knuckle is."

The young man in the Kreutzmeyer T-shirt sliced the meat.

"Here you go, bud," Cliff said.

"Thank you kindly."

"You betcha."

Stepping inside, Chuck reckoned that the barbeque joint had not changed in thirty years or more, or at least in as long as he could remember. The building was made of corrugated tin situated on a concrete slab with a ceiling fan above every other table. The same Audie Murphy movie posters as he remembered from before the conflict hung on the walls. The same farm implements, the same yokes and plows and hog scratchers hung above the front door. Chuck liked the way the place looked. It looked old. But it looked old in the right way. It looked old and well-kempt, old but not dirty. It looked like people imagined a famous barbeque place to look, and Chuck remembered once hearing Kreutzmeyer say that renovation could actually be a liability. It could change the flow of air. It could take the magic out of the barbeque, so he had decided to leave everything the same as it looked the first time Kreutzmeyer's graced the cover of *Texas Traveler* magazine.

Inside the corrugated metal barbeque joint, the three men followed the line and got potato salad, baked beans, pickles, onions, and jalapeños. Then they took a table in the front, close to the door. The two businessmen discussed a project over lunch, and Chuck ate and minded his own business. Minding one's own business, Chuck thought, was simply part of the job. So after he had eaten, he sat there satisfied, full from all of the barbeque, and stared out the window.

Kreutzmeyer's truly was the best barbeque in the state, and he was thankful that the barbeque joint was in his home county. He knew that folks in Luling and Lexington and Schulenburg would all argue that their barbeque was better, but Chuck knew different. Sitting there at the table, Chuck thought about how he could have driven Cedric and his guest to Kreutzmeyer's, or any other barbeque place in the Hill Country, faster than he had got them here in the boss' helicopter once you considered the time it took to run the punch list, get them loaded in the chopper, and get clearance to take off, but it was all about impressions. He knew that his boss wanted to impress the Yankee businessman, so he had asked Chuck to fly them to Kreutzmeyer's, which Chuck had done by taking a wide, ambling route so that they would be in the air longer.

Now Chuck had nothing against Yankees, or at least he had had nothing against Yankees since Vietnam. One of his closest friends in the Nam was a Yankee copilot from Trenton, New Jersey, a man who had a foul mouth and a quick wit who had saved Chuck's ass no fewer than three times. His Yankee buddy had made him feel like he had risen from the grave each time, for he knew that he should have been dead on all of those occasions.

Chuck had gone to Vietnam dipping snuff and listening to Lefty Frizzell and Bob Wills and returned from Vietnam with a head full of Jimi Hendrix and the Doors and memories like two years of brown acid. Merle Haggard was singing "The Fightin' Side of Me" on the radio at Kreutzmeyer's, and Chuck wished it would end. He had no use for nationalist bullshit at this point. Not just American bullshit. Any nation's bullshit. He wished he could hear Hendrix play "Voodoo Chile" instead. He wished he could become lost in the mad left-handed progressions and the strange fugues of a Hammond B-3 organ, to become lost in music, to become music, to leave memory and consciousness behind, but this was not his barbeque joint, not his place, not his place to speak, not his place to act. He would sit there and drink sweet tea doing his best not to pay attention to the talk about mineral rights and leases and pipe. He would do his best not to listen to the bullshit of men with draft deferments. Bone spurs for Cedric and he imagined college for the man from Boston. O'Clery spoke well and gave no indication that his life had been anything but pampered. At the very least, he had not given off the vibe that he had spent any time in jungle boots having to use his toothbrush to clean his gun. When O'Clery lit his cigarette, he did not hide the flame, nor did he hide the ember, which led Chuck to figure that the man had not spent a single minute in a combat zone.

A lot of folks had tried to avoid the war, but the thought never crossed Chuck's mind. He had heard of an ol' boy who put jellybeans in his underwear for his physical to show that he was crazy, but he was then ordered to eat the damn jellybeans. The boy, for that is all he was, couldn't escape the draft because he was poor. He was sent to Fort Hood, where he ended up with a First Cavalry patch on his sleeve and then, after a week in Vietnam, a flag upon his casket. The kid thought too much to survive the war. At least he hadn't had to live through most of a tour and die at the end. Chuck wished the damn bullshit song about running down my country, hoss, would end. He wished "Purple Haze" would blaze from the speakers so that he could simultaneously remember and forget.

The barbeque was good. It was really good. The bark on the brisket was smoky and crisp, the meat tender, the beans well-seasoned, the potato salad homemade and fresh, and the slices of onion sweet. He thought the pickled jalapeños mild, though the Yankee in pinstripes coughed and slipped a chewed-up pepper into his napkin. Chuck noticed this but did not consider it a lack of masculinity. He'd probably do the same were he ever to encounter Oysters Rockefeller.

"How'd you like it?" Cedric asked his northern visitor.

"Good. Very good. Thank you for lunch."

"You betcha. I reckon we need to make ourselves scarce. You 'bout ready, Chuck?"

"Ready when you are."

All three men used the restroom and then headed back out to the helicopter.

"How long you been flying these things?" the Yankee asked.

"A few years, I reckon," Chuck said.

The Yankee gave him a nervous smile.

"He flew one in the war," Cedric said, putting his hat in his lap.

"Y'all hold on tight," Chuck told them. "Hold on real good."

The chopper rose off the ground and soon was flying high above Waylon County headlong in the direction of the sun.

February 15th

★ ★ ★

rank Hardy and Ivy Lee Jones walked into the Hoggly Woggly to buy Valentine cards and candy for one another at a discount rate. It was February 15th, and the heart-shaped boxes of chocolate and the little packets of chalky pink candy with words like 'love me' and 'be mine' stamped on them with Red Dye #40 were now fifty percent off. Frank and Ivy Lee always celebrated Valentine's Day on the fifteenth because a day was a day was a day. They liked the sentiment of Valentine's Day, but they also knew that they could celebrate the same exact sentiment on the fifteenth for considerably less money and then go to any restaurant in town assured that they wouldn't have to wait for a table.

"This heart is still kinda high," Frank said with a frown.

"We can wait until tomorrow if you want. Everything'll be eighty percent off."

"Our kind of love can't wait till tomorrow. And besides, I'm not that cheap."

Ivy laughed as a form of rebuttal.

"Now, Ivy, you might think I'm tight as Dick's hatband, but that ain't even close to the truth. I just want us to be smart with whatever money we've got. I'm looking out for our future. I want us to be comfortable all of our lives. And pinching them buffalo nickels when we can will allow us to be just that."

Ivy looked at him in amusement.

"Are you hungry?" Frank asked. He was a big man with a bushy mustache and hands the size of anvils.

"I could eat in a little while. Are you gonna take me out for a romantic Valentine's dinner?"

"Sure am. How about Kreutzmeyer's Barbeque?"

"Frank, baby, I do like Kreutzmeyer's, but I don't think it's the kind of place you take your wife for Valentine's Day."

"Well, why not?"

"For one, I just got my hair done. I don't want it to smell like smoked ribs."

"They got good ribs there. And good bullets too. And I like any woman that smells like barbeque. It kind of turns me on."

Ivy batted her eyelashes and ran both hands through her flaming red half-dome hairdo.

"Well, Frank, I would like to think that I'm the only woman for you. I hope you don't fall for any ol' woman that smells like brisket and smoked sausage. And besides, I think that also makes you sound kinda like a cannibal, which isn't very cute."

"But baby, I love you so much I'd drink your bathwater."

"Yes, but I'd hope you wouldn't eat me."

"Just the white meat."

Frank gave Ivy a kiss on the cheek. He was a funny one, she thought. He was all bark and light on the bite, which was good as far as she was concerned. Marriage past fifty was more about getting along than getting between the sheets, so she was fine with all of that.

"We could go eat pork tacos up at the gas station," Frank said. "They got that good Jalisco-style salsa too. And they got a quiet little booth next to the automotive rack where we could eat. It has a nice view of the highway."

"Now you're pulling my chain. And besides, if the booth is occupied, we would have to wait on the curb outside for a while."

Frank just grinned.

"Ivy Lee, once the table was ready, the gas station attendant would step out the front door with the cowbell clanging and say, 'Hardy, party of two' and we'd sit down at that booth by the transmission fluid, just like at any other restaurant. Well, I can already tell by the look on your pretty little face that you ain't going for that idea. And I know you don't like Chop Suey Louie's Kung Pao Palace either, which is too bad because their sweet and sour pork is so good it'll make you weep. So, Ivy Lee, why don't we go to the Wailin' Biscuit Café for our romantic Valentine's Day dinner?"

"I guess we could go get a chicken fried steak. It's not like Waylon County has some fancy French place to go to and get all romantic, and the only Eye-talian place within twenty miles is an all-you-can-eat buffet. And I don't want to get romantic at a table next to a little league team filling their bellies with ham and pineapple pizza."

"Then the Wailin' Biscuit it is," Frank said, holding out his elbow like he was escorting the homecoming queen.

Frank was Ivy Lee's ninth husband. Alejandro, her eighth husband, would have taken her to Kerrville, where they would have slept at a bed and breakfast and dined at a fancy restaurant on the Guadalupe. At that fancy restaurant they would have eaten chardonnay garlic mussels and sipped flutes of dry Champagne, and he would have told her sexy things in Spanish although the only words she understood were "¿Dónde está el baño?" and "una más cerveza." Watching his sexy mouth move was good enough for her. She never understood what he was saying, but it really didn't matter much. After that, he would have ravaged her beneath the sheets while listening to Santana's *Abraxas* album on the portable stereo he took with him everywhere.

However, Ivy Lee came to understand that Alejandro carried the portable stereo to a number of motel rooms in four contiguous counties, where several other women, mostly redheads like her, but strawberry blondes as well, also fell under his spell and made love to him to the rhythm of "*Oye Cómo Va.*" He could have at least played a different album for each one of them out of common decency, but he had not, and Ivy Lee could not bear the jealousy and shame and had to split the sheet. And now Alejandro was gone.

As for her other husbands, including Joe Ted, who was number five and number seven, some would have done better and some would have done worse than Frank on Valentine's Day. Steve, who was number four, would have been laid out drunk on the floor by the time Ivy Lee got home from work, and she would have likely had to clean up a trail of whiskey vomit, and Harlan, with stink bait on his pants, would have cooked blackened catfish for her and given her a candy bar he bought at the minnow shop. George the Hairy would have forgotten the holiday altogether.

Ivy thought about telling Frank about her Valentine's Day greatest hits to give him some ideas about what she preferred, but she imagined it wouldn't help their marriage at all. It would only pit Frank in competition with men that no longer mattered, and such talk could cause nothing but resentment, jealousy, or outright combat, three outcomes that Ivy no longer had a stomach for. Luckily, she had finally learned her lesson and made a vow not to discuss any of her previous husbands with her current one. However, by not sharing her tales about the battlefield of love and marriage, Ivy imagined that Frank must have thought her life had only consisted of an uneventful childhood and many years of working at the grocery store, but then, many people's life stories probably sounded like that, so Ivy did not fret over it. Occasionally, she did share expurgated tales of her life while sitting on the couch with her feet propped up so Frank could paint her toenails. When she did tell a story, she did her best not to mention the husbands by name or make a value judgment about any of them. She simply treated them as characters in her story. Granted, it was not like discussing her previous husbands would have somehow violated the charter of their marriage, for this had not been included in the vows they exchanged before the Justice of the Peace, but it seemed the courteous, thoughtful thing to do.

After paying for their Valentine cards and heart-shaped candy boxes in the fifteen items more-or-less line at the Hoggly Woggly, Frank escorted his wife outside, opened the passenger door to his big heavy-duty pickup truck, and helped Ivy Lee inside. She liked that kind of chivalry and adoration, and that was perhaps why she was so wildly in love with Frank. Well, that is not completely true, she thought. She loved the purity of his heart, his honest concern about her happiness, and, though she appreciated how he worshiped her, his almost irrational adoration is not what had won her. Growing up, she had had a dog, Fido, and he had loved her from within his very marrow, but he also licked his own ass and balls, and that kind of unexamined love was not what she wanted. She loved Frank because he was a good ol' boy with a good heart and was generally as calm as a chamomile bubble bath.

Frank put the truck in gear just as Possum Jones and Tammy Wynette began singing a duet on the stereo. After turning the music down a notch, Frank drove Ivy across town toward the Wailin' Biscuit Café, the parking lot of which was mostly empty since it was a Tuesday, and Valentine's Day had fallen on a Monday. But then Frank kept driving. Ivy Lee was touching up her make-up when she noticed that the truck was heading out of town.

"Frank, you passed the Wailin' Biscuit."

"Well, I'll be durned."

"Aren't you going to turn around?"

"Eventually."

"Frank, baby, you just passed the city limit sign."

"Yes, ma'am. That is correct."

"I thought we were going for chicken fried steak."

"Chicken fried steak is not romantic," Frank said without takng his eyes off the road.

"Then where are we going?"

"France."

"France?"

"France. Where the ladies wear no pants. France."

"France?" Ivy asked with twangy inflection.

"Well, not exactly France. We're going to Paris."

"Paris?"

"Paris. We're going to eat snails under the Eiffel Tower," Frank said with a grin.

"You can't get no more romantic than that."

"I don't think so either. And I done booked us a room at the Versailles Palace Motor Inn."

"But I have to work tomorrow."

"I already cleared it with your boss."

"Well, you are a real romantic, Frank Hardy."

"Yes, ma'am, I reckon I am."

Ivy Lee Jones reached her hand into the Hoggly Woggly bag, pulled out a box of chocolates, opened the cellophane wrapper, and slipped a pink-cherry-filled chocolate into Frank's mouth.

"You're going to ruin my appetite, Ivy Lee," Frank said.

Ivy ran her hand across Frank's thigh.

"I think not," she replied. "I think you'll still be plenty hungry."

Frank laughed and turned a little red, his cowboy boot pressing harder on the accelerator, the truck heading just a little bit faster toward Paris, Waylon County just a little farther behind them now.

"Frank, I have to say that you surprised me. This isn't the way we normally spend February fifteenth."

"No, ma'am, it isn't. Although we may always be looking for a bargain in the great flea market of life, our love comes at a premium."

Ivy Lee Jones beamed as she held onto her man. Frank smiled proudly with a big, strong hand on the steering wheel, the truck heading up the interstate toward Dallas where they would follow a smaller highway up to Paris, where unbridled romance was waiting just for them.

The Ties That Once Bound
★ ★ ★

"Sobriety doesn't suit you," Josephine said, twenty years since divorced from Gilbert. She was wearing a silver dress with a string of pearls, and her blond-highlighted hair was worn up to accentuate the slenderness of her neck.

"I never thought so either. But the court ordered me to dance the twelve-step, and I reckon I learned to cut a pretty good rug."

Gilbert, in a charcoal gray coat and a blue silk tie, stood an arm's length from her. He was nearing fifty, but his hair was still full and indigo dark.

"Well, you don't look happy," she said.

"How is happy supposed to look?"

"More excited about life."

"If I was any more excited about life, I wouldn't know what to do with myself."

He held his right palm upward and rotated his body slightly as if to encourage Josephine to look all around her. Their daughter, in a long white wedding dress, was dancing with Clifton, her lawfully wedded husband, on the dance floor of the Victorian cattle baron mansion they had rented for the wedding and reception. Old friends, the men in blazers and cowboy boots and the women in cocktail dresses, mingled and danced and drank.

"The wrinkles on your face tell the tale," Josephine said. "They all trail downward, which means you're unhappy a lot more often than you're happy. If that weren't the truth, it wouldn't be written on your face."

"You don't know."

"I'm your ex-wife."

"Ex-wife is right. If you understood me better, we'd still be married."

"I still can't believe we reached this day. Here we are at Sandy Ann's wedding. It all happened so fast."

"I know. Life happens fast. And by the time you think you have it figured out, you are about out of time."

"I know it. And there's our daughter dancing with her new husband. It's great, but it's still kind of hard to believe. It somehow doesn't all seem right, though I know they are happy and everything is so new and beautiful for them."

"How's Joe?" Gilbert asked.

"He's doing fine. We had our twelfth anniversary the other day."

"That's good. It sounded like you were gonna cut bait a while back."

"I thought about it. But I'm glad I didn't. We're doing pretty good. And it's fun to sign greeting cards with 'Jo and Joe.'"

"Well, you look good."

Josephine glanced at the dance floor, where her husband was spinning the flower girl to the tune of the "Tennessee Waltz." And then she fixed her eyes on Gilbert, who was standing dead still in front of her.

"Thank you," she said, though her mouth seemed reluctant.

Josephine had not seen Gilbert since their daughter was in kindergarten. The last time she saw him, he was in the back of a sheriff's department vehicle on his way to the county jail. He was wearing a blood-splattered white T-shirt, and the blood on his shirt was hers. He had busted open her nose.

But she had provoked him. She had gotten in his face and bared her teeth. She had escalated and escalated and escalated. Every time he had tried to disengage, she started screaming more. Maybe she had wanted him to hit her. Maybe she had wanted to see how far he would go, to dare him like he was a dog at the end of his chain. Normally when an argument reached that point, he grabbed his keys, slammed the front door, and headed off to a beer joint. But that time he hadn't. He had cuffed her across the nose. Drunk and bleeding fast, she had called the law. No man in Josephine's family would have ever hit a woman, though some of Gilbert's people would, and apparently Gilbert would as well, though he only hit her that once. Josephine's father, who passed away a couple of years ago, would have shot Gilbert and fed him to the buzzards had she not begged him to spare her ex-husband's life.

Once Gilbert was off probation, he left Texas and never came back. For the last several years he had owned a bar in New Orleans, a place that opened at ten in the morning and was famous for its crawfish Bloody Marys. And though Josephine never tried to keep Sandy Ann from seeing her father, she never encouraged nor facilitated her daughter's visits any more than law or decorum happened to dictate.

"Waylon County hasn't changed much since I was here last," Gilbert said. "The only thing different is that everybody's older."

Josephine tilted her head.

"Me especially," Gilbert said. "You know, I never did apologize. I'm sorry I hit you. I never hit a woman before, and I never hit a woman since. Don't know what the hell I was thinking. Took me twenty years to see you face-to-face and apologize, but here I am."

"I forgave you years ago. I couldn't carry that with me. I couldn't carry that hate. It was too heavy to carry very far down the road."

"Well, thank you. Thank you for your forgiveness. It's been eating at me for years, and I didn't want to write a letter or call you on the phone."

Josephine smiled, and Gilbert smiled back.

The DJ played a hip-hop song, and all of the young people got on the dance floor and moved around. The older people returned to their tables or went over to the bar for another drink. Josephine's sister, Annie, came and got her from where she was standing there with Gilbert, and the two of them walked over to a table where their aunt and uncle from the Panhandle were drinking iced tea.

The next song was by George Strait, and the older people returned to the dancefloor. Josephine danced with Joe, who was wearing a black Stetson and a tuxedo jacket. They danced the Texas two-step with the comfort and ease of long-time partners. Joe put his mouth to Josephine's ear, and she laughed, her tongue showing slightly between rows of straight white teeth. About that time, a tall man in a herringbone blazer patted Joe on the shoulder, the two hugged one another, and then they walked over to the bar, leaving Josephine laughing behind them. Josephine returned to her table and poured a fresh glass of Champagne before visiting a few guests and then placing herself in Gilbert's line of vision. He walked toward her, leaving two steps between them.

"Back in the old days we were Bonnie and Clyde," he said. "We were dangerous."

"Yes, we were."

"We didn't give a damn."

"No, we didn't. We raised our glasses high and didn't worry about tomorrow."

Gilbert smiled shyly.

"I don't raise my glass too high anymore. To tell you the truth, I don't raise it at all because I don't know when to stop."

"I understand."

Gilbert nodded slightly toward the side entrance.

"I'm over you," she said.

"I'm not over you."

"I know it."

Gilbert walked around the edge of the dancefloor, shook a few hands, and slid out the side door. Josephine got a new glass of Champagne and walked out the front entrance. Soon she found Gilbert behind the mansion leaning against the red brick wall.

"I just want to talk to you," he said.

"I know it."

And then he kissed her hard on the mouth, and she kissed him back, her arms around his neck. Gilbert ran his hands all down her body, a wild, mad memory of better days.

"I shouldn't have done that," Josephine said.

"I know it," he replied.

She stepped back, and they looked into each other's eyes.

"We should go somewhere, Jo. For old times' sake."

"I can't do that."

"Everybody's in there having fun. Nobody would be the wiser."

"I probably shouldn'ta drank this much."

"Come on, let's go. For old times' sake."

Gilbert reached gently toward her, and her face took on a blank expression as if she were recalling something, as if something deep inside had surfaced. And then she shook her head from side to side like she had just woken up from a terrible dream, and before Gilbert could withdraw his hand, Josephine had already reared back and hit him square in the face with her left fist, her wedding ring cutting the bridge of his nose, blood dripping from his right nostril.

He didn't even flinch. He just stood there looking at her.

"I'm glad we got that over with," Josephine said.

"Me too," Gilbert replied.

"That was good, though. Really good."

"Like Bonnie and Clyde."

"My mama said you were no good the day she met you."

"Your mama was right."

"And my daddy was going to put a bullet in your head."

"Well, he should've probably done it."

"Maybe so."

Josephine gave Gilbert a dirty little smile and headed toward the front door, empty Champagne glass in hand. Gilbert walked across the parking lot and climbed into his big, late model pickup truck. He started the engine, rolled onto the highway, and drove out into the darkness of the big Texas night with blood dripping down the front of his starched white shirt and the past upon his mind.

Settler's Rest

★ ★ ★

The Texas sun was burning like a jalapeño-bacon grease fire, and there was nary a cloud in sight that bright August afternoon. The funeral procession, which was led by a low-slung hearse and two black limousines, mainly consisted of four-wheel-drive trucks and the occasional town car driven by someone who should have surrendered his or her license a decade ago. A couple of miles down the state highway, past the little town of Warnell, the gloomy caravan turned onto a narrow, chugholed blacktop and then took a dogleg left, passing through the wrought-iron arch at Settler's Rest Cemetery. Byron Herblight, decked in a dark gray suit and a subdued psychedelic necktie featuring cosmic sea turtles swimming in a swirling, inky universe, was sitting in the backseat of the second limousine contemplating the fragile, fleeting nature of life as well as the horrifying permanence of certain punctuation errors.

He wondered, as he had every other time he had passed under this somber arch, how anyone could allow words to be forged in iron and put on display without so much as a proper proofread. Byron, who worked at the James S. Hogg Document Production and Data Transmission Building at the Texas State Capitol complex in Austin, spent most of his days editing and revising congratulatory missives and gold-leafed certificates destined to adorn the office walls of some of Texas' finest, most upright citizens. Thus, punctuation and spelling were the air he breathed.

As the vehicle in which he was traveling rolled across the gravel road past dozens of headstones, Byron considered the apostrophe in Settler's Rest, for its placement suggested a single solitary settler, and it was abundantly clear that a great many settlers, as well as several generations of their descendants, had been buried here over the years. Honestly, Byron did not even care for the word "settler." If he had his way, the burial ground would have been named Pioneers' Rest, for "settler" somehow implied a lack of volition.

And although much of his family was interred here at Settler's Rest, Byron had never even entertained the thought of being buried within eyeshot of that detestable apostrophe, regardless of the fact that his grandfather had offered a plot for both him and a guest. No, he would rather have his ashes loaded into a space capsule and jettisoned into orbit or even have his mortal remains entombed beneath the cafetorium stage at Warnell High School, where his life had recently been affirmed when he was presented with the Alumnus of the Year Award, than be taunted by that dreadful apostrophe for all eternity.

And then he spun his mind to the matter at hand. His great-aunt, Libbie Perkins, would soon be committed to the earth. He always loved his Aunt Libbie, and he was proud that she had chosen him to be one of her pallbearers, for she had many nieces and nephews and other relations upon whom she could have bestowed that honor.

Aunt Libbie always wore pink dresses and offered visitors iced tea and chess pie whenever they came to call. She also taught the middle school boys' Sunday School class for half a century, where she exhibited both the patience of Job and the stomach of a billy goat. Yes, Aunt Libbie endured decades of the odd, awkward jokes that resulted from the strange synaptic miswirings of the adolescent brain as well as managed not to faint or even list at the awful olfactory sensations that regularly assaulted her senses in the youth hall there at the House of the Lord. Aunt Libbie, Byron reflected, had always been good-natured and funny, and those who knew her best knew her to be the finest of fundamentalists, the kind that reveled in a slightly naughty allusion and would even drink a margarita when away on vacation. Byron always loved Aunt Libbie, and he knew that she loved him, too.

The chauffer driving the hearse that was leading the procession parked in the gravel, and the cars and trucks that followed came to a halt. Men never seen beneath the wide-blue sky without a beat-up straw hat or a feedstore cap stepped out of their vehicles bareheaded in reverence. Women most often seen in tube tops or spaghetti straps which revealed the hearts and dolphins and roses tattooed upon their deeply tanned skins were wearing dresses long and dark enough to make a Branch Davidian proud.

Byron and the other five riding with him, strong, wide-shouldered men who hung sheetrock or laid brick, climbed out of the limousine while the driver in his black coat and captain's hat waited behind. The day was brutally hot, the sort of day Texans talked about with filthy alliteration often involving their favorite fricative, the letter F. Byron could taste the dust in his mouth, and he could hardly see through the lenses of his pence-nez glasses.

While he was walking toward the back of the hearse, he could tell that something was awry. The preacher and a few others were milling around Aunt Libbie's plot scratching their heads and looking around in a bewildered, abject state of confusion. The preacher, an affable fellow with a penchant for using the word "saith," reminded Byron of a squirrel he had once seen running around in a state of absolute befuddlement searching for a large tree that had recently been cut down.

"They forgot to dig the hole," Larry, Byron's big, brawny cousin, said.

Larry's eyes cut toward his brother, a former football captain known simply as The Anvil. Byron, who, out of nervous habit, was tugging at the rubber band that held his ponytail, imagined that Larry and The Anvil would soon be pounding Snuff McGee, the hard-drinking gravedigger, into a putty similar to that used on the fenders of rusty old muscle cars.

"I'm so sorry," a trim young woman in large round spectacles cried as she stood in front of Uncle Edmund's wheelchair, which was situated in front of his wife's undug grave. "It's my fault. I accidentally told the gravedigger to put the hole in the wrong place."

Larry and The Anvil looked at the young woman, who had just started working at the funeral home, and their shoulders began to relax slightly. These two large men, after all, were virtuous adherents to the Texas tradition, and Byron knew quite well that they would do no woman harm in word nor in deed, though he imagined that they still might pummel the gravesmith nonetheless.

Uncle Edmund sat in his wheelchair staring into the heat of the day, and one of Byron's female cousins, a tall woman named Carrie, placed a handkerchief over his bald head, which was quickly beginning to burn in the cruel Texas heat. Makeup ran down the women's faces, making it appear as if they were melting, and sweat soaked through the men's church clothes in the most unflattering of ways.

About that time everyone came to realize that the hole had mistakenly been dug some six rows away, at the future grave of Libby Perkins, the wife of Edmund's third cousin, Pete, who was already occupying his plot. Libby had moved to Washington State with her daughter upon her husband's passing, and being in less than sterling health herself, had elected not to fly down for today's funeral. Byron wondered if someone would broach the topic of burying Libbie in Libby's plot and vice versa, but he doubted that neither Uncle Edmund nor Cousin Libby, who had surely heard reports of Edmund snoring so loudly that Aunt Libbie ended up deaf in her left ear, would be too amenable to an eternal wife swap.

The young funeral director, who reminded Byron of a sexy librarian he once dated, called Snuff McGee on his cellphone while everyone stood anxiously around her. Byron, however, knew that Snuff would not answer, for the day was Saturday, and Snuff was likely in the clutches of a powerful hangover, the kind that makes a man feel as if he has been eaten by a coyote and defecated off a cliff, to paraphrase a saying in the local vernacular. Yes, Snuff was likely suffering from a powerful case of brown bottle flu and slumbering like the residents of Settler's Rest, though there was also the possibility that he had not yet even gone to bed and was still swilling barley pop and listening to Lynyrd Skynyrd at top volume on his eight-track player, rendering him, in either case, incapable of hearing his telephone. And even if the funeral director was able to contact Snuff, Byron wondered if everyone would, or even should, wait there in the heat to watch him claw out a grave with his backhoe.

"Y'all all go on," Cousin Larry said. "Y'all all go back to the church house and eat the barbeque of mourning. The Anvil and me will wait here with the hearse until Snuff McGee shows up and digs the hole so that we can give Aint Libbie a proper burial. Apparently things gotta be supervised around here."

The preacher nodded in agreement, and it was, in Byron's opinion, a sound decision indeed, for there were numerous octogenarians and even a nonagenarian or two congregated there in the hundred-degree heat.

"Would you like all of us pallbearers to stay here and help bury her?" Byron asked Larry.

"Nah, don't worry about it. Y'all go ahead and ride back to the church. Our sweet Aint Libbie wasn't big as a minute. I'll bet she didn't weigh a buck-oh-five dressed to the nines in a corsage and Sunday shoes. The Anvil and me can carry her little pink coffin and lay her down to slumber."

The preacher and everyone else got back in their cars and trucks ready to head to the church fellowship hall, so Byron climbed into the limousine, albeit reluctantly. The driver, seeing that he had all four of his remaining passengers, followed the gravel road toward the Settler's Rest arch. On the way back to town, Byron thought about spelling, punctuation, and life it-self. He thought about apostrophes and unfortunate homophones, and he wondered upon the strangeness of life as he adjusted the half-Windsor on his somber psychedelic tie, where the cosmic turtles swam the chiaroscuro universe in a perpetual state of suspended animation.

A Psychobilly Prayer

★ ★ ★

Hildegard of Limburg woke up in her whitewashed cell at the old monastery in Erfurt where Martin Luther once wrestled with the Devil. Next to her bed, less than an arm's length away, rested her lap steel guitar and small tube amplifier, both of which she had brought from her home in Central Texas. The morning sunlight poured in through the window, and Hildegard, no longer able to sleep, washed her face in an ancient basin, slipped on her gingham dress and finely tooled cowboy boots, and stepped out of the room and onto the cobbles of the courtyard overlooking the ruins of the medieval library. The monastery where she slept had been secularized years ago, and the former cell, now called a guestroom, still carried a feeling of ascetic simplicity.

That evening she would be playing a concert in Saint Augustine's Church, silhouetted by the kaleidoscopic beauty of the lion and parrot window above the sanctuary. Hildegard, when asked what she played, simply told her interlocutors that she played honkytonk versions of medieval hits on her lap steel guitar. This summer she had been invited to play concerts along the Luther Trail, where the audiences were always thrilled to hear her perform on lap steel as well as to hear her speak to them in her native Texas-German, a language from a speech island in the Texas Hill Country which in many ways resembled nineteenth-century German yet also featured English loan words such as *der Mesquitebaum* and *die Cotton* as well as locally coined terms such as *das Panzerschwein*, or armored pig, the Texas-German word for armadillo. For German audiences, Hildegard

219

was at once a glimpse of their linguistic past as well as of an isolated community that, through creativity and fluency, had adapted their language to a strange, hostile new world far, far from home. These audiences were fascinated by this walking anomaly, this woman who played the music of medieval and Renaissance Europe on an instrument more often found in a Texas dancehall than in an historic stone church and who spoke their language in both the manner of the past and in a way they had never before heard in their lives.

Hildegard walked to a nearby café with window boxes filled with petunias for a breakfast of a soft-boiled egg, rye bread, butterkäse, and salami, and she wished that she would have not decided to wear cowboy boots, for their riding heels were not designed for cobblestone, though, like many a Texan in Europe, she wore them anyway. She should have worn her Mary Janes, she thought, and saved the boots for her concert, but she guessed she would never learn.

Hildegard, after all, had actually lived in Europe in her younger days, though, during a cold, lonely winter in France, a bottle of absinthe and Hank Williams had persuaded her to go back home to Limburg, Texas, the place where she belonged. And here she was back in Europe, and though she was not necessarily where she belonged, she was older, and hopefully a little wiser, and, at the very least, where she wanted to be at the time.

From a tucked-away table near the window, Hildegard quietly drank her coffee and watched the people pass by outside. She saw men in gray suits and muted ties and women in dark dresses and scarves. She liked the monochromatic scene. She liked how the limestone buildings across the street, buildings darkened by lignite soot, served as a backdrop. And she liked the tilt of the sun and how it made her realize that the Northern Renaissance artists were not painting from artifice but from life, for the slant of the sun seemed the same as she remembered in the paintings of Bruegel, Dürer, and Cranach.

While she sat there enjoying her breakfast, a punk rocker in leathers and spikes, with hair the color of jungle birds, passed by the window in the direction of the door. The punk stepped into the café, and Hildegard thought he looked like a rough, jackbooted version of the psychedelic angel in van

Eyck's *Dresden Triptych*. After scanning the room, the punk took a seat at the table next to Hildegard, pulled a French cigarette from a hard pack, and lit it with a stainless-steel Zippo. He ordered black coffee and a roll.

"Hello," he said.

"Hello," Hildegard replied, wondering where this was going to go.

"I saw your picture on the placards. You are the American that is playing tonight."

"Yes, I will be playing tonight."

Hildegard noticed on his jacket an anarchy symbol and a button with a picture of an American flag on fire.

"I am coming to the concert," he said. "I like the steel guitar. I like the country music. I like Johnny Cash. Do you know Johnny Cash?"

"I know his music, yes."

"I like Johnny Cash and psychobilly music. I like that music. I play bagpipes in a psychobilly band. We play tonight, but late, much after you play."

Hildegard wondered if this man had been watching her, was stalking her. These were concerns. Real concerns.

The man took out his phone and walked over to her table. Although quiet music was playing in the café, he clicked to start a video on his phone.

"This is my band," he said.

Hildegard watched and listened. The drummer played like a middleweight boxer thrumming his opponent, driving the beat, driving the sound, a mad cowboy waltz with a Stratocaster's twang hanging in the air as if in a desert waste, the doghouse bass thumping, the singer singing in a wide Texas drawl, though a well-tuned ear could hear that the singer was not an English native, but a German speaker. And then a bagpipe was injected for a solo. It was piercing, immediate, almost chaotic, and it was good, really good.

"I like it," Hildegard said. "Great bagpipes. Never heard bagpipes played in country music, but it's good."

But then, she thought, few people had probably ever heard medieval compositions, plainsong and polyphony from centuries ago, music originally played by musicians who had turned to dust generations ago, performed on a lap steel guitar. Her music, Hildegard thought, was the other side of the same coin. Hildegard imagined that the young cowpunker had already gathered that, and that this common denominator was the reason he was now standing before her.

"Don't mind Uwe," the waitress, with magenta hair and a diamond stud above her lip, told Hildegard. "He is my favorite *Stammgast*. He means no harm. He comes here many days. He often speaks with the musicians. He is harmless, even if he doesn't look like it, even though his nose is pierced like a bull."

Uwe smiled, revealing a couple of missing teeth, and his deep blue eyes twinkled.

"After you play, you should come sit in with us," he said. "You would have fun, I think. A new experience. How often have you played Johnny Cash songs with a psychobilly band in a basement bar in the old DDR?"

"Never."

"*Genau.* That's why you should join us."

"I'll think about it. I might be tired by then, and well, you know, I have a bit of jetlag."

"We can sleep when we're dead," Uwe said, "but I will not pressure you. However, the invitation is there. I have a ticket to your concert, so if you want to go, you can tell me afterwards, and if you do not, *kein Problem*."

Hildegard finished her coffee and paid her check. She smiled at the man with the jungle bird hair and walked to the door. On the street she breathed in the air, looked straight ahead and walked without smiling, as she had seen so many passersby do. She wondered about the young man and his motives. He was simply a musician, like her, she imagined, someone who loved music so much that he would loiter around a place in order to meet a traveling musician he wanted to play with. She understood that.

So often she had played alone these last several years. In her limestone house on the Roemer Escarpment, she played her music, far from any road, any other person, and the solitude gave her strength. It gave her energy, allowed her to grow however she wanted to grow, to explore however she wanted to explore because there was no one to approve or disapprove of the music she made other than herself. The solitude was her strength, her secret.

That afternoon she quietly strolled the streets. She visited the twin cathedrals and the Merchants' Bridge, with its half-timbered houses and artisan shops. Her day was quiet, like days at home, though with a more tangible sense of melancholy, mortality, and *Sehnsucht.*

When the time to play approached, she returned to her cell, showered, and put on the black A-line dress and turquoise necklace she always wore when she performed. She then walked across the courtyard to Saint Augustine's Church. She spoke briefly with the man who had booked her, a tall, pleasant man in bifocals and a dark gray suit, and then she discussed logistics with the soundman.

As she waited in the sacristy with a cup of hot tea, she could hear footsteps echoing from the nave. She could hear people filing in for the performance. She could hear people speaking in hushed tones that echoed through the church. In the sacristy, she sat and set her mind for her performance. And she considered the wooden panels around her, wondered about how for hundreds of years clergymen had sat in this very room, had prepared for the feast days, for sacred rituals, and now they were gone, had disappeared, with many of their bones perhaps resting in the crypt below her.

When Hildegard was introduced, she stepped out of the sacristy and walked over to the pulpit, the heels of her boots resounding off the stones, echoing in the apse. The sound excited her, for she knew that her lap steel would have a round, full sound in this sanctuary, where music, more holy to her than prayer, would soon be played.

She bowed as the patrons clapped, and she looked across the audience seated in the pews of the ancient church. She saw elderly pairs and clutches of matrons, male couples in fine clothing, and a small group of students most likely from a nearby gymnasium. On the back pew closest to the door sat Uwe, whom she had met that morning, his hair bright and wild in this room filled with people dressed in slate and black, people with dusky blond, flat brown, or graying hair. Looking across the audience, Hildegard, though she had met him only once, recognized him immediately, but then, most anyone would, for he was like a macaw living among sparrows and wrens and thrushes. He sat alone, the only person on his row, though the rows around him all were full.

Hildegard placed metal picks upon her right index finger and thumb and placed her gleaming steel bar upon the strings with her left. She played the old music from medieval days, when music was a subject akin to mathematics in the great universities of Europe. She played the patterns found in codices, in palimpsest fragments, in half-charred books of prayer. She played plainsong and polyphony. She played them all with a Texas accent. She played the sound of the wind rattling the mesquite trees, the call of the mockingbird, the cry of the panther. She played the evensong of locusts and the low of the longhorn, the solitude and distance.

In the back of the church the man in leathers and spikes sat with his eyes closed as if in prayer, lost in the music it seemed, transported wherever the glissandos would take him, transported by the sound of the steel guitar, by the vibration of phosphor bronze strings within the cathedrals of his eardrums. And when the concert ended, the people clapped and smiled, and Hildegard thanked them for coming.

"*Danke schön*, y'all," she said. "Thank you for attending. Thank you for having me."

After she switched off her amp, she stepped into the nave, where she mingled and nodded and answered questions. And when every member of the audience had left save one, that man, the man in the back pew, rose and approached her.

"Beautiful," he said. "Beautiful. You play so very well."

"*Vielen Dank*," she said. "You are very kind."

"This evening, if you would like, you can come play with my band. We would love to have you."

"I don't know. I love the offer, but I don't know."

"If you change your mind, we'll be at a bar called Chinaski's Place."

Uwe's voice echoed across the nave, and the two of them stood there in silence until his words had disappeared. Hildegard thought about returning to her cell, to silence, and wondered if that is what she wanted. Interaction exhausted her, for she was used to her home alone in the Texas wilds, and not speaking with anyone, much less dozens of people. But then, any night she wanted she could sit alone and read until she fell asleep. And, besides, it was small talk that sapped her energy, and there would be little chance of having to endure small talk if she was sitting in with the band.

"I'll go with you," she said.

Uwe smiled widely, showing his missing teeth.

"Let me fetch the van," he said, "and I will come for you."

Within moments, Hildegard already regretted that she had agreed, that she had made an impulsive decision. She was alone in another country about to get in a van with a man she did not even know. But there was no turning back now. She would ask for a cigarette and smoke it in the van, prepared to use it as a weapon if she needed to. She had lived in a city before, after all, and knew how to take care of herself.

Uwe pulled up in a white panel van. He opened the sliding side door and placed her amplifier on the floor. Hildegard climbed in the front seat with her lap steel in its gig bag between her legs.

"I am glad you will come," Uwe said. "I do hope you enjoy playing with us."

Hildegard smiled and watched the road as Uwe drove to a more industrial part of town. On a street corner she saw teenagers huffing silver paint from a paper sack, one of them, a thin boy, pale and glazed, had blood dripping beneath his nose. They passed graffiti and soot and broken concrete, barbed wire rigged over windows.

Uwe stopped at the bar called Chinaski's Place, where a tall blonde in a latex dress greeted them in a baritone.

"*Guten Abend*," she said.

"Hello, Irma," Uwe replied. "This is Hildegard. She'll be playing with us tonight."

"Good evening," Irma said, turning to Hildegard. "You are from Texas. I saw your picture in the newspaper. Welcome. I hope you have fun here."

"Nice to meet you," Hildegard said, and then she and Uwe descended the stairs into the bar, Hildegard carrying her lap steel and Uwe her amp, a bagpipe case upon his back.

Smoke billowed out of the basement as if from hell, and Hildegard could hear loud voices, the clanking of glass, and raw music blaring from the speakers. She did not know if this was a good idea. Soon after they reached the bottom of the stairs, Uwe handed Hildegard a beer and they toasted with a *Prost*. The band was already set up, and the two of them wended their way through a labyrinth of flesh to get to the stage.

Women that looked like Marlene Dietrich in conchos and spurs sat at the bar smoking Lucky Strikes. A man with a pompadour in a bright red nudie suit stood near the PA. There were punkers and bikers and waifs and stoners. They all spoke in German, loud and hearty and sure. Hildegard met the drummer, a lanky shirtless man covered in tattoos of wagon wheels and six-guns who had Sitting Bull tattooed on his left bicep and the words "Qui cantat, bis orat" upon his heart. She met the bass player, who wore a porkpie hat, and she met the lead guitarist, whose eyes were glassy and his face thin. He was wearing an unbuttoned pearl snap shirt with the sleeves cut off.

The drummer tagged his snare, and then the crowd roared. They cheered from the rough wooden tables and moved closer to the dance floor. The band played "Ring of Fire," with Uwe on vocals, sometimes singing in German and at other times in English. The band played hard and fast and the crowd moved to the music. They laughed mad-eyed and called and shouted. They raised their fists when Uwe played a solo on his bagpipes.

Hildegard sat in the eye of the storm in her chair on the stage. She had never played in such a place. Uwe sang another verse and the chorus, "*Ein Ring aus Feuer, Ein Ring aus Feuer.*" Uwe nodded her in, and Hildegard played a solo, the drums slicing the night, the sunburst Gibson wailing, the doghouse bass leaving space for her to explore. Hildegard played like the world was on fire, like wildfire on the prairie, consuming the cactus and mesquite. She played like a twister ravaging the plains, *Ein Ring aus Feuer, Ein Ring aus Feuer.*

People danced and screamed, "*Schön, schön,* go go go." And she played and played and played. And Uwe smiled the fearless smile of a man that probably enjoyed a good fight, his hair bright, his face glimmering with sweat, and he nodded for Hildegard to keep on playing, to take the crowd to ecstasy, to travel the wilderness of sound to the desert of consciousness, to the Wild Horse Desert of the heart. And she played as if possessed by a miracle, a miracle where each and every person in that smoky basement were one, where no one was alone. Hildegard felt the holy unifying presence of music, a psychobilly prayer, and she slid her steel bar and plucked the strings, the whole place enflamed in this ring of fire.

226

The Angel, the Devil,
and Saint Nicholas
★ ★ ★

Saint Nicholas, an Angel, and the Devil sat at a table inside the KJT Hall taking shots of slivovice one after the other. The slivovice came from Jan Jelinek, a Czech handicraft exporter who traveled to Texas every December to sell traditional wooden ornaments at the Old World Christmas markets. He had been coming to the Saint Nicholas Eve celebration in Krasna Lipa since the Velvet Revolution, and he always smuggled plenty of that strong, clear, homemade plum brandy to America to share with his friends. At present, Saint Nicholas, the Angel, and the Devil were sitting around a plastic bottle with "*Dobrá Voda*," or "Good Water," on the label, though the water happened to be fuel-grade Bohemian moonshine.

The hall, which had a long wooden dance floor and naked beams along the ceiling, was empty. The children had already come to the KJT for Mikuláš, as the holiday was called, and now were gone. They had come at dusk to recite a poem to Saint Nicholas, receive their chocolate, and go back home at a reasonable hour so they would not be sleepy at school the next day.

"Why don't we have another shot?" slurred the Angel.

Her flowing dress and long blond tresses were impeccable, and her gauze wings remained straight despite the fact she was leaning back against them in her chair. Her face, no matter how beatific, how beautiful and blue-eyed and rosy-cheeked, could not disguise the fact that she was absolutely hammered.

"A little one couldn't hurt," Saint Nicholas said. "I mean a *maličký* shot. Just a little-bitty *maličký panáček.*"

Saint Nicholas straightened his miter, groomed his white beard enough that it was not in his mouth, and poured another round. He accidentally splashed some slivovice on the front of his red velvet robes, but that was hardly a concern since he already looked unkempt due to the creamy mustard he had gotten on himself while eating a smoked sausage.

"Let's save the slivo for later," the Devil said. "We can hardly stand as it is, and we promised to visit some children's houses."

The Devil slid his shot glass toward the center of the table, the chains he was wearing rattling as he moved his arm. The Devil's skin was colored with soot, and his hair and coat were made of buffalo hide, a costume that had been in his family since the turn of the twentieth century. The curled ram's horns on his head were a bit off-center, but he was, by a wide margin, the most sober of the three.

"Why do I always have to be the responsible one?" the Devil asked.

"Because you're the oldest," Saint Nicholas said, stroking his white beard as if it were real.

"Happy Mikuláš," Jan Jelinek said after joining them at the table. "I bring this bottle from Czech Republic. Drink."

Jan Jelinek poured each of them another shot. He was quite a bit older than the trio, and his chestnut hair was silvering at the temples. Jan had straight, symmetrical features, an affable smile, and a smooth face that rarely required shaving. His eyes were bright, showing cunning when they flashed, and resilience when focused on a single point. There at the scuffed wooden table he poured each of them another round.

The Devil and Saint Nicholas both glanced over at the Angel. The Angel, Sunny Patek, had always been beautiful. She had high cheekbones, a light, healthy complexion, and flaxen hair, and it seemed that her expressive eyes, mischievous lips, and lithe dancer's body could make a man as crazy as a buck in the rut. Saint Nicholas, who on any other day was known as Justin Zima, had been playing Saint Nicholas the last four years hoping for a chance to take Sunny out. His buddy, Billy Beranek, currently clad as the Devil, wanted her, too.

Justin and Billy, who had been close since elementary school and even roomed together in college, would never let a woman get between them. And even though they both had an eye for the same petite blondes, they had never fought over a woman. Justin and Billy had known Sunny Patek since middle school, had spent endless hours with her, and yet never had they truly competed for her affection. Their friends and families said that the three of them were like brothers and sisters, and Justin and Billy, tacit with their true intentions, had always played along hoping that it would lead to something more. Yet after all of these years, it had led to nothing. Both of them had held her hand for a fleeting second, had held her hair while she puked cheap wine into the porcelain bowl during high school, and had warmed her with their letter jackets, but neither one had even kissed her, much less taken her on a true date. They had given her presents and birthday cards. They had called to make sure she had made it home safely when they stayed out late. But as soon as either one of them advanced, Sunny retreated, and as soon as they retreated to lick their wounds and refortify their pride, she advanced again. Now both young men had returned from college determined to finally impress her. And though Justin and Billy never talked about it, each one planned to make her his own.

College had not worked out for Sunny. She had gone to school at Texas State, where she learned a lot about mixed drinks and cultivated an appreciation of tubing the San Marcos River, but she had not attended a lot of class, and now she was back home in Waylon County. She had never told her parents why she couldn't make the grades, but it seemed that they had a good suspicion. They did not get angry, nor did they subject her to a sermon. They just defunded her, saying that if she wanted to go to college, she would need to pay for it. In the year and a half since she dropped out, she had not managed to save enough to get back to school, and with her little business of selling flowers out of a vintage hippie van, which she called "Scarlet Begonias Mobile Florist," starting to gain momentum, she had decided to postpone school for the time being.

"*Na zdraví*," Jan Jelinek yelled, and the shot glasses were raised into the air.

After the shot, the Devil and Saint Nicholas staggered to the restroom, the white-walled door of which had the word "*Muži*" painted at eye level.

"Hell, Saint Nick," the Devil said, standing wide-legged at the trough urinal.

"Hell what?" Saint Nick replied, a high, clear arc projecting beyond his robes and splashing onto a glacier-blue toilet mint.

"Tonight's the night," the Devil said.

"The night for what?"

"Tonight's the night I get her."

"Ain't no way you're gonna get her. Apparently you done caught a case of the delusional disorder. I read about that in my Intro to Psychology class, and it looks like you done caught it."

"I'll take her home with me tonight. I guaran-damn-tee it. And you cain't catch delusional disorder. It ain't like cat-scratch fever or the mumps or something like that. You should've paid better attention in class. All I can say is that there ain't no way on Earth that Sunny would ever decide to be your girlfriend."

"Listen here, Devil. You clearly underestimate my otherworldly charm. Tonight's the night I make her mine."

"Yeah, right. You ain't got a snowball's chance in Marfa."

They both laughed merrily and crossed streams as an act of goodwill.

The Devil and Saint Nicholas both zipped up. Saint Nicholas then stepped over to the sink and turned on the hot water. He ran a palm over a lump of cheap bar soap and rubbed both hands together beneath the water. The Devil headed toward the door.

"You ain't washing your hands?" Saint Nicholas asked.

"Didn't piss on 'em," the Devil said and pushed the bathroom door open.

The Devil and Saint Nicholas walked back over to the table where the Angel was sitting with Jan Jelinek. A Czech Christmas song about rocking little baby Jesus played over the speakers. There were a couple of scratches on the album, but that was not surprising considering how many folks taking shots of the Christmas spirit had dropped the needle into that album's groove over the last twenty years.

"All right, sweet little Angel," the Devil said. "We have houses to visit."

"Let's have one more round before we go," the Angel said.

"School tomorrow," the Devil told her. "Kids are waiting for us."

230

He reached a soot-covered hand out for hers. She took his hand with the tips of her slender porcelain fingers.

"Jan, we'll be back," Saint Nicholas said.

Jan Jelinek gave a half-cocked smile, the smile of a man who knows he has been momentarily outmaneuvered. He knew, after all, that an ordinary man could not travel the town in the company of the supernatural. No mortals were allowed to follow. And he had time. He would not fly back home to the Czech Republic until after *Tři Králové*, Three Kings Day.

"Janečku, I'll be back," the Angel said, drunkenly adjusting her wings. "I'll see you when we get back, you little cutie pie."

The Devil and Saint Nicholas cast one another a sideways glance that scarcely concealed their disapproval of Jan being lavished with such terms of endearment. The Devil, perhaps to make Jan believe that he and Sunny were attached, had now interlaced his right hand with her left, his dusky digits contrasted by her translucent white skin. With his free hand, the Devil slung an empty gunny sack over his shoulder to indicate that he was ready for departure. Then the holiday troika locked arms at the elbow, stepped out of the old social hall, and swerved their way between the painted wooden church and the bone-white rows of headstones in the kirkyard to the residence of Pepa Dvorak, whose surname had lost its hook a century ago, though it was still found on the marble slabs in the cemetery.

The Dvorak place, which was an old clapboard affair from the early twentieth century, had Bohemian lace curtains on the windows and a "*Vitáme Vás*" welcome mat in front of the door. A flickering hurricane lamp in the bay window led the trio from the street to the front porch, where they gave one another a quick appraisal.

"You look a disaster," the Devil said, straightening the Angel's halo with one hand and clutching the mouth of his gunnysack with the other.

The Angel just smiled a glowing smile. Then, before anyone could knock, Pepa Dvorak came out the front door in a camouflage T-shirt, jeans, and cowboy boots.

"Glad y'all could make it," Pepa said. "But I thought y'all woulda been here a good while ago. Figured y'all woulda made it a little bit after dark."

"Got detained at the KJT Hall," the Devil said, "but we made it here.

Yessirree, we made it."

"Come on in," Pepa said. "The kids are waiting in the living room."

The Angel, the Devil, and Saint Nicholas entered the family's living room, where cape-mounted bucks hung on every wall. Two children, a little boy and a little girl, sat on the couch staring. The boy was probably six with dark hair and freckles, and the little girl, whose hair was light and longer, sucked her right thumb and clutched a pillow with her left hand. Both were wearing red and white shirts with a picture of Santa Claus on the front.

"*Hezký Mikuláš*," Saint Nicholas said, lowering himself to a knee to talk to the children. "Happy Saint Nicholas Day to you. Have you been a good boy this year?"

The little boy looked over Saint Nicholas' shoulder at the Devil, who was sticking his tongue out and contorting his face. When the boy's eyes got wider, the Devil started rattling his chains. The Angel gave the Devil a quick elbow jab to the ribs. Then she placed an open palm beside her mouth and moved closer to his ear. The Devil stopped rattling his chains and gently moved his wooly head toward the Angel's lips.

"Don't make 'em cry," the Angel said, her breath warm on the Devil's skin. "They're little. Save it for the big ornery ones."

The Devil's face looked enraptured, in clear contrast to the visage of Saint Nicholas, which had begun to sour upon seeing the Devil in such apparent ecstasy, though the patron saint quickly managed to regain his patent jollity and redirect his attention to the children.

"Do you have a song or a poem for Mikuláš?" he asked.

The little boy stood up straight on the couch. He then belted out "Jingle Bells" with a surprising amount of gusto. The little girl pulled her slobbery thumb out of her mouth on the chorus and joined him the best she could. While they sang their little duet, the children's mother snapped a picture and then made a video on her cell phone. Mikuláš, looking at the camera, smiled and offered each of them a chocolate bar, which they took with their eyes fixed on the Devil and his burlap sack.

"Happy Mikuláš to you, good children," Saint Nicholas said.

The trio made their way to the front door. On the way out, the Devil bumped into the coffee table, and the Angel used a floor lamp as a walking cane as she stumbled toward the door. Before reaching the threshold, Saint Nicholas looked at himself in the mirror above the couch and tugged at his robes and beard to ensure that everything was straight. Then, once the holiday visitors had made it out the door, they found Pepa Dvorak leaning against the porch rail holding a bottle of whiskey. He handed it to Saint Nicholas, who took a pull.

"Damn," Saint Nicholas said. "That'll put hair on your chest."

Saint Nicholas handed the bottle to the Devil, who took a swig without comment and then handed it to the Angel. The Angel turned the bottle up and took a long, slow gulp. She, in turn, handed the bottle back to Pepa.

"That was a shot for the first leg," Pepa said. "Now a shot for the other."

Pepa passed the bottle to Saint Nicholas, and it circuited back around. When the bottle returned to Pepa, he took a quick pull and laughed.

"Thank you for coming," he said. "*Děkuju.*"

"Don't mention it," Saint Nicholas replied. "*Není za co.*"

The trio spilled off the porch with the Angel in the middle and the Devil and Saint Nicholas holding either of her hands. The whiskey was enough to warm anyone up, but extra warmth was not necessary, for the weather was so nice that the lantana and Copper Canyon daisies in the Dvoraks' flower beds were still in full bloom.

Saint Nicholas, the Angel, and the Devil walked up the road to Jerry Kovar's house. The house was an immense two-story made of Hill Country limestone and had a large balcony in front, which was bordered by wrought iron railing decorated with Texas stars. The whole house glowed red and green from the chili pepper lights that followed the eaves and columns of the place. A Cadillac with dealer plates and a "Kovar Cadillac" insignia below the left tailfin was parked in the driveway.

Although they were trying to be quiet and discreet, Jerry Kovar intercepted the trio at the top of the driveway. He was wearing a black polo shirt and a pair of golfing pants. "Kovar Cadillac" was embroidered on his shirt where the left breast pocket would normally be. He was holding a Limburger Bock sheathed by a red "Kovar Caddy" koozie.

"Glad y'all made it over," Jerry said. "There could be a goddam alien attack, and Little Phillip still wouldn't notice that y'all were here. He's in his bedroom flopped on a military-grade beanbag chair playing video games. When he's in there machine-gunning everything in sight, he doesn't notice anything around him. It's just him, the screen, and his crazy-ass thumbs."

"Glad we could come," Saint Nicholas said.

Jerry Kovar smiled at Saint Nicholas, though his eyes were on the Angel.

"Listen," Jerry said. "I don't want y'all in there coddling him. The little asshole is in trouble at school for calling all the other kids assholes, and we can't have that. He shouldn't be calling 'em assholes. Not in elementary school anyway. He got himself in trouble, and he'll have to sit around with his thumb up his ass during recess for the next week, or at least until the teacher gets tired of looking at him sitting there next to her. I need y'all to make an impression on the boy."

"Hell," Saint Nicholas said. "Why don't you take those stupid video games away from him?"

Jerry almost laughed.

"He'd throw a shit-fit, a real Donald Duck. And I ain't got time for that. And his mama would protect him like a she-wolf either way. She'd aid and abet whatever assholery he was involved in. She'd say I was resentful because the boy wasn't my son."

He pulled a snuff can out of his back pocket, packed it with a quick flick of his wrist, opened the lid, and took a dip.

"Well, y'all," he said, spitting into the purple sage just off the porch. "I cain't alter the boy's behavior to any real extent in my current role, but I have a real good feeling that the goddam Devil can change the little asshole's tune."

Jerry pulled an exotic leather wallet out of his back pocket and handed the Devil a hundred-dollar bill.

"I need you to make a significant impression on the boy," he said.

"Keep your money," the Devil laughed. "This here's a public service. I'll go in there and visit with him. Maybe I can help change his tune."

"I hope so. Right now his mama is at exercise class, or so she tells me. She won't be able to intervene."

Jerry opened up the big oak door, and Saint Nicholas, the Devil, and

234

the Angel crossed the threshold. The trio walked into the entry hall onto the hardwood floor, where they met Sydney, the Australian shepherd, who sniffed everyone's crotch and wagged his tail.

"*Hodný pes*," Saint Nicholas said, petting the dog's head and then holding up two fingers to bless him.

"Phillip!" Jerry hollered. "Little Phillip!"

He hollered as loud as he could, his voice echoing through the large living room with its huge leather couches and longhorn rugs.

"Phillip, come on!" he said, "Mikuláš is here."

The trio stood in the living room. Above the fireplace hung a framed "Come and Take It" flag with fake bullet holes in it. Beneath the flag, an old Sharps .50-caliber rested on the mantel. After a few seconds of waiting, Jerry led them to Phillip's bedroom door, and without a knock or a word of warning, he opened the door. The Angel took a step back and let Saint Nicholas and the Devil enter first in case the boy was sitting around in his underwear.

When they entered the room, Phillip, who was short and stocky, darted his eyes toward the shaft of stark light shooting from the open door, but then his eyes returned to his glowing computer screen. He was playing a first-person shooter game, where he was charged with eliminating furry little prairie dogs dressed in World War I German helmets, which made them look a bit like squatty little unicorns. Phillip screeched arcane madness into his headset, an odd, indecipherable lingo that sounded strange coming from a voice so high and young.

"Hey, boy," Jerry said, tapping Phillip's shoulder.

The boy moved away quickly, repelling his stepdaddy's touch. Then, a few seconds later, Saint Nicholas gently removed Phillip's headset, though the boy immediately shoved it back on his head as if he could not survive without it.

"Son, you are on the high road to an ass-whipping," Jerry said, looking for a belt.

"Would you like to recite a poem for Saint Nicholas?" Saint Nicholas asked.

The boy turned.

"A poem?" the boy asked.

"A poem."

235

"Aren't poems queer?"

"They're not queer. Not all poems are queer."

The Devil chuckled at the conversation.

"Quit laughing," Phillip said. "Stop it now."

The Devil brushed buffalo fur out of his eyes.

"How old are you?" the Devil asked.

"Nine. Nine years old. How old are you?"

"More than five thousand years old. I was once in Heaven, but now I am the King of Hell. Do you have a poem for Mikuláš?"

"Poems are queer."

The Devil shut the bedroom door.

"Mikuláš, it looks like this one has given us no choice. I'm going to have to haul him off to Hell."

The Angel and Saint Nicholas stepped back by the door. Jerry stood by the closet with his arms folded in satisfaction. The Devil, for his part, moved slowly toward Phillip with his gunny sack wide open, his body crouched over like he was hunting snipe. Phillip hollered something precociously profane and then sprung from the floor with his headset still on. The Devil rushed him, taking him out just above the ankles, which sent him tail-first into the bag. The Devil then slid the bag over the boy and tied the mouth closed with the competence of a team roper. The boy kicked and hollered, but there was no escape. The Devil, having sacked his share of naughty children over the last couple of years, stood patiently beside his quarry and waited.

"Phillip, if you acted like a nice boy and didn't give your teachers and your stepdad such a hard time, you wouldn't be in the Devil's sack on the way to Hell. You were not even nice to Mikuláš. So I have to take you to the place they warned you about in Sunday school. I hope you like it hot."

"Asshole!" Phillip hollered, punching and kicking from inside the sack. "Asshole!"

"Holler all you want, Phillip. You're just a banty rooster in a sack."

"Let me go! Let me go!"

He kicked and kicked, and the Devil stepped back and watched as the boy tried to bust out of the burlap sack. The Angel, looking a bit disconcerted, leaned against Saint Nicholas, who put one arm around her shoulder and stroked her hair with the other. Jerry, the boy's stepfather, watched the convulsing sack with a lean grin on his face.

"Asshole! Asshole!" Phillip screamed.

"That's the King of the Assholes to you, boy," said the Devil.

There were loud machine gun sounds coming from the computer. Phillip's online avatar had just gotten eliminated by the general of the prairie dog army.

"Asshole! I was about to beat the record!"

The boy punched and kicked for a while longer, and when he finally settled down, the Devil picked up the sack. Phillip began to kick and scream once again, but with little effect, for the Devil kept the bag suspended off his hip, making it difficult for the boy to land a solid blow. Saint Nicholas opened the bedroom door, and then he, Jerry, and the Angel followed the Devil toward the front entrance.

"Off to Hell, boy," the Devil said. "No sleep there. Only fire and torment. No video games in the whole place. Just pain and suffering. Hot coals. Crying. Gnashing of teeth. All kinds of brimstone and biblical stuff like that down there."

The Devil stepped off the porch and onto the gravel road outside the house with the boy in the gunny sack over his shoulder. Saint Nicholas and the Angel staggered behind him, occasionally tripping over a rock or stumbling from too much slivovice. Jerry, who lived on this road, walked smoothly and calmly beside them in the starlight. The Devil, moving faster than the others, opened the churchyard gate with the tow-sack over his shoulder.

"Phillip," he said. "It's still a ways to Hell. We have to stop and rest."

The Devil, with a grin that looked like a lazy waxing crescent, dropped the sack next to a marble gravestone with the word Dvořák on it. The boy kicked and screamed and gouged for a good long while. Finally, after what must have been half an hour, the boy started to blubber inside the sack. He cried and cried and blubbered and blubbered, heaving and snorting and cussing. From his vantage point, the Devil thought that the boy must have rolled into the fetal position. Jerry stroked his chin in admiration and then nodded to the Devil, who untied the sack and stepped away as if it were full of rattlesnakes. Phillip, wild as a bobcat, piled out of the sack and, with fierce, crazy eyes, ran from the graveyard toward his house with incredible orientation.

"Thanks, y'all," Jerry Kovar said. "That oughta fix the little asshole's wagon for a while. If y'all are ever in the market for a Cadillac, call me. I'll cut you a helluva deal."

"Thank you, Jerry. Have a good 'un," Saint Nicholas said, and the trio traveled on.

A little ways down the road, the Devil and Saint Nicholas both looked back to see Jerry still openly gawking at Sunny, but considering that the Cadillac magnate was stuck watching his little hellion of a stepson, they knew that he posed no real threat to their courting efforts. Heading to their last house, the Angel walked on her own accord. Both the Devil and Saint Nicholas held out a hand for her, but she did not accept either one.

"It's nice to have Jan back in town, isn't it?" the Angel said. "When he comes here from Europe, it always means that it's the most wonderful time of the year."

Saint Nicholas and the Devil walked along in silence. An owl called somewhere in the distance.

"Sure, it's nice to have him here every year," Saint Nicholas finally said while pulling white beard hair out of his mouth. "He's a nice enough ol' boy."

"Oh yeah," the Devil said. "As soon as Jan gets to town, I know it's about time to fetch my horns and burlap sack from the back of the closet. And well, any ol' boy that shows up and fills you full of plum brandy is all right in my books."

After a few blocks, the trio reached Jimmy and Heather Novak's brick ranch house. As soon as the three figures reached the front porch, lights came on throughout the house. A dark-haired boy in a red cape, who must have been about eight years, opened the front door. When the trio entered the house, the boy ran past them and jumped onto a piano stool in the parlor.

"Jimmy Junior, do you have a song or poem for Mikuláš?" Saint Nicholas asked.

"Got a really big show for you, Mikuláš," the boy replied.

Jimmy and Heather Novak, the boy's parents, sat on the couch facing the center of the room looking like the subjects of a Grant Wood painting. Jimmy motioned for the visitors to take a seat.

"Sit down and enjoy the show," he said.

Before Saint Nicholas could take a single step, the Devil had already spirited the Angel to the love seat, where the two now sat side-by-side. Knowing that he had been outplayed, Saint Nicholas adjusted his miter and, with a hint of resignation, plopped himself down in a leather recliner. Once the three were seated, Grace, a little brown-haired girl in a tutu, came out of the kitchen with three Bohemian beers on a tray. She offered one to each of the visitors, all of whom accepted. She smiled and returned to the kitchen. The boy in the red cape gave the visitors a nod and a smile and began to play a rag on the piano. His fingers moved deftly across keys that tinkled and trilled beneath his practiced touch. About that time, the little girl in the tutu returned to the living room carrying an accordion. She played a funny little solo followed by a curtsy. Her parents and the three supernatural guests all clapped in admiration. Then a third child, known commonly as Boomer, came dashing in from the hall in peppermint-striped pajamas. Boomer slid across the hardwood floor like a Broadway star and began to sing. The other two backed him up doowop style.

"Mikuláš, Mikuláš, we love you,
And we have a song, woo hoo,
We hope you love our song so well,
And do not send us all to Hell."

When the song ended, the singers all came together in the center of the room and gave a bow. The Devil, the Angel, Saint Nicholas, and their parents all lavished them with a standing ovation.

"Wonderful, wonderful," Saint Nicholas said, handing each of the children a stack of chocolate bars. "You are all very good children. Great singers and musicians, too."

"Last year we all ended up in the sack," the boy in the red cape said.

"This year Saint Nicholas has nothing but praise for you."

"They're quick studies," their mother said.

"I can see," the Devil told the little performers. "I prefer good children.

239

It's easier on my back, and I don't get kicked in the kidneys through my sack."

Saint Nicholas turned up his beer, and the Devil did the same. The Angel swayed a bit, and then she put her full lips to the bottle. Once all of their beers were finished, the trio left the house and started walking back to the KJT Hall. When they arrived at their destination, Jan Jelinek was waiting over by the bar. He returned to the table.

"How was it?" he asked.

"It was a very good lesson as usual," the Devil said, putting his arm around the Angel's waist. "Good children got chocolate. Bad children got a trip to Hell. If all of America took up our customs, juvenile delinquency would decrease fivefold in the United States."

The Angel stole a side glance at Jan Jelinek, who was now sitting at the scratched-up wooden table behind the big plastic bottle of slivovice. The holiday trio now headed for the restrooms, with Sunny, the Angel, heading toward the one marked *"Ženy,"* and the Devil and Saint Nicholas headed to the one labeled *"Muži."*

"Hell, Billy," Saint Nicholas said, almost missing the trough. "Keep your mitts off of Sunny. She's drunk."

"Keep my mitts off of her? So you can paw on her?" the Devil asked before losing his balance and splashing off the floor for a second before he could resharpen his aim. "We ain't never argued over a woman in all our lives. So let's not argue over this one. Hell, there's a million girls out there."

"Then let me have a go at Sunny."

"Nah. Cain't do it. Let me take a run at her," the Devil said, straightening his buffalo wig.

"Cain't do it either. Tonight's the night."

"Well, we can do it like gentlemen. We been best buddies since we were damn near shitting yellow, and it don't look like neither one of us is gonna concede at this point. Let's just duke it out, and whoever wins gets first shot at her. No hard feelings after it's over with."

"I think it's preposterous to fight over a woman," Saint Nicholas said, his beard now yellowed by lager. "Preposterous. Did you hear me? Or did you not learn that word in freshman comp?"

"Never in my life would I believe that my best friend was a chickenshit."

Saint Nicholas hit the Devil between the eyes right there in the middle of the john. The Devil's head popped back, and then he pushed Saint Nicholas hard with both hands, causing him to bounce off the wooden wall and bang into the trough. While Saint Nicholas was trying to collect himself, the Devil zipped up and kicked him behind the knee. Saint Nicholas' head banged into the shelf where folks put their beers while doing their business, and then he turned and punched the Devil in the left eye, which began to swell up almost immediately. After that, the Devil ducked low and came up hard and fast, his chains ajingling as he hit Saint Nicholas square in the nose.

"That hurt," Saint Nicholas said.

"You think that punch to the eye tickled?"

They stood looking at one another.

"I reckon we both got our asses kicked," Saint Nicholas said. "I can't believe we did that. Best friends since we were little fighting over a woman."

"Well, let's call it a draw."

"If it's a draw, then why don't we try to date her at the same time, like them Europeans in the dirty movies do?"

"If she won't date one of us, I doubt she'll date both of us."

"Well, maybe not."

The two washed their hands and faces in the sink and walked back out into the social hall. The Angel, Sunny Patek, was snuggled up next to Jan Jelinek at the table. Saint Nicholas and the Devil both bristled at the sight.

"Jan, take your paws off of her," Saint Nicholas said. "She's drunk."

Jan gave him a puzzled look.

"Your hands," the Devil said. "Take your hands off her."

Sunny stood up.

"Wait a minute. I get to choose who I'm with, not y'all. I've had a few drinks. But I still get to make my own decisions."

She sat back down and rested her head on Jan's shoulder.

"So we both chase you around since middle school, and you end up with him?" Saint Nicholas said, touching his nose to appraise whether or not it was broken. "He ain't been here a week. And he'll be gone a month from now."

Sunny smiled and put on some red lipstick, though with limited success. Jan straightened her halo, which littered glitter on her hair and shoulders.

"I love you two guys," Sunny said. "I have always loved you. But I don't want to be with you. If we have a relationship and it goes wrong, then we have to see each other at the Hoggly Woggly, at church, and at the post office. We have the same circle of friends and will be at the same dances. Krasna Lipa is too much of a fishbowl for me to date anybody from around here. It would be too uncomfortable if the relationship didn't work."

"But what if it did work?" the Devil asked.

"The odds are against it working. How many people does a person date before finding the right one?"

"You could try us both and increase your odds of finding the right one," the Devil said.

Jan Jelinek poured a round of shots.

"Boys, let's have a drink," he said.

The Devil and Saint Nicholas sat down, albeit grudgingly.

"*Na zdraví*," Jan said.

Everyone raised a glass and tilted it back. Then Jan checked his watch.

"We should probably be going, gentlemen," he said, standing up and holding out a hand for Sunny.

"So you're going back to his hotel room?" Saint Nicholas asked.

"I will neither confirm nor deny that. You can use your imagination. But I will say this. Right or wrong, whether I go to Candy's Motel with him or not is none of your business."

Jan Jelinek took his bottle of slivovice in one hand and the Angel in the other. Outside, he started his rental car and the Angel got into the passenger seat. The headlights came on, and the car disappeared into the Hill Country night. The Devil pulled a flask out of his vest and handed it to Saint Nicholas. Saint Nicholas took a pull.

"We ain't trapped in no damn fishbowl," he said.

"Far from it. We're cosmopolitan."

"Just like the folks in Europe."

"You want to go to the Old Coyote Bar and troll for ladies?"

"Don't see why not."

The Devil and Saint Nicholas shook hands and smiled. The night was still young.

A Lost Cause

★ ★ ★

"I ain't gonna stay silent no longer," Royce Granger hollered from the back of Robert E. Lee's horse, his left hand wrapped around the general's waist and his right hand waving the Stars and Bars. "I ain't got no use for that lug nut in Washington any more than y'all do. He's just a loudmouth Yankee, and he ain't got no character. And I like black folks as good as anybody, and that black man that was killed by that skinny white cop deserves justice, but ain't nobody gonna take down this statue."

Beneath him, a crowd largely comprised of young people stood assembled in the Texas heat. Most were white, but some were black, and Royce, from his vantage point on the back of the general's horse, only saw a couple of people he recognized in the entire crowd. He figured most of the protesters were from Austin, since it wasn't that far away, and he would be damned if he let a bunch of kale-eating millennials pull down the only statue of any consequence in all of Waylon County.

"That statue is a monument to racism," someone in the crowd hollered.

"To me it ain't," Royce replied.

"To us it is," someone yelled.

"To me it's a tribute to slavery," the first someone screamed. "It has to come down."

"To me it stands for bravery, and it ain't going nowhere."

"Racist!"

"I ain't no racist," Royce said with his flag held high. "And my family didn't own no slaves. They were poor dirt farmers like anybody else. They picked their own cotton. They grew their own food. They fought for their country no different than the soldiers in Vietnam."

"But that was different!"

"To hell it was different. It was the poor fightin' for the rich like in any other war. The rebels fought like they were told, and though they were out-numbered and out-provisioned, they still fought for the lost cause."

"Tear it down!"

"Over my dead body!"

"Tear it down! It makes us feel bad. Destroy it!"

"It's part of my identity!"

"Destroy it!"

"It's part of my heritage!"

"Destroy it!"

"You're not erasing my family's past!"

A dozen or so men began to pull at the statue, and though he could have, Royce did not poke anyone with his flagstick.

"Tear it down," someone screamed, and then there was a chant two hundred people strong.

"I'm for you more than I'm against you," Royce hollered, holding tight to Robert E. Lee, "but I ain't gonna let y'all go around destroying every-thing my people are proud of. You're not going to take away the spirit of defiance, the spirit of rebellion, the spirit of the downtrodden, the spirit of the underdog."

And the horse named Traveller rocked beneath him. The verdigris horse rocked and rocked and there came the sickening squeal of bolts being up-rooted from the concrete. Royce held on tight as he, the general, and the general's horse came toppling to the ground.

Down from the Mountain
★ ★ ★

Handley Robertson stepped out of his trailer and looked up the steep grade of the mountain to the timberline, where the tall white dome of the observatory, like an idol to some ancient god, rose above the piñon pines and Emory oaks. The day was blue and clear, and Handley blinked as he tried to adjust his eyes. Daylight, he well knew, always required adjustment, for he was a nocturnal creature and spent most of his nights exploring the mystery and poetry of the universe through elongated tubes and refracted mirrors on top of that mountain, where he spoke in the arcane language of numbers and theory while drinking pot after pot of coffee. And though Handley truly enjoyed his colleagues, his work, and the deep, dark sky, he still required the occasional afternoon among the trees to maintain order, harmony, and clarity in his mind.

For the last several years, Handley had lived alone in his trailer, though he was friendly with the family that lived next door, which consisted of Johnny Ray, who worked as a mechanic, his wife Phyllis, and their two children. Handley and the Rays lived in a small compound near the base of Mount Locke, a community comprised of the astronomers, maintenance staff, cooks, and mechanics needed to support the great telescopes above the Davis Mountains. Most of the staff had children, and for these children, the mountains were their playground, and when they were not at school below in Fort Davis, they were running wild among the trees.

One of those children, though she now rejected being called a child, was Astrid, Johnny and Phyllis' daughter, and she had recently dyed her hair multiple colors trying to match the hues of the Andromeda Galaxy as seen through the Hubble telescope. Astrid wore seven-studded earrings to represent the Pleiades, the first star cluster she was able to identify as a child, and though she was friendly, and pretty as well, people did not always know how to take her when she traveled into town.

Astrid was sitting in a wooden deck chair on her front porch reading a world mythology book when Handley stepped outside.

"How goes it today, Handley?" Astrid asked.

"Doing fine. Doing fine. How about you?"

"Getting ready for the solstice."

"It'll be here shortly."

"I'm having a friend up from Marathon to celebrate."

Handley smiled.

"That's good," he said.

"My friend is a pagan like me. We're going to eat special solstice food."

"I don't reckon I know what that would be. I'm usually up at the eighty-two-inch working on the solstice. Midnight dinner is usually a hamburger or something. The cooks don't change the menu up too much for celestial holidays."

Handley winked, tipped his cowboy hat, and walked down the path from his trailer. He was a little sleepy because of javelinas rooting around under his floor early that morning, but he was often tired, so he took it as a matter of course.

When he was young, around seventeen like Astrid now was, he had also tried different religions on for size, but none seemed to fit. He was washed in the blood back home in Waylon County, and to some degree that blood had never washed off. He had read about Buddhism, Hinduism, Islam, and the Tao. He had quoted the texts and talked about them often, but never had he converted to another religion, though many faiths had somehow come to inform his own.

He believed in God, and he felt that the religions represented the many faces of God. The face he preferred to worship was that of his raising. Still, Handley felt a certain kinship to Astrid, for he understood her search for meaning and truth, a search he felt was much like his own at her age, when

246

each religion was like a novel new toy, a wonderful package to unwrap and explore until he came to understand it. He doubted Astrid would remain a pagan for too long. Paganism was simply an enjoyable toy to play with on her quest for knowledge and understanding.

Handley, with a sure and nimble step, followed the trail to the big volcanic rock where he liked to sit and think. Today he thought about exoplanets, planets that circled other stars in other solar systems, of which thousands were surely inhabitable, if Earth-like is the criterion upon which inhabitable is defined. But then, there were many kinds of bodies on the periodic table of exoplanets. There were Terrans and Subterrans and Neptunians. There were Miniterrans and Jovians. Life, as humans understood it, could likely be supported on the warm Terrans, but who was to say that forms of life not yet encountered by humanity could not exist on a huge, gaseous Jovian or on a Neptunian planet? He thought of other life forms on other planets, and he wondered what manifestation God would use to present himself on these distant planets. He wondered if the almighty would imbue the souls of our extraterrestrial kin with feelings of peace and tranquility once they came to acknowledge and accept the great one and his presence. Surely, he would do as he had done on Earth. Surely he would make manifest his true love for all beings so that all could come to know him.

There on the mountain, Mexican jays passed through the pines, stopping to look at Handley a moment. He always liked these big blue and white birds, for he appreciated their curiosity. He also liked how they resembled the northern jay yet were clearly a species all their own, a unique species that never failed to remind him of how lucky he was to live in the borderlands.

Handley thought about whatever crossed his mind, worries surfacing from the depths and then submerging when fantasies arose, his thoughts rising and falling with the current in his river of consciousness. He thought about Paloma, the woman he loved, and how she did not want this life, would not have this life, and considered Handley too confined by his ways, too rigid and unyielding. She did not want to endure years with a man who would always work the night shift. She did not want to live on the mountain. She wanted to live near her family in town, to see her brothers and sisters and *primos*. She wanted to play with her *sobrinos* and have children of her own, children who would live among their cousins and enjoy festive holidays and birthday parties in the park. She wanted to dance and sing and laugh without care. Handley loved Paloma, for she had a good heart, and he knew she truly loved him, but he also loved the stars. He needed them. He needed them as much as he needed anything.

Handley heard light footsteps coming down the path. The birds, as was their custom, called out in warning. Having lived here for what must have been a decade now, Handley knew most of the animals on the mountain, knew where they lived, when he would most likely see them, and how they would behave.

"I thought you would be here sitting on your favorite rock," Astrid said, walking up to him in a pair of low top All-Stars. "And I was right."

"What are you up to?"

"Just hanging out. Any big news up the hill?"

"Just studying supernovae. They're moving fast. Redshifting out into space, expanding into dark energy. The world's getting smaller. The universe is getting bigger."

"The other day I was reading about how the universe is expanding at a crazy pace, that it's even expanding faster than y'all expected. That's really cool."

Handley fastened the top button of his western shirt and glanced down at his work boots for a moment.

"Yeah, it's interesting," he said. "Watching the reading on the spectrograph is incredible, surprising. I would even say mind-blowing."

"What did people say when y'all brought that stuff down from the mountain?"

"Nobody wanted to believe it. It would mean a change to the model of the universe most scientists believe in. And, of course, other folks have their own belief systems, and nothing we say on the mountain will ever mean anything to them either way."

Astrid lit a clove cigarette and took a long drag. Handley considered saying something to her, but he didn't. He just watched her move the cigarette to her painted lips with her pale, slender fingers. Astrid was a lot like he was twenty years ago. He had to try everything for himself, and nobody could tell him different. He probably had a right to tell her something, considering that he had lived next door to her since she was a little girl, had played frisbee with her and her older brother, and kept an eye out to make sure they were safe.

As long as he had known Astrid, Handley had always told her about the stars and planets, had shown her supernovae and binary stars and neighboring galaxies through the telescopes near the visitor center. He had taught her things about the sky that most people did not learn until college, if then. He had taught her that what appeared intuitive was not always right. He had taught her that the full moon was not the best time to view our planet's satellite, for it appeared flat. He was, perhaps, a greater influence on her life than he would have ever anticipated himself to be. Astrid always looked up to him with those big brown eyes. He admired her youthful enthusiasm and hungry mind, and she, from what he understood, admired the tiny threads of universe he could unravel for her.

Handley thought about time. He thought about a binary system twenty thousand light years away. He thought about the time it took for that light to reach Earth. He thought about what it was like to look at the sky, to realize that each star he saw was a different distance away, and although he was seeing many stars at the same time, what he was seeing were events that happened thousands of years apart. These objects all seemed somehow synchronous, in harmony, because their light arrived at the same time, though the events the light represented were far, far distant from one another in time.

"So have you decided where you are going to college?" Handley asked.

"I think so. I've narrowed it down to a couple of schools on the East Coast and one in California. You know, I never wanted to leave the mountain, but it looks like I need to. If I want to be an astronomer like you, I'll have to go down the mountain."

"You'll make a good astronomer. I know that."

"If it looks like I won't, I'll start my own band or something. I'll call it Astrid and the Exoplanets or something like that."

"You'll be good at whatever you decide to do."

Astrid took a deep haul from her cigarette, blew a smoke ring, and then began to speak.

"Well, I guess I had better blaze," she said with a smile.

Handley smiled back.

"See you later," he said. "Don't take any wooden nickels."

"I never did," she replied.

"I know it."

Handley thought about time and space and distance. He thought about the billions of years of history, the formation of stars and planets, the birth and death of heavenly objects, the merging of galaxies into one over periods of time beyond the imagination. He thought about the milli-wink of time humanity has inhabited the Earth, and the unfathomably short time we have, each star shining concurrently, but from a different place in time.

Easter Fires
★ ★ ★

The smoke billowed white from the grass fire up the way. The fire was burning low and cool but traveling fast from what Oma could tell. The volunteer fire department, operating from their brush engine, was fighting the best they could, but other departments from surrounding counties would have to assist if the fire was going to be contained. From the front porch of her clapboard house, Oma could see that several acres had already burned and that the winds of April were nourishing the growing fire that was consuming the granite hill in the near distance. The fire was still relatively far away, but it was close enough to make her worry. If it came down the slope, crossed Krieger's pasture, swallowing his acres of alfalfa along the way, she would be very concerned, but she did not think the fire would jump the road. Surely the volunteer fire department would use the road as a fire break and contain the blaze. But if the fire did advance, lighting up the brush along Oma's fenceline and sweeping the cotton field in its hungry march toward the house, she would have to decide what to do. She imagined that she would load her grandchildren, the dog, and any moveable heirlooms into the truck and evacuate.

Evacuation was not her style. She came from pioneer stock, and her ancestors did not evacuate. They fought the Comanches when they had to and made peace when they could. They had survived smallpox, the harassment of Confederate irregulars, and the pressures of two World Wars, when their loyalty was questioned because they still spoke their mother tongue, the tongue of the Fatherland. Her family had also stood their ground during drought, when they had to sell their cattle before the animals all dropped dead from hunger, and the family had lived through torrential springs when the Blazeby River and its tributaries had overflown their banks.

But her grandchildren were raised in Houston, and they did not speak the mother tongue. In fact, the only words of German that Frida and Steve seemed to know were "*Oma*" and "*Danke*." And they were not tenacious and tough like their ancestors. They were wonderful children, smart children, polite children, but still they asked that the crust be removed from their peanut butter sandwiches, and they would not explore the farm too much because they were afraid of snakes and didn't want to get stickers in their shoelaces. So they stayed inside and played video games in the living room. Oma did not know how they were able to hook up all the cables to play the games on the big screen television, but at least they were clever and industrious enough to do so.

The present year of drought had left the land parched. Otherwise there would be no grass fire in April. There would be bluebonnets and wine cups and blanket flowers, but there would be no fire. Frida and Steve, aged seven and five, were staying with Oma for Easter while their parents were in New Orleans for the long weekend. Oma had scolded her son and daughter-in-law for not spending Easter with their children, for they were providing a poor example, but neither of them had been too affected. Candace, her daughter-in-law, had been raised in the North and was a bit too secular for Oma's taste, but that was none of her affair, and she steered away from that topic whenever it arose, out of both civility and the need to see her grandchildren.

After checking on the fire, Oma stepped back inside the house, quietly closing the front door behind her. She then walked through the living room, past the eight-point buck above the mantel and the cuckoo clock on the wall, over to the kitchen, where Frida was sweeping the floor and Steve following her around with a dustpan. Oma always assigned her grandchildren a task or two when they visited, and she had been tickled earlier when Steve told her that he loved visiting the farm, even though there were more chores to do than at home. And then Oma laughed again when Frida said that there were more rules, too, but that it was no big deal because if she and her brother did what they were supposed to, Oma's flyswatter would remain on its hook by the kitchen door.

Earlier in the afternoon, Oma had baked Steve and Frida a peach cobbler made with peaches from a friend's orchard out in Fredericksburg. She had frozen the ripe fruit last summer in order to make cobblers whenever her grandchildren came to visit. And that morning Oma had taken the children to town. They always enjoyed their trips to Limburg, walking along the Marktplatz, and peering into the whitewashed Vereinshalle. They enjoyed seeing the limestone facades of the old mercantile buildings along Hauptstrasse and visiting Bauer's General Store, where Oma would always buy them a croquet set, a tetherball, or some other such game to play in the yard. The children liked to play the games, they really did, but they did not like to stay outside for very long, and they would end up playing horseshoes or badminton or washers for about ten minutes before going back inside to shoot space aliens or jump around a fairyland searching for troves of gold.

After walking around town, Oma took her grandchildren to the Wal-Mart on the state highway, where they bought two dozen eggs and an egg-dying kit that included little decals of cartoon characters she had never seen before. At that time, Oma could see smoke far away, but the fire had not overtaken the granite hill beyond the family place. Upon reaching the caliche road that crossed her property, Oma could see that her bird dog, Bruno, was close to the house, and she was glad of that. If they needed to move fast, she wanted the dog to be nearby.

Come sundown, Oma and the children went to the dining table to prepare it for making Easter eggs. Oma placed an old copy of the *Waylon County Messenger* across the table and then put half a dozen coffee cups filled with water on the paper, and the children dropped a dye tablet into each cup. In the country, the night is dark, much darker than Houston, and the children, finally deciding to look out the window, looked out into the night where the fire was burning bright and high upon the hill.

"What is that fire, Oma?" Steve asked, his big eyes almost reaching the bangs of his pageboy haircut, a Star Wars T-shirt on his back.

Oma did not want to alarm the children. She had been trying to put to-

253

gether a response to the question, were it asked, all day, but she was having a hard time with it. She did not want to lie to them, but she did not want to frighten them either. Then she remembered an old story she had heard her whole life. She remembered the story of the Easter Fires. One spring night in the early days of settlement, Comanche warriors lit signal fires on the limestone hills of what would be known as the German Belt, and in order not to scare her children, a creative young German mother told them that the fires were lit by the Easter rabbit to boil water for the Easter eggs. This story, more than any other, seemed to be the best one.

"The Easter bunny and his jackrabbit friends are on the hill making Easter eggs," Oma said. "They are boiling water to make their dyes. They are boiling bluebonnets to make blue dye, Indian blankets to make red dye, and black-eyed Susan petals to make yellow dye."

"Can we take the telescope to the porch and go watch them?" Steve asked.

"We can't do that. They would stop making eggs. They eat carrots, so they have wonderful eyesight. They can see us from incredible distances. If we took the telescope to the porch, they would put out the fires and go away. They are magical rabbits, and we would spoil their magic by trying to watch them dye their eggs."

"Are you sure?" Frida asked. She had long blond hair and wore a ruffled dress for all occasions. Oma had tried to get her to put on jeans so she wouldn't scratch up her legs in the brush near the fenceline, but she was not having it.

"Positive," Oma said. "Are you ready to boil some eggs?"

"Yes, but why are we boiling eggs if the Easter bunny is already doing it?" Frida asked. "Won't he be bringing us eggs?"

"We are doing it because it's fun. It's fun to paint eggs."

"Are these dyes made from wildflowers?"

"No. Just food coloring."

"It would be nice if they were made from wildflowers."

"This is not a great year for wildflowers. It would have been difficult to get enough to dye the eggs this year. It has been really dry."

"But the Easter bunny is making dye from wildflowers."

"Yes, but he and the jackrabbits are all magical. We are only human."

A fire siren sounded outside. It traveled high and wide across the fields. It made a long, lonely distant sound, though it was hardly distant. The truck was close. Too close. Bruno howled and howled.

"Oma, why are there fire trucks coming?" Steve asked.

"The Easter bunny always feeds the firemen the night before Easter. The volunteer firefighters always invite the rabbits to their big fish fry out in Laubensbach every year, so the rabbits always invite the fire department to their egg coloring party the night before Easter."

"Bunnies are vegetarians," Frida said with some authority. "They are vegetarians like my mom."

"The rabbits don't eat fish at the fish fry. They eat the salad. The firemen always make giant bowls of salad. The rabbits eat the lettuce and tomatoes."

The fire was getting closer. Oma could smell the smoke inside the house. While the children dyed the eggs, she stepped out on the porch for a minute to see what was happening. The fire had reached Krieger's alfalfa fields. More sirens sounded outside. She wondered if they would be asked to evacuate. The children dyed the eggs all sorts of colors. Some eggs were red, others blue. Some were yellow on one side and purple on the other. On some, they had drawn designs with a white crayon, and now the designs showed up beautifully. Steve had dipped a couple of eggs into every color, which left them a murky, unattractive gray. Those would be prize eggs, Oma thought. The dark gray eggs looked like rocks, so they would be harder to find than the yellow or blue ones.

The children, without being prompted, cleaned up their mess after they had dyed all of the eggs. They had been raised to be self-reliant, and Oma appreciated that. She let them clean the best they could. She let them pour the used dye into the sink and put the now-colorful newspaper into the trash, and then she cleaned up behind them without a word. After they were finished, the children kissed their Oma on the cheek and headed to the guest bedroom to sleep.

"*Gute Nacht*," Oma said.

"Good night," the children replied.

Oma then stood on the porch and watched the fire. She could see the silhouettes of the firefighters against the flames. The flames illuminated the arcs shooting from the hoses of the brush trucks. The water looked like rainbows of flame in the night. Oma hoped that the fire was not so large that it made the Houston or New Orleans news. Then her son and daughter-in-law would be worried. Waylon County had no television station, and they probably would not have watched it even if it had. As far as they were concerned, the only news coming from Limburg and its surroundings had to do with bratwurst-eating contests and high school football.

Oma went inside and sat on the couch to watch television. Every now and then she looked out the lace curtains to see if the fire was being contained. She dozed for a short while around two, but she was awake again by three. Around dawn, she walked out onto the porch. Though coals glowed here and there, the fire had been contained. Smoke blew over the fields. According to legend, or at least the stories of her own parents, the Easter Fires brought fertility to the land from which they could be seen. The smoke and ashes brought abundance to the soil over which they passed. Oma felt that, in this case, the smoke and ash brought fortune, for her family's land had been spared. She knew the Kriegers across the road would be fine as well. They had good insurance, and they were so wealthy from oil leases that the loss of a little alfalfa would not matter much to them.

The fire, Oma thought, had strangely reminded her of wonderful times. When she was a little girl, Easter Fires had been built all around German Texas, and the pioneer mother's tale had been shared around many a family table. But the fires had been forbidden for many years now. They had been forbidden ever since the drought of the nineteen-fifties culminated into a burn ban that was never lifted.

Oma was in a strange way glad that the fires had occurred and that she could share the old story of the Easter Fires with her grandchildren. It put them in touch with their family's past and rekindled her own memories of fond times. Oma took the basket of eggs from the kitchen, and in the pale, holy light of Easter's early dawn, she walked out into the fields to do the work of the Easter bunny and his jackrabbit friends.

Her grandchildren would not rise any time soon. They never had been early risers, and that was fine with Oma. However, this morning they surprised her. Not long after she sat down at the kitchen table for a cup of coffee, the children in their pajamas and tennis shoes came rushing for their Easter baskets. They would hunt for eggs, and then the three of them would get dressed and go to church. Oma looked across the field at the brilliant sunrise that had been intensified by the ash and smoke. This was a beautiful dawn. Such a beautiful dawn. Oma smiled in reflection. Her life, she thought, was truly filled with abundance and joy.

Acknowledgments
★ ★ ★

"Baby Head" *New Texas* (July 2019)

"Down from the Mountain" *descant* (2020)

"The Flag Salesman" *Cowboy Jamboree* (Fall 2018)

"The Flag Salesman" *Red Dirt Forum* (reprinted Summer 2019)

"He Drank His Coffee Black" *New Texas* (forthcoming)

"Honkytonking with the Silver Strings" *Panther City Review* (2018)

"Ink upon the Furrows" *Texas Observer* (October/November 2018)

"The Lord Ain't Willing, and the Creek's Done Rose" *The Blue Nib* (2020)

"The Most Famous Person in the Room" *Red Dirt Forum* (Spring 2020)

"The Pregnancy Test" *Panther City Review* (2018)

"Skunk Scent" *Panther City Review* (2019)

"Third Fiddle" *Dead Mule School of Southern Literature* (January 2021)

"Under the Banner of Willie Nelson" *Red Dirt Forum* (Spring 2020)